A note from the author:

A true story

Operation Underpants almost caused a major security scare in the United Kingdom

My good friend Russell Smith, while holidaying in the UK with his wife Merrill Smith, had been taking some photographs for the cover of this book. Seeing a UK military base surrounded by barbed wire he decides 'This will make a great shot', only to discover that army security didn't take kindly to their bases being photographed. Things only got worse. 'What's your name,' said the burly military security officer. 'Smith' said Russell. 'Oh yes and my name is Jones' – what's the name of this make-believe book of yours?' 'Operation Underpants,' continued Russell.' To which the officer said. 'I don't think you appreciate the seriousness of this, Sir.' I am pleased to say however that Russell was eventually released, minus the particularly good photos, but at least he got to keep his camera. 'Watch out for the tanks', yelled the security officer, as Russell wandered in a daze across the road after his brush with British terrorism laws. Looking up he saw two large military tanks baring down on him. And in Russell's words – '*They missed me by "that" much.*'

Please don't tell – let's keep it our little secret. But if Russell was a true friend – he would have been arrested and his story reported in the national press. Great publicity for *Operation Underpants,* but instead 37 friends on Facebook had a good laugh. Only Russell!

Other Books by
Mark A. Biggs

Above and Beyond

OPERATION UNDERPANTS

Mark A. Biggs

mbkbooks

MBK CONSULTING

Copyright

Copyright Mark A. Biggs 2016

Paperback ISBN: 978-0-9924293-5-5

E-Book ISBN: 978-0-9924293-6-2

A CIP catalogue record for this book is available from the National Library of Australia.

First Published in Australia 2016.

Second Edition September 2016.

by

mbkbooks
MBK Consulting
5 Elizabeth Close
Drouin Victoria 3818
Australia

www.mbkconsulting.com.au

Dedication

To my beloved Lacy

Front cover photograph: Ingrid Bergman – Pixabay CCO Public Domain &
Edna Collings

Continuity editor Colleen Crookston.

Cover Design by Craig Braithwaite – Aussiepics: www.aussiepics.com.au

PROLOGUE

The outbreak of death

This latest outbreak of the Ebola virus was the most significant since the disease first appeared in 1976 in two simultaneous outbreaks—one in Nzara, Sudan and the other in Yambuku, Democratic Republic of Congo. The latter occurred in a village near the Ebola River, from which the disease takes its name. Although devastating, the pattern was familiar; the outbreaks occurred in countries with weak health systems and a lack of infrastructure resources—places like Sierra Leone, Liberia, and Nigeria. The outbreak was declared a Public Health Emergency in 2010. With the frequency of international travel and business, even the poorer parts of Africa were no longer self-quarantined due to poverty. Following the initial two hundred deaths, and with the risk of the virus spreading to other parts of the world increasing daily, the world woke from its slumber to first contain and then to eradicate the disease.

The World Health Organisation, aka WHO, was working in Africa not long after the first confirmed reports of Ebola in 2009. Its initial responsibility was to trace the disease back to its source and identify the species of Ebola. WHO would produce modelling to map and predict the spread of the disease, liaise with the affected countries on containment and treatment and with the world community to assist the affected countries.

From the very beginning, this outbreak seemed different. Casualty rates for Ebola are generally high, ranging from twenty-five to ninety percent, with the average sitting at fifty percent. Even when advanced Western medical hospitals had been established, the casualty rate remained alarming at ninety percent plus. It was, until this point, believed that if people survived the illness they developed a natural immunity to the disease, which would protect them from a future attack. Of the Western medical staff that had become infected and survived, ninety percent had a relapse of Ebola a few months later and died. Unlike their Western counterparts, the African patients who had become infected and survived developed immunity to the disease. Another factor that made this outbreak different was that WHO investigations can normally trace the outbreak back to a single source, even identifying the individuals who had transmitted or brought the disease into another country. On this occasion, however, there appeared to be three simultaneous outbreaks. A final difference was that, although the virus was definitely Ebola, it was not one of the five known strains.

By the time the outbreak was contained in early 2010, twenty-five thousand people on the African continent had died as had twenty-five Western medical staff. The Public Health Emergency was in its monitoring phase when the first reports of an Ebola outbreak in London were confirmed. As there was a significant gap in time since the death of the last returning health worker from Africa and the outbreak in Britain, it was felt unlikely that the two incidences were linked. With the death toll now at eight, British authorities and WHO worked around the clock tracing the origins of the disease and any possible connections between the infected people.

The first people known to be infected were David Carlisle and Trevor Ingram. David was from New Quay in Wales and Trevor from Margate East in Kent. David, a teacher at Aberaeron Primary School, about fourteen kilometres from his home, had felt unwell that morning. Another cold he told himself as a sore throat took hold—no point going to the GP. The National Health Service (NHS) had, over the preceding five years, been pushing to reduce the use of antibiotics dramatically. GPs had been quite successful in educating their patients that, if they had a cold or flu, antibiotics were of no use and the best thing they could do was to go home and rest. The results had been a significant reduction in people—other than those needing medical certificates for time off work—attending their GP with cold or flu-like symptoms.

By the second day, David felt very unwell, his body had begun to ache, and he had headaches. He had decided he would have to visit the GP if only for a medical certificate. By the time he arrived at his doctor's he was running a fever. The doctor later told the authorities that he had asked screening questions, such as had David recently travelled overseas, but the responses gave him no cause for additional concern. David was prescribed Panadol to bring down the fever and asked to come back in a couple of days if things had not improved. It was fifteen hours later, at about one in the morning, when he started to vomit blood. His wife, in a distressed state, called for an ambulance. A triage doctor asked the same screening questions. Presenting with a high fever, flu-like symptoms, stomach pains, and vomiting blood, David was diagnosed with a suspected undefined infectious disease and barrier nursing protocols were implemented. His wife however went home and continued her social interactions, now somewhat restricted due to her need to be with her husband.

A health alert for GPs and the general public did not occur until David Carlisle's death and when the test results confirmed Ebola. It would be unfair to say Britain went into panic for it did not. However, with the first symptoms of the disease— fever, fatigue, muscle pain, headache, and sore throat—almost undistinguishable from common illnesses, the primary health care system was placed under considerable pressure.

It was shortly after Trevor Ingram's death, and with three new infections linking back to him, that Britain declared a Public Health Emergency. The circumstances, for all intents and purposes, met the four decision criteria:

1. Is the public health impact of this event potentially serious?
2. Is the event unusual or unexpected?
3. Is there the potential for international spread?
4. Is there the potential for travel and trade restrictions?

For health authorities the race was on to find the source of the outbreak. The incubation period for the Ebola virus is between two and twenty-one days but, even after extending their target range to eight weeks, it seemed unlikely that David and Trevor had met either directly or through a third party. Of the other deaths and infections, each could be traced back to them. This made two simultaneous independent common sources of the outbreak, however improbable that seemed. Although investigators were confident David and Trevor were the source, no one could determine how they contracted the virus. Neither man had recently been overseas or had contact with animals, other than each having a domestic cat. At best the WHO investigators determined that both men could be described as unremarkable; middle-class men going to work each day to pay off a mortgage and in apparently stable relationships. They had questioned the respective wives intensively, to the point of causing unwarranted and unwanted distress, over any possible extra-marital sexual activity and drug use. Nothing.

What was of interest to the investigators were the common features of both men. They were both in their early thirties, married but with no children, were teachers, and male. Frighteningly, all those thus far infected with the virus had been Caucasian males between twenty-five to thirty-five years of age.

The first reported case - that of David Carlisle, occurred in mid-September 2010; ten days later he was dead. The fifteenth and final death occurred in mid-November 2010 and with it the disease vanished as abruptly as it had started. One hundred percent of those infected had died. Only one healthcare worker, a female doctor who treated Trevor in the emergency unit, had become infected, which gave confidence that the pandemic protocols worked well. In January 2011, some forty-two days after the final reported infections, the UK was declared Ebola free.

The virus, like the African outbreak in 2009, was not one of the five known species. It was, however, a likely variant of the African strain and biologically at least it was likely that the two outbreaks, in Africa and the UK, were in some way linked. The UK outbreak belonged to what became known after the Africa outbreak, as the Zaire—AAA species. While the UK Ebola was Zaire—AAA it behaved differently in the way in which it attached itself to particular antibodies. However it was too early to say anything with any certainty. As with the African outbreak, initial testing showed traces of plant DNA.

With the outbreak over, the statisticians started to work, poring over infection rates and disease modelling. To the fore in everybody's minds was how unexpected it was that an Ebola outbreak in the UK should be independent of an African link. The review and modelling highlighted two significant conundrums.

First, with the number of people infected, one would have expected the infection rates to be much higher before the outbreak was contained. The infection patterns were not as traditional modelling suggested. Investigators expect either a steep increase in the number of people infected, followed by a gradual decline, or multiple peaks in the number of people infected. The pattern would depend upon the infection and the way the infection was transmitted. Ebola is a highly contagious person-to-person transmission; cases are expected to present over more than one incubation period and, until effective controls are put in place, one expects to see multiple peaks before a gradual decline. Health authorities knew, in truth, an outbreak of a highly infectious disease, like Ebola or Bird Flu, in the UK would be very difficult to contain quickly, but in this outbreak the pattern peaked in infections (fifteen deaths over a couple of weeks) and then nothing. The transmission stopped.

Secondly, the infection data confirmed the anecdotal picture that emerged during the outbreak; the virus targeted predominately younger Caucasian adult males. The statistical confidence rates suggested an infection pattern of mainly males was unlikely to be caused by chance. But, then again, viruses, particularly new strains, tend to have a mind of their own. The only known female casualty was the emergency triage doctor who saw Trevor when he was first admitted to hospital.

After the UK was declared Ebola free, the next virus scare came just one month later, this time in the United States, from a town called Jacksonville in Georgia. Georgia is the ninth most populous state in the United States, with approximately ten million people. Within the demographics of Georgia, nine percent of the population is Hispanic and Latino. Despite this low representation in the population, and an even lower representation in Jacksonville, within a period of three weeks, seven male Hispanics were seriously ill with H5N2, also known as Bird Flu. What had scientists baffled was the H5N2 virus had not, until then, been known to make the jump from bird-to-human, and from human-to-human transmission. Like the UK Ebola virus, H5N2 was highly unlikely to have originated from the United States, yet none of the victims could be linked to Asian travel and there were no reported cases of human H5N2 Bird Flu elsewhere in the world.

Epidemic and pandemic planning swung into effect almost immediately after the second case of H5N2 had been verified. All people leaving and entering countries around the world were subjected to body temperature checks. Such a rapid escalation of response was driven by health, security, and intelligence experts who believed there was a probable link between the UK and USA virus outbreaks, although this was not shared with the public. In both cases the specific virus was not common to the country and both predominantly targeted specific genders, ages, and ethnicities. When the emergency was over, other similarities were also confirmed. The H5N2 had not transmitted beyond the initial victims and it vanished as quickly as it began. The most telling link, however, was the presence of plant DNA in both the UK Ebola and USA H5N2.

Authorities were convinced that this was more than a health emergency and, in all likelihood, was a matter of national security. Although generally believed impossible, authorities wondered if a biological weapon had been used on the United Kingdom and the United States. If true, it was a biological weapon that could target specific genders, races, and ages. Was the fact that the transmissions stopped after the initial infections a weakness in the weapon or a demonstration of the control? With no one claiming responsibility for the attacks, the answer perhaps lay in the African Ebola outbreak. It had the presence of plant DNA but its infection behaviour was different. If a definite link was established between Africa, UK and the USA, authorities could be fairly confident that terrorists had control over the transmission. The consequence of a terrorist or organised crime group having such a weapon was too catastrophic to contemplate.

In a nondescript office of DSTL (Defence Science and Technological Laboratory) hidden deep underground in the dark recesses of Porton Down, Wiltshire, England - algorithms worked their mathematical magic, crunching and churning its daily feed. '**Data Match**' suddenly flashed up on the screen. — Key words found: *DUVAL-CLAUDE- CLIFF.*

Chapter 1

Home

Max

Life is a relentless march of time. In its wake everything is changed but still seems to remain the same. It feels like only yesterday— but also a lifetime ago— that I stood on the deck of a battleship in times of war, on the convoys to Russia, was married and raised a family. Each morning I would rise full of anticipation, in search of adventure and excitement, but complain bitterly of having no time. As years came and went life changed. I became a grandparent and then found retirement, or did retirement find me? Yet free time was still elusive. Finally when the chaos slowed, old age and frailty had become my companion and time a burden.

I had taken again to checking the newspaper each morning; a ritual of my lifetime stopped only when Olivia, my wife of 63 years, and I were first confined by our children to this nursing home. Was it a desire to be needed or a fantasy for a life now lost that caused me to peruse the paper in search of a secret message? Why after all of this time would there be one? For a short period each morning, as I scanned the papers, I was transported back to those days now long ago. In that dream my body no longer ached, my balance was steady and my mind was sharp. In that fantasy, I didn't fear the prospect of dying the slow, cruel and painful death of old age—but saw instead the resurrection of a dormant soul.

With the paper read and breakfast finished, the seconds, with great effort, became hours and soon midday would bring the second highlight of my day—lunch. I knew that I must not complain, for I was luckier than most; the love of my life was here with me. But we were prisoners, not through locks and doors, but through bodies and spirits that no longer heard or responded to the call of adventure. Nowadays, I was elated if I responded to the call of nature without a mishap, let alone responded to escapades, but I scanned the paper for a sign of adventure nonetheless.

Growing old is peculiar to the individual. For some, eighty-seven is frail, while others jump from airplanes at ninety-six. Being old is nothing more than a lottery of when venerability ends and degeneration wins. Reduced mobility, increased unsteadiness, falls, near falls, confusion, uncertainty, incontinence and social isolation... Oh, what a mouthful, made worse when the mind is sharp and you see and feel the decline.

I had always thought that it would be a gradual waning—but you're independent one day and frail the next. The swiftness exceeded my wildest expectations, unlike the gradual decline of sexual desire. We still had sex, the reduced mobility and fear of falling not yet an insurmountable barrier. The fear of falling came from sneaking to Olivia's room at night... Oh, did I neglect to say? No one expects a husband and wife to move into a nursing home together so we had adjoining rooms. Or, we would have, when Betty next door shuffled off her mortal coil. She's a tough old bird so there was no expectation of it happening any time soon. In the meantime, if the twinge of sexual desire moved my penis, the wheelie and I had to navigate the corridors. But mostly the erection came from holding on to go to the toilet. In truth, it was not sex that drew me to Olivia's room at night. I added sex in defiance, to cry out: *We oldies still do it! WE HAVE SEX!* Perhaps it was to cause offence to our children who would be revolted by the image. *OLD PEOPLE HAVING SEX!*

When you have been with someone for nearly sixty-three years there's an intrinsic security, an inner peace, which comes from sleeping together. When on my own, my thoughts and dreams were disturbed by vivid memories from a distant past, haunting the relentless minutes and hours of the night. The empty room, filled with anxiety and fear of its own choosing, a recent experience for which I had no control.

After a lifetime of playing the doddering old vicar, even as a young man, I had long since forgotten where the acting ended and the truth began. When staff members caught me and my wheelie visiting Olivia, prowling the corridors at night, it was with ease that I slid into my role. They saw only a doddering old Max and when they asked me to go back to my room I'd tell them, feigning mild confusion, 'I'm going for breakfast.'

'It's almost midnight,' Nurse Ratched replied, while gently encouraging me back to my room. While on my nightly clandestine missions I imagined all nurses as Nurse Ratched, a character from the novel One Flew Over the Cuckoo's Nest—but, in truth, most were gentle and kind, although sometimes a little impatient.

There was no rule to stop me visiting Olivia, it's just nursing home convention. The only people staff-members expect in the corridors at night are dementia guests who wander in search of lost moments, for memories that are gone again in an instant. And so they'll wander, in search of nothingness.

I didn't complain when sent back to my room but was annoyed for being sloppy and being caught. Providing I had not fallen asleep, the nightly raid on Olivia's room was my game of youth, the last vestiges of rebellion. When all went quiet, I was transported back in time, sneaking out behind enemy lines, evading the Gestapo or the Russians. It's a small consolation but, when I was discovered, it was mostly on the return journey. The evasion skills had not totally left me yet. The night-time visits were not an overnight affair—sharing a single bed in comfort, at any age, is a pleasure only enjoyed for a short time. After an hour, maybe two, I fled the scene and my memories of a wonderful past. Wheeling my way back through the corridors, time moved forward, and I reluctantly returned to the realities of the present.

I was not the only guest moving through the corridors at night. As statistics command, men die earlier than women so there are fewer men than women at these 'Hotel Royals.' Of these men, there are fewer still who are inclined to or can offer "services". An interesting observation; those providing amenities are not always the ones you expect.

One enduring myth is women don't enjoy sex in the way men do and an even greater myth: older people don't anticipate sex. Age is liberating. Sexual taboos that often accompany youth and adulthood are forgotten. Consenting desire with foreseen pleasure becomes a rightful end in itself. The sexual acts—even the sex of your partner—are irrelevant to anyone but those engaged in the play. Of all of the sex myths, one that does hold truth is that older women don't openly discuss sex in the way men do but even this is only partially true. At our Club Paradise the women had a women's only book club—secret women's business I called it. It was through the book club that the taboo of talking about sex faded away. Here under the guise of literary reviews women read passages of erotic encounters that stir the loins. Olivia sometimes read aloud to me excerpts from their latest books:

Then as he began to move, in the sudden helpless orgasm, there awoke in her new strange trills rippling inside her. Rippling, rippling, rippling, like a flapping overlapping of soft flames, soft as feathers, running to points of brilliance, exquisite, exquisite and melting her all molten inside. It was like bells rippling up and up to culmination. She lay unconscious of the wild little cries she uttered at the last. But it was over too soon, too soon, and she could no longer force her own conclusion with her own activity. This was different, different. She could do mothering. She could no longer harden and grip for her own satisfaction upon him. She could only wait, wait and moan in spirit as she felt him withdrawing, withdrawing and contracting, coming to the terrible moment when he would slip out and be gone. Whilst all her womb was open and soft, and softly clamouring, like a sea-anemone under the tide, clamouring for him to come in again and make a fulfilment for her. She clung to him unconscious in passion, and he never quite slipped from her, and she felt the soft bud of him within her stirring and strange rhythms flushing up into her with a strange rhythmic growing motion, swelling and swelling till it filled her cleaving consciousness, and then began again the unspeakable motion that was not really motion, but pure deepening whirlpools of sensation swirling deeper and deeper through all her tissue and consciousness, till she was one perfect concentric fluid of feeling, and she lay there, crying in unconscious inarticulate cries. The voice out of the uttermost night, the life! The man heard it beneath him with a kind of awe, as his life sprang out into her. And as it subsided, he subsided too and lay utterly still, unknowing, while her grip on him slowly relaxed, and she lay inert. And they both knew nothing, not even each other, both lost.

'Very raunchy, Olivia,' I proclaimed. 'I've never read *Lady Chatterley's Lover*, but I think I might enjoy this book. It's a classic!'

It was our anniversary tomorrow, not for our wedding, but it was two years since we had the pleasure of moving into this 'Club Med ... ication,' our 'La Abattoir,' for discerning men and ladies.

Our two children, Melissa and Gordon, visited today as they did on a weekly basis. Gushing, smiling, hugging and wondering why or how we cling to what must be a miserable existence. We have never wanted to live with our children. Caring for aged parents is not part of the Australian culture. Long before we came to the nursing home, and while still living in our own house, Gordon suggested we sell up and help build his new house, onto which we could build ourselves a granny flat. Better still, we could help both the children build houses and have a granny flat at each location. They said that this would help them share our care arrangements—guaranteeing a Rolls Royce of support and attention from the family. It was a compelling argument. After talking it through, Olivia and I came to the conclusion that we would prefer the company of people of a similar age and that we would move into a retirement home. I am ashamed to say we also feared that our care may not be the children's primary motivation. Although I spent the best part of my career as Minister in the Anglican Church, we, unlike many of our colleagues, were not short of money. The source of wealth, so we told the children, was a modest portfolio of shares purchased fifty years ago. Over time the shares had grown by the miracle of compounding dividend reinvestment and were now worth a tidy sum. Until two years before, we were enjoying our retirement and spending what the children believed was their inheritance. Our suspicions of the family's "care" motivations were not helped by Jane, Gordon's wife. On occasions too numerous to count she reminded us that it was our responsibility, as parents, to leave the children an inheritance. It was, and I quote, 'Irresponsible to squander money in the way you do.'

We had recently seen a film, *Mrs Caldicot's Cabbage War*. The son, following the death of his father, persuades his mother to give him power of attorney. The son then sells his mother's house, puts her into a home, and takes off with the rest of her savings. This story, despite a happy ending, did nothing to ease our harboured fears.

Chapter 2

European Odyssey

'Well that's lunch, the second highlight of my day.'

'Sometimes you complain too much Max,' Olivia replied before bidding me a good afternoon as she headed off to book club.

With Olivia gone I settled into my favourite chair for a quiet afternoon nap. With the anniversary of moving into the home only a day away, sleep did not come easily. My mind was filled with thoughts and memories of the circumstances which conspired to bring us here.

So much had changed over the last three years; we had gone from being eighty-five-years-young to eighty-seven-years-old. Before the nursing home, retirement had been fulfilling and not without the occasional derring-do adventure. Perhaps our greatest passion, especially in those early years, was riding our vintage motorbike and sidecar exploring and terrorising

Australia, the United Kingdom, Europe, and the USA. We were a sight to behold, the two old farts, the doddering old vicar astride his motorbike and his nutty wife in the sidecar, her hair flailing against the wind. Although the events that would bring us to the nursing home were yet to occur, Olivia and I recognised during our eighty-fourth year that the days of riding the bike were drawing to a close. These thoughts would align with other circumstance and so, to celebrate our eighty-fifth birthdays (we are the same age, with birthdays just one month apart), we wanted one final trip.

The dream was to ship the 1948 BSA A7 motorbike and sidecar back to the UK for an epic ride across Britain and Europe. Our swan song; the farewell ballad of Max and Olivia. We still intended to travel within Australia, but those long-haul flights were becoming difficult. This last trip would be an opportunity to say farewell to colleagues and people who had become friends over a lifetime. Some I met while serving together on clandestine missions in WW2 and others were part of Cold War activities. Most shared in the secret side of our lives as we shared in theirs and it was for these people that, each morning, I still searched the newspapers.

The planning for the odyssey happened from our Maldon home shortly after our eighty-fourth birthdays. Maldon is a small town in Victoria, Australia. It's notable for its nineteenth-century appearance arising from the gold rush days. With a population of just over a thousand, it provided an ideal hideaway where people pay little attention to your past or day-to-day activities. As I have done for most of my life, I wore a dog collar from the moment we arrived, which was some twenty years before. We took the opportunity and joined the BSA motorcycle association, which had quite a following in Western Victoria and was one of the reasons we chose Maldon for our retirement hideaway. I wore my dog collar even when riding—always with the sidecar —and wearing my leathers I played the eccentric old vicar. I displayed little mechanical aptitude for my bike, despite, in truth, being reasonably skilled. My apparent ineptitude and need to pay for repairs was a notoriety I was pleased to wear. Olivia's favourite line was, 'Oh, if something breaks, I call for a man,' despite both of us being far more competent than we made out.

The odyssey was to take us from London to Cornwall and then up to Scotland, visiting secret places from WW2 and the Cold War on the way. From the UK, we would travel to Brittany and, after a detour through Paris, on to Holland. From there we'd make our way to Poland and Walbrzych near the border of the Czech Republic. Leaving Poland, the plan would be to travel through the Czech Republic, en-route to Germany. Then, from Germany, we would cross the Alps into Switzerland, before the autumn snows, travel through to France and finally end in Spain. This was a daunting enough trip for persons of any age, let alone two octogenarians with a 1948 motorbike and sidecar. It was during the planning for this trip that our children first mentioned the need for a power of attorney. *What happens*, they said, *if you are ill while away, or you have an accident? Who will make decisions on your behalf, take care of things back in Australia, or even get you back to Australia?*

The motorbike and sidecar was packed carefully in a crate and travelled to the UK by cargo ship. It cleared Customs and the forwarding agent had it waiting at Heathrow airport the day of our arrival. I still remember it clearly—Olivia's eighty-fifth birthday.

To help us recover from the long haul flight we normally spent one night at Heathrow. This time, however, two nights were in order; the privilege—or is it consequence?—of age. We chose our much-loved hotel, the Renaissance on Bath Road, a favourite because we liked the name. Renaissance: a revival; a definition that summed up our dreams perfectly.

The early part of the European odyssey was a reminiscence for another time. My memories were drawn to that time six weeks into the trip. We had spent four days exploring a network of secret tunnels buried deep within the mountains on the border with the Czech Republic. Locating the Janus Key was the true purpose of our trip and a matter of national security. The search had taken longer than we expected and we wondered, at the time, if our information was wrong. Seeing the Janus Key again, which had lain undisturbed for nearly sixty-three years caused an uneasy feeling which swept through us both. Holding it once more brought back the memories of travelling to Russia on

Convoy JW59, retrieving the key from a brothel in Murmansk and taking it back to the UK and our headquarters in the village of Cliff where it remained until 1945. With the war nearing the end, a decision was made to hide the Janus Key. I, myself, hadn't hidden it in the tunnels near Walbrzych from where we retrieved it, but I had been entrusted with the names of two people, each of whom knew one piece of information. The combination of these two fragments led us to the key's location. As guardians, Olivia and I understood the secret of the key—what it could do and why it should remain hidden until called for.

Leaving the tunnels, our plan had been to cross into the Czech Republic and on to Prague, a 207 kilometre journey, to meet a contact waiting to take delivery of the item. Ever since arriving in Walbrzych though, we'd had a suspicion of being followed. This was confirmed on our second day when the same black Mercedes Benz followed us out into the countryside. It was not difficult to lose the tail but we knew we needed to be extra careful.

Having retrieved the Janus Key from the tunnel, rather than heading into Prague, we detoured back to Walbrzych and manoeuvred through the narrow laneways, courtyards and tight spaces until we were confident we were not being tracked. I stopped briefly for Olivia to scramble out of the sidecar. I then continued my circuit of the back streets of Walbrzych. Olivia, remaining vigilant to evade any unwanted company, made her way to the post office, sending the Janus Key, once again, en-route to a small and nondescript cottage in Cliff, Cornwall, courtesy of the mail service. I picked her up in a quiet street, confident we had been unseen. After the safe disposal of the package, we stopped for a coffee before starting the ride to Prague.

I remember it as if it were yesterday. It happened just outside of Walbrzych. How, I don't know. We'd had no signs of being followed and we hadn't seen any vehicles. Without warning the left wheel of the sidecar came loose and, a split second later, the left-front fork of the bike gave way, sending it and sidecar cartwheeling down the road. With each impact the bike and sidecar, now separate missiles, flew back towards the heavens before coming to rest. Plywood and metal scattered across the scene like seeds blown in the wind while Olivia lay injured and unconscious in what was left of the sidecar. Ten metres away, my body remained motionless in the vegetation. Although I have no recollection of the event, it was reported that I somersaulted over the handlebars, slid across the gravel and then tumbled down the road. It was a catastrophic accident for anyone but particularly for people our age.

We learnt later that, despite the accident occurring on a major road, it was some time before we were discovered and help arrived. Amazingly, other accidents had closed the highway in front of and behind our crash site. If it were not for the distinctive motorbike and sidecar, it may have proved more difficult for the authorities to identify us. All of our possessions—passports, money, clothes, even the number plates from the bike—everything was missing, presumed stolen. Twenty-four hours of investigation drew a blank. Police are reluctant to make identification appeals to the public because of the distress caused to family members by discovering, through the media, that something tragic has befallen a loved one. It was with hesitation that the police made an appeal to the public for any information about Olivia and myself, which would help identify the elderly couple travelling by vintage motorbike who had been involved in a serious accident. The calls flooded in and the story of us, the eighty-five-year-old husband and wife riding across Europe, went viral. If the coincidence of two separate accidents on the same stretch of road with a third—ours—in the middle raised suspicion of a coordinated strategy against us, our age quickly dispelled such thoughts.

It was many months later, when we were back in Australia, that our contacts in Cliff told us of Inspector Axel and his investigation.

Inspector Axel of Interpol had been delayed for over an hour by an overturned vehicle which blocked the road in both directions while he travelled on DK35 from Prague to Walbrzych. When the road was again open, he was surprised to see what appeared to be the police clearing the site of another accident some two kilometres further on. Then, a further kilometre up the road, was another overturned vehicle.

It was the following day, and now back in Lyon, when Inspector Axel first saw the news report of the accident involving an elderly couple—apparently riding through Poland on a 1948 motorbike and sidecar.

Due to the terrain, the rescue helicopter has been forced to land at the Hotel Eden to evacuate the yet to be identified accident victims, he learned from the news reports.

Inspector Axel recalled seeing the Hotel Eden while waiting for DK35 to be opened. He remembered because Eden was not a name that would ordinarily be associated with Poland.

The news report concluded by asking anybody who knew the identities of an elderly couple riding a black 1948 BSA A7 sidecar to contact Polish authorities. He had thought this strange. It wasn't the accident that sparked his interest, but the call to help identify the couple. *Why didn't they know who they were? Where was their identification?*

Three accidents, a road blocked in both directions and an anonymous couple. When taken together the events were an unlikely coincidence, Inspector Axel had reasoned. Why go to such lengths to target an eighty-five-year-old couple? The circumstances, he had believed, warranted at least a cursory glance.

When police need to make inquires across multiple countries, Interpol is the agency to which they turn. It was fortuitous that the request made by Polish authorities to assist in the identification of motorbike accident victims went to Inspector Axel.

Identifying us hadn't taken long. The public appeal for assistance generated substantial leads and within twenty-four hours Inspector Axel had contacted Jane in Australia and she had positively identified the motorbike. Generally this is where his involvement should have ended, but, after detailing his suspicions to his superiors, it was agreed that he should make further inquiries.

Inspector Axel spent the next two weeks examining credit card and mobile phone data to help unravel our movements across Europe. Because people are creatures of habit, generally daily movements and even purchases can be predicted with a high degree of certainty. Credit card companies employ algorithms and data mining techniques to identify variations from the holders' established parameters. In plain English, they are looking for variations of routine. These deviations may indicate fraud or a marketing opportunity due to changed circumstances. Amazon famously sent a young lady maternity advertising before she knew she was pregnant. Her regular purchase of ladies' sanitary items had stopped and Amazon rightly predicted this change was due to pregnancy. Mobile phones switch to the nearest telecommunication tower as people travel, and this information is recorded and kept by the provider, offering a visual representation of a person's movements. In an average week these are remarkably consistent and repetitive.

They travel the same way to work, have one or two favourite coffee shops and visit the same friends and locations. If web browsing is included, in combination with phone and banking transitions data, the predictive capacity is impressive. Before going on holiday people explore various options on the web, purchase airline tickets, hotel reservations and hire the car, all on their credit card. Once on holiday the mobile phone and credit card record the route travelled. There are predictable patterns and routines for people on holiday. For example, when tourists stop in a town, their mobile phones will generally show travel to and from major tourist sites within the vicinity. The digital picture expected is a *cloverleaf* as people travel out to sites then back to the hotel, rather than the linear travel lines of our daily routine to and from work. Unpacking the digital story, for an experienced investigator, is to understand the 'why'. Is the footprint consistent with the story? If not, why not?

One of the first things Inspector Axel established about us was that we almost always purchased petrol on the credit card. Sometimes we purchased fuel two or three times a day, these purchases following the mobile phone footprint. What really piqued his interest was something a less experienced detective may have missed; on three separate occasions fuel was purchased following a number of days where, according to our mobile phone records, we stayed in range of a single transmitter. The first such occurrence was in Brest, the second in Antwerp, and finally in Walbrzych. Such departures are easily explained, but it was a variation from routine. *Is it possible they were trying to hide their digital footprint?* Inspector Axel had written in his final report. It was our stay in Walbrzych that convinced the Inspector that all was not as it seemed. Our mobile phones had been stationary and our credit cards unused for long periods of each day. Yet, most evenings the motorbike was filled with petrol—a pattern repeated four days in a row. He concluded, rightly, that we had been riding somewhere and choosing to leave phones and credit cards behind. Such caution, he reported, seemed strange. However, because we had been travelling by vintage motorbike and sidecar, he believed we would have been memorable to people we passed. It would take only good old-fashioned police work—talking to people—to unravel our movements.

The serious accident, coupled with the image of me, Max—a doddering old vicar riding with his wife of over sixty years—captured the hearts and imaginations of the public; the media loved it. Social media became awash with reports, personal accounts and sightings of us. The romantic images of the trip, a trip brought to a tragic end, made us instant heroes. People wrote to the newspapers, posted on Facebook, tweeted and blogged any sightings and personal encounters with us, the two old farts, as we came to be known.

By applying a degree of healthy scepticism to media reports, a bit of guesswork and by cross-referencing the accounts with digital records, Inspector Axel pieced together our journey to Walbrzych. He had hoped either to confirm or dispel his hunch that we travelled to locations outside of Brest, Antwerp and Walbrzych when mobile phone records had us staying put. He was pleased and disappointed. No sightings from the surroundings of Antwerp or Walbrzych, but we had been seen in Lannilis and Landeda, some thirty kilometres from Brest. These reports served only to increase his suspicions as notes in his diary revealed. *The more I think about it, the more I reconciled myself to seeing shadows. Was I like all the others? Romanticising the tale, but going even further and adding secrecy, mystery, and intrigue?* As he was an experienced investigator, we can only guess that he tried to dismiss the conspiracy but found himself drawn even closer to the story.

To satisfy himself once and for all, Inspector Axel had examined the police reports for a week either side of our visit to Brest. He focused on a ten-kilometre radius around Lannilis and Landeda. Unfortunately, two days after we left Brest, eighty-seven-year-old Mr Pierre Gicquel of Lannili drowned in the estuary of Aber Wrac'h. Mr Gicquel, according to the local papers he read, had been a leading figure in the French Resistance during the WW2, risking his life on clandestine operations helping allied service personnel escape to England from the beaches nearby. The article concluded that his death was being treated as a tragic accident.

Inspector Axel, perhaps because he didn't believe in coincidences, became certain that our visit to Lannilis and the drowning of Pierre Gicquel, were in some way connected. If true, he later said, it was also likely that the three crashes near Walbrzych were not accidents and the theft of our possessions meant someone had been seeking something. His final report contained handwritten notes showing his thinking during the investigation. *What were Max and Olivia doing in Walbrzych? Where did they go each day? Were they searching for something? Did they find it? Did the thieves get it? What was it? Was Pierre Gicquel killed for it? Is this somehow connected with the war?*

Most police, unlike the way they're portrayed in the movies, are happy to share information. The Polish and French authorities had listened with interest to Inspector Axel's story and were swayed to expand their investigation into the accidents and death. If inadvertently you investigate a person or persons of interest to one of the spy, security forces, undercover, or specialist police units, a call is quickly received. The Agency at Cliff ensured all was quiet. Requests for information, military records, banking, and credit history were sent with no hindrance. No one of significance appeared interested in either Olivia or me. My Ministry of Defence (MOD) service record had no links to Special Forces, SOE, SIS, or MI9; nothing out of the ordinary or remotely secret. As far as Inspector Axel could tell, my Coastal Forces vessel, ML 243, was not linked to clandestine sea operations to Brittany. Olivia's military service was, as reported in the media, as a pay clerk. He did write however, *because*

Olivia and Max were stationed in different parts of the UK, it is difficult to see how they met during the war. But he added, *that did not account for holidays, leave, mutual friends, and many other explanations.*

Having drawn a blank on us, Max and Olivia, Inspector Axel delved into Mr Gicquel's past. His wartime involvement with the French Resistance was well documented and, after the war, he was decorated for services to the Free French. The remainder of his life, from a media or authorities' perspective, was uneventful. He had no contact with police, was a life member of some local community groups and there was nothing suspicious or unusual in his finances. However, the night before we were seen in Lannilis, Mr Gicquel received a phone call from Brest originating from a public phone booth. CCTV footage of the booth was inconclusive, *it appears the caller was trying to hide his or her identity from the cameras,* he reported. Further examination of phone records uncovered another payphone call—this time two weeks earlier—from the UK, but no CCTV footage.

In his personal diary and not included in the official report, Inspector Axel wrote that he *felt confident Max, Olivia, and Mr Gicquel knew or knew of each other. If a betting man, I would lay money that they met in WW2. The drowning was most probably not an accident and, while I do not suspect Max and Olivia of murder, I feel the death was probably a result of the visit.*

With no new information, and us now back in Australia, his suspicions were insufficient to warrant re-interviewing. One year after the accident, the file was closed. The Coroner determined Mr Pierre Gicquel's death a tragic accident. The loss of Pierre Gicquel must have weighed heavily on inspector's conscience. *'I should have done more,'* was the last entry of his personal diary.

Chapter 3

Sentenced

I must have drifted off into a deep sleep at this stage in my remembering, because, with a sudden jerk, I woke to find that I had been dribbling.

'Hello Max,' said one of the nurses, while wiping away the saliva that had accumulated on my chin.' She was slightly blurred as seen through my half open eyes still heavy with sleep.

'I didn't mean to startle you, dear,' she continued. 'You go back to sleep now.' With those words she slipped quietly away leaving me in my chair.

I had been dreaming of our European trip, the motorbike crash and the murder of Pierre. This was not the first time the memories from the past had visited to haunt my sleep; it had become an unwelcome feature of my long nights alone. It was an unusual occurrence for my daytime naps, however.

Having been awoken, it felt as though I had been sleeping for hours but, looking at my watch, I saw only fifteen minutes had passed. *Another fifteen minutes, I thought, then I will get up, before Olivia returns from book club and accuses me of trying to sleep away what remains of my life.* Closing my eyes, I relaxed once more, settling back into my favourite chair.

A vague reminiscence from the Prague hospital was my first memory after the accident.

The beginnings of coherent recollections didn't start until I woke in a London hospital after being medevaced from Poland. It was three weeks later when the police, on behalf of the Polish authorities, who had been unable to interview us due to our injuries, came to take our statements. We both genuinely have no recollection of the accident so telling the truth was easy. For the rest, we told of our travels but confused times, places, and sequences. Interviewed separately, our plan was to continually accuse the other of 'Senior Moments.'

'Olivia forgets things. Yesterday, she went to buy a bottle of wine to have with dinner, but she became lost. Couldn't find her way back to the hotel. It's happened before. A couple of times she has even gone into the wrong hotel room, when she forgot our room number. Well that's what she told me. From now on, when she goes out on her own, I'm going to put a sign around her neck, like Paddington Bear. If found, return to…!'

The policeman smiled knowingly.

'Yesterday Olivia was here, in hospital.'

'Yes,' I said, 'we were both in hospital; we have been here about four weeks.'

After what seemed an eternity—two months in hospital, and then two months in rehabilitation—medical clearance was given to travel home to Australia. But, before leaving, a call had to be made to headquarters in Cliff using a public phone box.

'Can I speak to Robin?'

'She's not here.'

'I want to speak to her brother, Robin.'

The password satisfied, we learned of Pierre Gicquel's death and, because of the accident, we assumed Pierre told his killers what he knew before he died. A good man and a trusted friend, we prayed his death was quick and painless. He knew only the name of the town near where the package, the "Janus Key", was hidden—it was our contact near Antwerp who knew the actual hiding place but not the town. Neither bit of information was of use without the other. The would-be assassins had to wait for us to recover the key, but their attempt to steal it had failed.

Our departure from London caused a flurry of excitement and, at the airport, the media and well-wishers gathered to bid a warm farewell. We were deeply moved, if not a little embarrassed, by the outpouring of affection. Twenty-one weeks ago, aged eighty-five, we had arrived at Heathrow to embark upon an epic journey to retrieve the Janus Key. We were still eighty-five, but we were no longer the same people. The trip and the accident had taken a heavy toll; our bodies were damaged and struggling to recover. Perhaps they never would but, worse than that, with the death of friends, our spirit was broken.

The flight from London to Australia was long and in my opinion had become longer, proportional to our age. Our arrival in Melbourne was a total contrast to our departure from London. Our welcome committee consisted of two: Gordon and his piranha wife, Jane. Although it was four months since the accident, our health and mobility were still seriously affected. With neither of us able to drive, it was decided we should stay with Gordon and Jane for a month before returning to our home in Maldon.

Before the end of the first week, to our dismay, a letter arrived. Some anonymous person recommended to the police that we have our drivers' licences cancelled. According to the letter from Vic Roads, we were to undertake a medical assessment, the result of which would determine if a driving test was required before our licences could be reinstated. Jane had us booked in for both the licence test and the medical assessment almost before we finished reading the letter. The result was a forgone conclusion: 'Full driving assessment required.' It was decided by the family that we should await the outcome of the driving test before returning to Maldon. Despite us being angry with Jane for writing to the police—for who else could it be?— it would be difficult in Maldon without a car or family to help us. The driving test was scheduled for three weeks hence.

Melissa came to dinner the second week of our return to Australia. Gordon, Jane and Melissa all explained the difficulties they faced as a family after the accident. With no power of attorney they had been unable to make important decisions, medical or financial, to help us. The travel insurance company wouldn't talk to them and this meant they had funded the first month of our hospital care themselves. What made them really annoyed, however, was that they had spoken to us about this very thing before we left on what they called an absolutely ridiculous trip.

'It would be in everybody's interest if you give joint power of attorney to all three of us. Before any decision can be made on your behalf, all three of us would have to agree. And anyway,' said Jane, 'we'd only exercise the authority in emergencies.'

We signed ... it was the worst decision of our lives.

Since moving in with Gordon and Jane we were reminded with regular frequency of our frailty. This assault on our confidence increased from Jane in the lead up to the driving test. Helping around the house or garden was prohibited. Outings such as shopping were permitted but punctuated by regular stops so we can "rest". Walking sticks must be used in case of falls. Our morning greeting went something like this:

'You're looking very pale, are you feeling okay? I think you should take it easy today.'

Even knowing that Jane was deliberately trying to erode our confidence and wellbeing it was surprising how quickly we succumbed. It's easy to be waited on, particularly when not allowed to do things yourself. Help for us, however, came only if we played helpless.

My description of Jane as a piranha is neither kind nor generous; it illustrates a total and utter lack of regard for piranhas. Piranhas scavenge on dead carcasses; Jane excels in eating live meat. Many years ago I nominated Gordon for an Order of Australia Award for being married to Jane. The application was rejected; Olivia said the assessment committee probably believed it was a bogus nomination. I disagreed; it was rejected on the grounds of category. Instead of the Order of Australia, I should have applied for a bravery award.

Our wellbeing was nearing its lowest point when Jane, with glee, took us to the driving test in Moonee Ponds, a suburb in Melbourne, famous because it's the home of Dame Edna and her gladioli. An automatic car was to be used for the test although we always drove manual cars.

'There's something special about changing gears; real driving,' Olivia used to say.

With us not having fully recovered from the accident, driving an automatic was the best and only chance to pass. Living in Maldon, with a population of one thousand, but taking the test in the capital city, made the task of passing a hundred times more challenging than it would have been in Castlemaine.

Castlemaine was the main regional centre near Maldon and usually where driving tests were conducted. We were far more familiar with Castlemaine than with Moonee Ponds but knew that there was absolutely no chance of Jane taking us there. A test in Melbourne was the only offer and, if we were to escape, pass we must, and pass we would. *At least one of us.*

The day started well; the weather was fine and the test time was a perfect nine-fourteen in the morning. Peak hour traffic was over and the lunchtime rush yet to start. Driving test thus far: Max and Olivia one, Jane zero. The day became even better once I successfully lowered myself into the driving seat of the little Subaru Impreza in which I was to take the test. After a brief car familiarisation we were set to go. I remembered to put the seatbelt on, always a plus. Foot on the brake, start the engine. No problems. D for drive. Mirrors. Indicate. Head check. Move off from the curb. Bugger, no indicators. The windscreen wipers moved instead, a mistake explained by our always owning European cars where the indicators are on the left. The driving assessor didn't appear fazed in the least.

'European car,' she said.

I smiled my acknowledgment, engaged the indicator, and switched off the windscreen wipers.

Tremors of apprehension caused my heart to race; you have to be a human date-and-time clock with radar eyes to drive in Melbourne. It's a hostile environment but don't be confused, this is not because of vehicle and pedestrians. Melbourne is a city of continual speed zone changes. Some are permanent, 50 kph on roads unless otherwise indicated; while others are dependent upon the day, date, and time. School Zones for example are 40 kph from 8.00 am until 9.30 am, and after 9.30 you drive at whatever speed the road was before the school zone sign. That is, of course, except on school holidays or weekends when the school zone speeds don't apply. Some shopping strips also have time related speed zones, which, to increase confusion, are not the same speed as the school zones. To know the correct speed you must read the small print under the sign. This sort of works well when familiar with the road but is an impossible nightmare when navigating a road for the first time. To maximize every possible chance to raise revenue by catching unsuspecting speeding drivers, the government adds seven speed zone changes in five hundred metres. Finally, to record the trip for prosperity, mobile speed cameras, which allow a three kph error, are waiting to snap your picture and issue the fine. An expensive photograph I hear you say. No. If you want the photograph of your recklessness you must pay extra.

It's a delicate balance: driving with caution making sure you exceed none of the variable speed limits and driving with confidence, so as not cause mayhem from being too slow. As time passed, we navigated the quieter streets, two school zones and a shopping strip. I felt my confidence grow and my old self return. Driving became enjoyable again and, in that moment, that split second in time, I relaxed; a sensation not felt since returning to Australia. I even started a conversation with my assessor.

We moved from back streets onto a major road with two lanes used by trucks but not trams. Again, all good. To add another level of complication for the unsuspecting country driver, when driving in Melbourne, some streets are shared by cars, trucks, trams and push bikes. The shared car and push bike lane can, at certain times, be used for parking cars, requiring push bikes and trucks to travel on the tram line, while also keeping clear of trams. But the gods had smiled and Jane's pact with the devil had fallen on deaf horns, as this was not a challenge that fazed me.

'Turn right at the traffic lights please sir,' said the assessor.

It is not a difficult manoeuvre, although a little more warning would have been appreciated. The move was from the left lane to the right lane and then finally into the turning lane, all before reaching the traffic lights. Traffic was not heavy but it was consistent. My pulse rate climbed; some anxiety is good and it takes my concentration to a hundred percent. I contemplated the move. Mirrors. Indicate. Head check (indicate for a minimum of two seconds). Truck, but safe gap. Merge over while maintaining progress. Mirror. Check indicator is off. The traffic lights turned red as I prepared to move into the turning lane. Mirrors. Truck behind. Second gear—*SHIT!* As I thrust my left foot to where the clutch should be, I hit the brake pedal with considerable force. The car nosedived to an instant stop. The truck had closed in behind the car—more than it should; it had no chance of stopping and slammed into the rear. My foot now firmly planted on the brake pedal, a David and Goliath battle that lasted but a fraction of a second, we were concertinaed into the car in front. A symphony of smashing glass, crushing panels and airbags followed. We were surprisingly unhurt except for pride.

'I take it that's a fail,' I said sheepishly.

The assessor was not amused.

The crash kept the local papers and current affairs programs entertained for days. Archive footage of the accident in Europe and pictures from Moonee Ponds accompany sensationalised headlines: 'The danger of old drivers.' 'Keep our roads safe.' 'Over 70—not fit to drive.'

The local tabloid ran a series of articles recommending everything from compulsory driving tests for those seventy years and over, to banning older people from the road altogether. One article by a medical boffin suggested brain deterioration in older drivers makes them a danger to all other road users. Road safety experts produced pretty graphs with complex tables to prove the point. What's really amusing however, following the Global Financial Crisis, countries around the world, including Australia, are progressively lifting the retirement age to seventy and beyond. The expectation is for people to work well into their seventies. 'Don't discriminate against older workers' has even become a TV ad campaign run by the Australian government. A beautiful irony. We want you to work and be independent of the pension, lifters not leaners, but you can't drive because you're brain dead, a danger to society.

After my failed test, Olivia declined her driving assessment and expectations of moving back to Maldon slowly diminished. After overhearing Jane's interview with a local tabloid, the fight rekindled in our bellies.

'They are not safe to be on their own,' she said.

It was two, maybe three, days after the driving incident when we hatched, as Baldrick from *Blackadder* would say, our 'Cunning Plan.' The plan was brilliant in its simplicity: annoy Jane into demanding we leave. To make life in her home unbearable, we would become the teenagers or hotel guests from hell. And so we did.

Unbeknown to us at the time, our behaviour only succeeded in a hastened secret family meeting. Secret from us, that is. The unholy trinity, Gordon, Jane and Melissa, unanimously agreed that we were incapable of living on our own. Gordon, much later, perhaps in a moment of guilt, recalled what transpired at the meeting.

'They are incapable of making rational decisions; I can give you plenty of examples of their deteriorating mental state, lapses in memory and unacceptable social behaviour,' Jane had said.

'Despite repeated reminders, they leave all of the lights on. They used blow heaters in their room and put the central heating on during the day. Can you imagine our power bill? They complain there's nothing to eat and they are bored. It's like having children in the house. On one night we came home to find them watching TV naked. Naked, can you imagine the sight, bodies like old prunes. Mum could have tucked her breasts into her socks, if she was wearing any. I'm still traumatised. Worse, we were expecting a guest, my boss. The evening had to be cancelled. They're losing their minds. There's nothing for it, they need care.'

The best solution, agreed the trinity, was a nursing home. The house would have to be sold to pay for it—but in secret.

'There's no other way,' said Melissa. 'The house must go. They can't know until it's sold; if they do, they are just as likely to run naked down the street screaming obscenities.'

'We also need to take control of the bank accounts, to pay for the retirement home, the rest can be equally shared between us, so we can visit and give them the best care,' suggested Jane.

According to their plan, we were to remain with Gordon and Jane until the house was sold. Being the kind, caring and considerate family they are, (I say this with some sarcasm) all agreed the plan was in our best interests. Using their power of attorney, the house was put up for sale and most of our money secretly transferred to new accounts—accounts controlled by them. The price asked for our home was a bargain; it was sold within two weeks.

The next family meeting did include us. Summoned, like convicted prisoners being led to the dock, we were seated solemnly at the kitchen table. The tense silence was cut by Jane who, without pausing for breath, declared our home had been sold and settlement was to be in three weeks. We were speechless and the surprises continued to leave us shocked and dismayed.

'You will be moving to a retirement facility and we will manage your money,' they said.

Graciously or begrudgingly, I'm unsure which, a weekly allowance was to be given for what Jane described as 'those little things, bits you require at the facility.' Most of our savings, including the proceeds from the sale of the house, was needed to pay for our care—or so they said.

'The only suitable nursing facility,' said Melissa, 'is an hour and half's drive away.'

Sentence pronounced, we left the dock not knowing if our prison was a retirement village or nursing home. They were to visit once a week; was this a promise or threat? But the truly frightening part: we were to leave on Monday 16 March—in only five days' time.

It's difficult to describe the range of emotions: numbness, despair and, finally, wretched acknowledgement of the inevitable surrendering of independence. It's not that moving into a retirement village or nursing home was necessarily the bad thing; it was the alarming realisation and unavoidable acceptance of our one-way journey. The final episode of life had begun with death at its end. In this new identity, nursing home resident, the uniqueness of contribution, adventures enjoyed and individual distinctiveness would be forgotten.

As with our parents before, we were destined to be remembered as old people in a home, a burden, an annoyance for a family compelled to visit once a week.

We felt bitterly betrayed, not only because our family believed we needed care, for in many ways they were right, but because of their misuse of their power of attorney to strip away assets and make decisions that didn't involve us. I will grant you one thing, they knew us well. We had no intention of leaving large sums of money to them and had planned to give it away progressively to charities and causes we cared about. Alas, too late, the money was theirs.

'Well, that worked well,' Olivia had said. 'Rather than annoying them into sending us home, there's no home! Max are you listening to me?'

My attention was drawn to the conversation but, still in deep contemplation, I'd replied, 'You are right, this has not turned out well.'

'Not turned out well? It's a bloody disaster, excuse the French.'

'There's nothing we can do at the moment. I've logged into the bank accounts and most of our money has gone. As they said, they have control of the finances. Perhaps we will be paid the allowance they promised. Our biggest problem, however, is to persuade them to take us back to our old home before settlement. Everything can go, the home the furniture the cars, but we must get the Box. Under no circumstances can anybody else find it.'

That evening, after the family meeting, we joined Gordon and Jane for dinner. Melissa, by this time, had gone and Penny, Gordon's and Jane's daughter, dropped in for the meal. Despite the day's events, Olivia and I agreed to be on our best behaviour; a departure from our recent conduct; often we were 'naughty' when Penny visited because we knew she quite enjoyed seeing her mother becoming flustered and angry as our mischief caused annoyance.

'You are right,' I said, seated at the dinner table. 'We are not the same after the accident, sadly and slowly we are coming to terms with being frail. A retirement village is perhaps best.'

'A nursing home,' interjected Jane.

'A nursing home,' I continued. 'It would help, moving into the facility, if we could say one final goodbye to our old home and its memories. To see it, just one more time.'

Perhaps it was the tone in my voice, the tear in my eye, or just that Jane had had her victory. For a second I thought she would agree, but sadly I was mistaken and with no energy left to fight, my eyes met Penny's.

We have two grandchildren, both now grown up. Simon is twenty-eight and Penny is twenty-three years of age. Like many grandparents we are blessed with a special relationship, aided I think, because their mother is such a dragon. It is wrong to rank bonds but, of the two, Penny is closest and dearest. She is bright, alert, considerate and the child we dreamed Jane of being when she married our son. From quite an early age, both Olivia and I believe she saw behind our façade, giving knowing smiles as if to say, *you're not what you seem.* She never said anything or asked any probing questions; it was just an air of understanding.

After dinner with Gordon and Jane, I spoke briefly and quietly to Penny in the kitchen. 'It's imperative and urgent that you come and see us tomorrow when Gordon and Jane are at work.'

Penny nodded in her knowing way and with a smile said, 'Ten o'clock?'

Penny arrived as agreed and seated around the kitchen table she, with a sigh, conveyed her disbelief and disappointment at what her parents were doing.

'We need your help,' I said. 'At our house in Maldon there's a package we hid many years ago. We would like you to retrieve it for us.'

'A package? That sounds very secret.'

'Secret is a good description. It's hidden in a concealed compartment built into the bookcase. You know the one; the bookcase against the back wall in the library. On the fourth shelf from the floor you will see a book called *Ruminations of a Rambling Idiot*. Directly above this book, on the next shelf, is a book with a plain spine. Pull the book from the top and it will open a compartment built into the bottom of the bookcase. In the compartment you will find a metal cash box. We need that cash box.'

'Will you tell me what's in the box?'

'Penny, we would like to, but it will only lead to more questions, questions we are not ready to answer. I promise you this, we will tell you everything. One day, one day soon. There's something else. You must keep the cash box safe until we move into the retirement village. Sorry, I mean nursing home. Don't bring it here.'

My dream flashes forward to the first Saturday in the home, when Penny came to visit. I see her telling Olivia and myself the story of searching the house, looking for the cash box. It was as vivid and clear as though it were yesterday.

'I think it was more than two years ago when I last went to your house. Sometime before you left for Europe,' said Penny. 'Seeing the house again brought it all back. All that time I spent with you and Gran seems just a heartbeat ago.

'Other old stately manors I've visited have been cold and uninviting, but your place was always warm and welcoming. A real home.'

Penny talked of a happy childhood, but Olivia and I knew she had not been particularly close to her mother and, during some of those difficult times, the growing pains, she had found comfort with us. It was in Maldon that she was able to play with old cars and motorbikes and experienced a freedom not found in Moonee Ponds. Many city kids found country towns boring but not Penny; Maldon had always been a blank canvas, full of adventure and opportunities.

In later life, Penny had often said, 'There was something exciting about staying with you, Gran and Pops.'

I think, in many ways, she knew that we had helped her find her way in life but what she may not have known was that she had given us love and with it renewed interest in life.

'The spare key was under the flower pot, where it's always been,' I recalled Penny saying. 'When I got the door open I was struck by the smell. It always used to smell sweet and homely but, this time, it was different; all smelling of damp and mildew. It felt sad, as if the house missed you.

'If I had not always felt safe in this place, I might have turned and gone out, but I knew you needed the box, so I went on. "*It's me,*" I said, just to make sure the house knew me. Maybe I imagined it, but I thought the sun just peeked out from behind a cloud to shine through the side windows. Things both looked and smelled better after that but it was still sad to know you'd never be there again.

'Following your instructions I went to the library. Seeing it again, it was not the romantic image of a grand library from a British castle or *Beauty and the Beast* that I remember, but it was an impressive collection of books nonetheless. The burgundy chesterfield was still near the open fireplace and I remembered sitting there reading with you two. We used to *save the world*, discussing everything from football to euthanasia.

'Looking for *Ruminations of a Rambling Idiot* was more challenging than I expected. A large title on a relatively small book spine meant the text didn't stand out easily from the other books but there, as you described, I found it. I reached for the book above and the secret compartment swung open.

'I knelt and looked inside and found the black cash box against the back wall. I tugged at the handle but it was locked.'

Penny later confessed to thinking that there must have been a key for the box hidden somewhere in the house. Even though we had not asked her to look for it, with all day to spare, she thought; *why not search for the key.*

She said, 'Going through the drawers and papers proved quite an adventure and I found a lifetime of stories and memories. It was interesting to see photos of you on your wedding day, with children and then as old people. It really got to me. I couldn't help thinking that soon you will be gone and I must spend as much time with you as I can. It also made me consider my own mortality and purpose in the world. I didn't find the key. But then I thought, *where is the last place you would consider looking for the key?* Near the cash box itself! I went back to the secret compartment and felt inside. Nothing. I used the torch I had to tap the rear wall of the compartment and heard a hollow sound. After I gave it another tap, the false back fell away and there was the key.'

'Max!' From a distance I heard my name being called; at first it was a soft 'Max,' like a word drifting in the breeze but, like an approaching train, it became steadily louder and louder.

'Max, Max. Wake up Max. Have you been asleep the whole time I've been at book club?' Without waiting for a response Olivia added, 'Don't you come complaining to me tonight that you can't sleep, not when you've spent an idle day sleeping and dribbling in that chair. It's not good and very bad for your brain.' Softening her tone she added, 'Come on, let's do a crossword together. I can tell you all about the new book we are reading. And no, it's not saucy.'

Olivia, as she did most afternoons, kept me occupied until dinner, after which I would retire to her room for a night cap before making my way to my own sleeping quarters, perhaps around 11.00pm. This was a late night for those in our resort… Or "Last-Resort", as I preferred to call it.

'Max, what would you like for dinner?' asked one of the kitchen staff, who had arrived at our table and was ready to take our order.

'For an entrée, perhaps your Mousserons de la Saint-Georges and then…' I paused as if to consider the choices. 'The Bœuf de Patagonie and to finish, Chocolat noir Guanaja.

'Perhaps,' I continued, 'the chef would match the wines to the meal. That would be truly appreciated.'

'He's in one of his funny moods again, is he?' said the patient kitchen hand to Olivia, ignoring my humour totally.

'If only it was funny, ha-ha,' replied Olivia. 'The burgundy pie for him, with the mashed potatoes, but no dessert.'

It was an uneventful dinner like the evening that followed and at about 10.30pm I made my way from Olivia's room back to my penthouse suite for another sleep disturbed night. It was gone midnight by the time I had struggled out of my clothes and found the sheets, my companions for the next seven hours.

The minutes ticked unhurriedly by while I lay on my back and stared inertly up into the stillness of the ceiling.

I remembered the Monday, the day we left to come into care.

With some sense of urgency, I saw Gordon and Jane bundle us into the car for the 110 kilometre drive to the facility, Bellbird Village. Arriving at the "village", Jane and Gordon took our arms, talking in loud voices as if they were deaf, and escorted us into the front foyer of the building where we were greeted by the Director of Nursing. To my surprise it was a new, modern and quite impressive facility. The astonishment was not so much about Bellbird Village, but that the family had chosen a nice place with our money.

'Good morning, I'm Jane, this is my husband Gordon and this is Max and Olivia who are moving into this beautiful facility.'

'Welcome,' said the Director of Nursing. 'I hope you had an easy drive and thank you for complimenting us on our home.

Max and Olivia's new home!' The word *home* was said with emphasis.

I smiled gleefully back at the nurse, knowing that she had been giving Jane a polite rebuke for calling our new home *a facility*. Disappointment was, however, not far away. Despite the home having adjoining rooms for couples, none were currently available.

It was the next Saturday before Penny came with the locked cash box. Together in Olivia's room, we shared a wee tot of Scotch whisky, a pleasure that had not diminished. I asked Penny if she found the key to the cash box (having forgotten to tell her where to look) and to my surprise she said, 'yes.'

'Did you open it?' asked Olivia.

'Surprisingly, no. I wanted to, but I didn't,' said Penny.

What to do... The options raced through my mind. Should we show her the contents and by doing so open a tide of questions?

Penny gave me the key and I opened the cash box which revealed two passports, one credit card and a sealed envelope. Penny looked upon the contents with a face that could not hide her disappointed. It was obviously an anti-climax after a week of waiting.

'Nothing very exciting,' I said, handing Penny one of the passports. Disappointment became surprise as she saw Olivia's photograph and then read the name, Olivia Breeze. Taking the second passport she read, Max Breeze.

'That's not your surname; Breeze! Is it? Who are you?' But before I could answer she added. 'I've always known that you two were up to something. Always.'

Thinking of Penny always makes me smile.

Now I looked over to the clock on the side table next to my bed. It was 3.30am.

Who are you? I said to myself. *Who are you?* A tear formed and trickled gently down my face and the memory of Penny faded to be replaced by the reality of another day. *What have you become?* - was now the question of my silent voice. With those words another tear formed and leisurely traced the contours of an empty face.

Chapter 4

Duval

Today was Monday 21, the third week of March and our anniversary, two years since moving to our Château d'If.

The day started like any other. I wheeled down to the dining room for breakfast and to read the paper. The dining room was relatively empty at 7.30 am and wouldn't spring to life until closer to 8.30. The aged, venerable, old, whatever name you choose to call us, tend to sleep in, not for rest, but so there's a little less of the day to get through. You can't say Bellbird Village is without activities but, even with an hour here or an hour there, mostly the days are long and the same. So, so long. The sense of purpose, meaning and urgency which drove you to rise early and face the world regardless of its adversities has long since gone.

Sometimes I still woke feeling as if I could conquer the world. I'd swing my legs from the bed and raise my body to its full height, only to find my balance faltering. As I swayed upon my feet, my confidence was drained and dimmed further with every rock. My head filled with giddiness; was it my health or anxiety that befell me? In the end it mattered not, for each day became another day of waiting for God and wishing time would end swiftly instead of loitering into a slow decline of mind and dignity. In what now seemed such a long time ago, I remembered being at home, a young man looking out upon the world, pondering its beauty and feeling, really feeling, the wonders of God's creation. Now, a lifetime later, my only ponderous insurmountable feeling was of fear, fear that Olivia would die before me and that I would be left alone.

How very selfish this was, as was my daily prayer for God to take me soon and take me swiftly. Whether there is an afterlife, I am ashamed to say, I no longer know with certainty. Even if this life is it and there is nothing else, it is not death I now fear, but the process of dying.

I have always been an early riser, enjoying a quiet hour sipping a cup of coffee while reading the newspaper. In keeping with my ritual, today I turned first to the notices section and scanned the death columns expecting the daily feeling of disappointment.

DUVAL Claude of Covent Gardens
Passed away peacefully
A private memorial service to celebrate
his life will be held at Cliff on
Monday 11th April 2011.

I couldn't believe my eyes!

While reading and re-reading, my heart began to race and, for a second, I thought it was a heart attack. Taking deep breaths to regain focus, I noted the sensation turned to that of excitement and then anticipation before giving way to uncertainty and trepidation.

A message from a life long ago stared back from the paper and with the top-secret code activated; Olivia and I must to get to the UK and a small Cornish village called Cliff. It was from here that our secret missions, both during and after the war, were controlled. Headquarters was a white house, one of only six dwellings in the village. It became a B&B after the war to hide the comings and goings of operatives. It was to Cliff we sent the key when last recalled to duty. This message meant only one thing: Janus was to be retrieved by us and reunited with its key. It had been decided during the dying days of the war that the Janus Machine must be separated from its key, for the safety of humanity. Although Janus could be used for great good, its original design and purpose was for pure evil.

Along with one other, we were the only people still alive who would know the final hiding place, albeit with the need of one other piece of information.

'The eleventh of April is only three weeks away. It's impossible,' I said to Olivia. 'How can we get to the UK, find the clue, retrieve Janus and then deliver it, in person, to Cliff all by the eleventh of April? It takes me a month just to get dressed and wheel down to the dining room, let alone to travel twelve thousand kilometres.'

In her calm, unflappable way, Olivia had just smiled and said, 'We can work it out tonight, when you come to my room.'

She has always been the cool headed one; I ran on pure adrenaline, doing everything at a hundred miles an hour, six tasks at a time. It was either fight or flight. Not with Olivia though; she was calm, controlled and methodical. But always late!

It being Monday, the next planned visit by family would be on Sunday, the twenty-seventh, and then not for another week. Thinking occupied the remainder of my breakfast. To escape unnoticed we needed the home to believe we were staying with family and for family to believe we were still at the home. No trace of our planning or intended movements could be left—this meant not using our own computers, iPads, or phones. All bookings and communications would have to be carried out using someone else's equipment and without their knowledge. Once our absence was noticed, because of our age, an extensive search would be launched by police and, with our colourful history, it might garner some local media interest. Worryingly, the story might also attract international coverage alerting our previous adversaries that we were on the move.

With the false passports and credit card that Penny had salvaged, we had the means to travel overseas but, without outside assistance in our current circumstances and conditions, it would be impossible. Penny's help might be needed and, at worst, it could be essential.

Before meeting Olivia tonight I needed to talk with Penny. Although it was probably safe to call her mobile from the nursing home, I couldn't risk the phone records being checked once we were reported missing. If Jane even suspected an escape, she might be suspicious of Penny's involvement and we wouldn't want her connected to our disappearance. Overly cautious? Definitely. Paranoid? Probably, but nonetheless necessary. The obvious solution that sprang to mind was to ring Penny at work using a pay phone from down the street. The problem; getting down the street. The answer; steal a motorised scooter from one of the residents—or guests, as Bellbird Village liked to call us.

Why I hadn't bought an electric scooter, I don't know, for the people who owned them absolutely loved them. For the mobility-challenged, the scooter gave a freedom no long available to those without wheels. I longed to go down the street at a time of my choosing. To read the paper and enjoy a real coffee from a café or any place other than here. Even as recently as the week before, I had refused a scooter. Was it pride, embarrassment at the loss of independence, fear, denial, or plain stubborn stupidity? On reflection; a combination of all the above. Sometimes I was miserable and, by making my stay at Bellbird more wretched than it should be, my gloom was justified. As a young man I had told the children that I was going to be a grumpy old man, and I was.

One of the fortunate truths of age is that we become creatures of habit. Vera, or Aunty Vera as she likes to be called, goes for an hour's ride most mornings and is always back by 11:00 am. She, unlike some guests, leaves the keys in her machine. By coincidence, 11:00 am on Mondays is also when Bellbird Village administrative staff have their office meeting. For about thirty minutes, you can almost guarantee that the front desk will be left unattended. Leaving Bellbird unseen was important; being caught coming back on the stolen scooter was not. If challenged upon return I knew better than to claim stupidity—the last thing I wanted was to be transferred to the Dementia Unit. A good lie, for which I had a lifetime of practice, could be constructed while terrorising the streets on the stolen four-wheeled chariot.

At 10.45 am, I watched Aunty Vera from a safe distance as she parked her scooter. Patiently, I waited and then waited some more as she dismounted. After taking her stick from the basket she moved, at an astonishingly slow speed, towards the power socket to plug in and recharge her wheels. She picked up the lead and stretched it towards the scooter. She fiddled with the plug… waiting… fiddled with the plug... At last, contact. No, something was not right. She went back to the wall. Ah, she'd forgotten to switch the power on. Agonisingly, she went back to the scooter again, this time checking that the charge light was on. All must have been well as she moved away from the scooter but then stopped and turned back.

Wait, I said to myself; *she's forgotten something else. No, she's forgotten what she forgot.* Unhurriedly she turned and made her way out of the parking room. I checked my watch and the time was 11.05.

This would be a quick and easy theft; a lifetime of skill and training told me that speed and confidence are the essential elements for success. After disconnecting the scooter from the power socket, I mounted my charge and turned the key on. *Bugger, where's the accelerator? No pedals, how ridiculous, it's only got two hand brakes.* I mumbled crossly to myself. Looking below the handlebars I discovered a green lever on the right and a yellow lever on the left. *Obviously, yellow is for reverse and green for forward,* I informed myself. Squeezing the yellow lever had no effect. Squeezing further brought no more result. Without warning the scooter leapt to life and bolted backwards. *Too fast! Brake, brake,* I told to myself. Pulling hard on the lever, in an effort to stop the scooter, made it instead accelerate rearward at ever increasing speed until... Bang! It slammed into two other scooters. The crashing, crunching and destruction of fibreglass was deafening. *Run away!* My instincts yelled. This time, after gently squeezing the green lever and patiently waiting for the motor to respond, I launched out of the automatic door and down the footpath. Relaxing a little, I put distance between myself and the village. I ventured towards my first ever road crossing. The secret, I had determined, was to maintain momentum: Not too fast and definitely not too slow. Leaving the footpath, the scooter behaved as if it had been thrown, with incredible force, onto the road. The relatively small curb sent the scooter rocking violently from side to side and, for an instant, I was almost thrown from the seat. Rather than riding and absorbing the gutter, the wheels smashed through the terrain sending shockwaves back through my hands. I was sure it would tip over.

Who designed these things? They have virtually no suspension. A death trap, likely to roll over on the slightest of provocation, I thought. On recovering from my initial shock, it was pedal to the metal, racing to and through the various obstacles in search of a public telephone and post office.

Penny, it is fair to say, was surprised by the call but did agree to visit tonight and break in through Olivia's French windows, which opened onto a small garden. In keeping with my paranoia, I asked her not to use her credit card or to buy petrol on the trip. Her mobile phone was to be left at home and, under no circumstances, was she to use the City Link toll road.

My final request was for her to download and then copy a program called iSunshare. She was to bring it with her tonight, which raised her curiosity even more.

With the phone call over, it was time to shuffle the scooter around, drive up the ramp into the post office and purchase a book of stamps. The twenty-minute return trip started well, with memories of motorbike riding rekindled by wind and sun touching the skin. Forgotten spirits of pleasure and joy were rediscovered as the world raced past; it was only at 15 kph but, on narrow footpaths, it felt like 115 kph. Without warning, the scooter stopped, coming to a halt halfway across a busy road. Traffic chaos followed the blocking of one lane. Trucks are an imposing sight when seen from the vantage point of what is really a motorised wheelchair on steroids.

Nurse Ratched was speechless, Aunty Vera distressed and the residents were evenly split between disgust and envy at my apparent rebellious behaviour. With little other excitement, the theft, scooter carnage and traffic jam would remain the topic of conversation for days.

At school, the headmaster calls your parents; here, at a nursing home, they call your children—both work with equal effectiveness. Over the phone a promise was made to pay for the damages caused by my excursion, a pledge made for improved behaviour and I was to be given a stern talking to on the next Sunday visit.

'Theft will not be tolerated,' concluded Nurse Ratched, pointing her dagger-like finger in my direction.

A grovelling humble apology was my only defence, accompanied by real dread; in just one day I had exhausted any goodwill harboured toward me at the home. If I was caught doing anything else, the UK would become an insurmountable obstacle and Janus might be lost.

If I thought Nurse Ratched's dressing down was intimidating, by the time Olivia said her piece, the nurse was only mildly unfriendly; a pussy cat.

Olivia opened her account with an attack of poignant humour, which spoke of my past failures. 'Another cunning plan Baldrick?'

That night, the dining room was a hum of excitement, of loud voices and quiet whispers. It was as if a bolt of rejuvenating energy had awoken many from a soulless slumber. There was even laughter, unfortunately at us and not with us, but laughter nonetheless. Olivia received looks of compassion, understanding and support, as though she was a mother responsible for a wayward child. After dinner, we made our way to the door ready to retire to Olivia's room for after dinner drinks in her luxurious royal penthouse suite. A hand gripped my shoulder and, in a quiet but firm voice, Jana, a fellow *'guest'* at our Hotel President Wilson, said in his rhythmic BBC accent. 'You can't fool me old man, something's afoot. You can count on me.'

Working to the agreed plan, Olivia left the curtains open and the lights on. It was close to 9.30 pm when a tap-tap tapping was heard on the French windows and past midnight by the time Penny left. During the visit, we shared some of our past stories and formulated another plan.

'Let's hope this idea is better than the one to convince Gordon and Jane to send us home... or stealing a scooter.' That was Olivia's final observation.

We decided that, over the next couple of nights, I would simply break into the administration office, use their computers to purchase airline tickets, hire a car, book accommodation and contact Cliff. We would tell the retirement home that, on Sunday, because of my indiscretion, Gordon and Jane would be taking us home with them for a month. At the end of their scheduled visit, Olivia and I would merely accompany Gordon and Jane to the car and wave goodbye. Then, rather than going back inside, we'd go up the road and wait outside house number thirty-five for a pre-ordered taxi. The taxi would then take us to the train station. From there, it would be by train to Melbourne, where we'd hide out in a hotel before taking a taxi to the airport and then a flight to the UK. All-in-all it was very straightforward. We debated the wisdom of writing under the guise of Gordon and Jane to inform Bellbird that we would be absent for a month. Doing this significantly increased the risk of staff talking to Gordon and Jane during their visit but, in the end, we determined this a risk worth taking. On Sundays, there is no administration staff on duty and the office is closed. It would be highly unlikely that any of the nursing staff on duty would have seen the letter and therefore raise it's contents with Jane or Gordon.

The letter to Bellbird Village was beautifully scripted by Olivia and included a further apology for the incident. Penny was to post the letter any time before Thursday using one of the street postal boxes in the city centre. Working in Hawthorn, some six kilometres from the CBD, and in keeping with the cloak-and-dagger world we were creating, she was to travel into the CBD during working hours without using her Myki travel pass. It was preferable that no one knew she was missing, so lunchtime was the best time and, of course, her mobile phone was to be left on her desk. At the end of the day she would follow her normal routine.

For a final act of intrigue, I handed Penny the Bellbird Village letter wrapped in a plastic bag, with instructions not to leave her fingerprints on it.

Before Penny left, we handed her another envelope, the one from the cash box, which contained a post office box key.

'Penny, the only secure way to communicate in the digital age is via post. In the next couple of days we will write to you and in the letter will be an envelope addressed to us in the UK. You're to use that envelope to send us this post office box key.'

As I said this, I pointed to the envelope in Penny's hands. She opened it to reveal the key and nodded.

I continued, 'If, for any reason, we don't pick up the letter in Britain, the return address will be to you.'

I could tell that questions were flooding Penny's mind because in rapid succession they sprang forth with urgency. 'What do you mean, if you don't pick up the key? And if it did come back what am I supposed to do with it? Why not take it with you?' And then finally, 'What is the key for?'

Inside I knew that Penny was the likely one to complete the mission and not us, but how could we expect help in ignorance, particularly if it placed her life at risk? After sixty-six years, the time was both right and necessary to share a little more of our story with her but not all of it. And so I began.

'Penny, I want to answer all your questions but it's not wise for you to know the whole story—not yet. You know some of our tale from when you brought us the cash box but, if it's okay with you, I will start again from the beginning. To tell you the truth, I can't remember what we've already shared with you. That was two years ago.'

Penny nodded and settled to listen.

'Olivia and I met during the Second World War when I joined an organisation called the Agency in 1943. The first time I saw her was at the headquarters, a private house in a small village called Cliff in Cornwall. She was a beautiful Wren working for a top secret organisation. She was an officer and I was an inexperienced ordinary seaman feeling out of place joining a group of seasoned sailors to be involved in all kinds of clandestine and secret operations. The men were all suspicious of the new boy and Olivia went out of her way to help me settle in. She gave me confidence before I was sent on my first mission. I think for both of us it was love at first sight. It's strange now but, in those days, ratings could not date officers.

We were breaking rules even then. The Agency was not my full time war role; I was assigned to other duties in the Royal Navy and only summoned to Cliff for particular missions. Sometimes I would go months without seeing Olivia.

'With the end of the war, our work with the Agency didn't finish. Times had changed and our relationship, which had been frowned upon, was now encouraged. The Agency had become paranoid about being infiltrated by the Russians. If an agent had a new girl or boyfriend, they wanted to know who initiated the relationship, just in case the new partner was a foreign spy. We were seen as a safe option.

'Olivia and I have, for the best part of our lives, continued work for them and a doddering old vicar with his faithful wife proved to be a most useful disguise.'

As I spoke, memories of a lifetime working together, often in dangerous situations, came flooding back. I recalled the friends we had lost, the places we had been, our wonderful marriage and subsequent life together. For a moment I had to stop talking as my voice choked and tears ran down my cheek.

'It's annoying how the slightest thing causes my voice to quiver nowadays.' After a cough to clear my throat and pausing to take a breath, I continued.

'You were spies?' interrupted Penny.

'I suppose we were. It almost sounds glamourous and on occasions it was, but, at other times, particularly during the war, it was deadly. This is one of those times.

'What we need your help with had its origins in the concentration camps of the Second World War; it was called, in German, *Projekt Janus* or Project Janus.

'It's not safe to tell you what the Janus Project was or what the Janus Machine did but it was for this left over legacy from WW2 that we returned to Europe for our eighty-fifth birthdays. Our mission was to retrieve a thing called the Janus Key and deliver it into safe hands. The motorbike accident was no accident; someone was trying to retrieve the key but it was, by then, too late. Thinking we were being followed, we mailed the Janus Key back to the UK. Who was trying to get it, how they know about it or how they knew we were trying to retrieve it, we don't know. Could be terrorists, multinationals or foreign governments; any or all would be interested and willing to kill for the secret or to keep it secret.

'All we really know now is, for the Agency to send the retrieval code, the message in the paper we told you about, something really serious must have or be happening. We don't know the exact hiding place of Janus but we believe it's somewhere in Scotland. The clue to its location will be sent to a post office box in Exeter. The key to this box is the one you are to post to us in the UK. Once we have what's in the post box we *believe* we will know where to look.

'Because of the previous attempt on our life, we don't want to carry the key unless absolutely necessary and, if we can't make it to the UK, we want to know that the key is safe. I can't tell you how, but we will leave you instructions. Knowing too many details of our trip may place you in danger; something we don't want to happen.'

'I need to pick you both up on Sunday. You can stay with me and I will take you to the airport,' Penny said in a slightly panicked but authoritative voice.

'That would be fantastic but our movements would too easily be traced to you. We don't want to place you in danger. Penny, people are willing to kill for our knowledge and also what they think we have told you. Already you know more than you should; our false passport names, where we are going and when you receive our letter, an address we will visit in the UK. We have to be really careful that we don't attract any more attention to you than we must. If anything was to happen to us, you will become the custodian of the key and we don't want the wrong people knowing that.'

'Do you think we did the right thing?' asked Olivia later. 'Involving Penny, I mean.'

'What else could we do?'

'We could not go?'

'Olivia, if I stay here I will die.'

'That's the whole point of these places Max. This is our hotel California—you can check out anytime you like, but you can never leave.'

'We are leaving!'

Chapter 5

The Grey Escape

After leaving breakfast and arriving at the rendezvous point at 9.25am I discovered that Olivia was, as always, customarily late. A couple of metres from the front office there's the public notice board highlighting the various excursions and activities on offer during the week. Waiting and reading the board attracts no suspicion and so I easily filled the time until Olivia arrived.

'Olivia, I was looking for you,' I said in a raised voice. Using my two walking sticks, I made my way over to the prearranged observation spot in front of the open administration office door. A fictitious conversation about the trip to the movies advertised on the notice board for this afternoon provided ample cover as we cased the layout of the office. I paid particular attention to the locks, room layout and the position of the computers and printers.

The administration area is located on the left hand side of the foyer as you come in through the main entrance. It's a large room with a reception window and counter linking it to the foyer. A number of desks furnish the room along with a printer and photocopier. At the rear is a door leading to the CEO's office, which is also accessible from the main corridor. It has a window to the outside but is private from the administration area and corridor.

The foyer, which doubles as the reception waiting area, is a large open space and a key pedestrian junction for the home. Corridors head off to the left and right. Going left you pass the administration area, the CEO's office and the Director of Nursing's office before coming to the accommodation areas. To the right is the main dining room, reading areas, a small chapel, a common room and then accommodation. I knew all this already, of course, but now I paid it particular attention.

From my vantage point, the lock on the administration door looked simple and easy to overcome with a credit card. I saw two computers, one on the reception desk and the other on a work bench farther to the back of the room. The main risk of breaking into the office appeared to be its visibility. Once inside, people could see us through the reception window although, at night, nursing staff don't generally walk past the window except during shift changeover. Unfortunately, the reception window was also visible from the corridor leading to the dining room.

People coming and going would see into the administration room if they purposely looked.

On finishing the surveillance conversation with Olivia, I made my way down the corridor and paused outside the CEO's office door. The office is accessible from the main corridor and from within the administration area. The lock on the door adjoining the main corridor appeared simple but would require specialist tools that I didn't have. The obvious plan was to use the computer in the CEO's office because it was out of sight of the reception window, but the only way to access the room was through the administration office.

The secret to planning and then executing a clandestine mission comes in two parts. First, do everything slowly, thereby maximising focus and speed. Many techniques are available to control the normal fight or flight impulse we all experience under stress; the management of this is the staple of secret agents. Over time we each find a technique or set of tools which work the best for us to enhance our calm and focus. For me it's colouring books. Before going on a mission or before spending an evening planning a mission, I would sit quietly focusing on colouring between, but never touching, the lines. Each stroke of colour was meticulously applied through slow, purposeful and controlled movements of the pencils. Breathing became one with the pencil, breathing in with one stroke and slowly out with the other, pausing briefly with each change of direction. If a colouring book was not at hand, doodling in the same slow and careful manner induced a tranquil unruffled state of calm and concentration. The second secret is to ensure that to all those around you, nothing seems out of the ordinary. With this in mind we joined the after lunch excursion, as advertised on the notice board, to see a movie, *Gulliver's Travels*, in 3D no less.

The timing of when to break into the office was the only decision remaining. There was no right or wrong answer with the outcome determining whether or not it was a good decision. Olivia and I discussed the two most obvious options; after the evening meal when non-independent residents are prepared for bed, or, alternatively, during the early hours of the morning when staffing numbers are low and the likelihood of anyone walking the corridors was slim. Each option had its own strengths and difficulties. In the early hours, any movement or sound would attract attention and, during the bed period, the building was a buzz of activity. After a lengthy debate, we settled on bed time, between the kitchen staff leaving (8.00 and 8.30pm) and the night shift arriving (10.30 and 11.00pm). Our plan left a narrow window, between 9.00 and 10.00 pm.

'There's no point waiting,' I said to Olivia, 'but everything would need to go perfectly.'

'Whatever you do, don't get caught. Not after yesterday. Remember, this is what you are good at and you've done it a hundred times before. Take your time and it will be a breeze.' She said and gave me a reassuring smile.

Doodling quietly and seated at the reading space provided an unobstructed view of the front entrance, dining room and reception area. The last of the kitchen staff bade me a *goodnight* as she left through the front door. I counted slowly to thirty. Adrenaline flowed through my veins and I felt invigorated; a sensation not experienced in many a year. My creaking old body stirred and woke from its long hibernation. The home buzzed with noise as residents and staff went about their business. With both walking sticks held in one hand and using the other hand to manipulate the credit card, a familiar clicking sound signalled that the lock was open. A check left and then right while slipping the credit card back into my pocket freed my hand to open the door.

'Are you okay Max?' a voice called from behind.

Trying to show no hint of surprise, I slowly turned to see Nurse Sian watching inquisitively. I took my hand out of the pocket, now holding a handkerchief, which I waved briefly in her direction before moving it towards my nose. Unhurriedly, I returned the handkerchief to the pocket and the second walking stick to my free hand. Clarification obviously at hand, Nurse Sian smiled enlightenment and hurried away.

After a brief pause and now with a little more foreboding, I proceeded with the break-in.

The door closed behind me and, for about the next three minutes, I was, through the reception window, on full view until I could find cover in the CEO's office. To my delight the CEO's office door was unlocked and swung open silently. Upon entering, I closed the door behind me giving me a sanctuary for the task at hand. I made myself comfortable at the desk and the CEO's computer whirred into life while I pressed F10 so that the computer would boot in Bios mode. After I inserted the iSunshare CD and selected the Boot from CD option from the Bios menu, a beautiful screen appeared with the title 'Reset Windows Password.' Scrolling down I chose "Bill's PC". Bill is the first name of the CEO. I clicked the reset password button and the password became blank. The computer was accessed. Time taken; ten minutes.

It was unmistakeable, the sound of a key being inserted in to the CEO's door which lead to the hallway, followed by the cluck of a lock giving way. The door handle turned and a crack of light penetrated the darkened room which moments before had been illuminated only by the light of Windows 7 emanating from the screen.

'Bill, Bill,' I heard Jana call aloud. The growing crack of light receded and then vanished as the door closed.

'Good evening Jana, how can I help you?' I caught the words being spoken in the corridor.

With the short conversation over, Bill opened the door to his office, intent, most likely, on catching up on some work in which he had fallen behind. The sense of unease was immediate; perhaps it was brought about by the door between his office and the admin being open, a door he always shut before going home.

I saw him as he peered out into the administration area but then apparently satisfied, he sat at his desk.

From my vantage point, hiding under a desk in the administration area, I saw his door being closed. With great effort I crawled out from underneath the desk and attempted to stand. Using the desk as a lever I hauled myself onto my feet only to see my two walking sticks still under the desk. In the next room I imagined the computer flickering into life and instead of starting in Windows, Bill would be welcomed by a screen that read:

'Insert Boot Disc.'

Struggling, I lowered myself down on to my knees, gripped the walking sticks and once more pulled myself up.

In my imagination, I saw Bill as he checked under his desk to where the computer lived, and observed the CD drive open. *Someone has been in the office and hacked into my computer,* he would think. At any moment he would, once again, open the door between the two offices but this time he would be looking for signs of a break-in.

I slipped out into the hallway and, in what seemed to take an eternity, moved out of sight from the reception window and then past the other entry to the CEO's office. I did not look back but knew that Bill would open the reception door and look up and down the corridors. Was I seen, or had I managed to slip away unnoticed?

'You're back early,' observed Olivia.

Slightly out of breath and pausing between words, I recounted the events of the evening. 'If it were not for Jana I would have been caught. Bill must have come back to do some evening work. Jana delayed him just long enough for me to get out but I didn't have a chance to restore his computer password. He will know someone was in his office.'

'Do you think Jana knew that you were breaking into the office?'

'I don't know but I think you should pay him a visit.'

'Good idea Max; do you want to come with me?'

'No, I can't. The break-in has taken too much out of me. I'm feeling just a little off.'

'You will be okay after a good night's sleep. I'll see you at breakfast.'

With my mind churning over what Olivia would say to Jana, I turned to leave the room.

'Max!'

'Sorry,' I said and gave Olivia the mandatory, but always welcome, kiss goodbye.

***

Olivia

Jana's room was one corridor away, a left then right turn. As with all places within our nursing home, it took only a minute before I was outside his door. So as not to alert the nearby residents, all of whom love a little gossip to fill what otherwise can be quite dull days, I gently knocked on his door.

'Come on in Olivia,' Jana called out.

He would have been a striking man in his day. Standing a little over 6 foot 3 inches tall, his face was dominated by sharp contours whose lines spoke not of age, but of profound wisdom. Sporting his long beard, it could have been Gandalf or Albus Dumbledore welcoming you. Looking around his room, I almost expected to see a pointy hat or a staff standing in the corner.

'Close call tonight Olivia.'

'Indeed it was Jana.'

'Tea?'

'White with none.'

While Jana slowly and methodically made the tea, I continued my inspection of his room. We spend a lifetime collecting. Trophies may represent our interpretation of success in a particular hobby or sport. There may be relics which hold intrinsic personal value, perhaps signifying learning or special recollections from important times, places, and people. Here, we had only sixteen square metres to house that lifetime of memories. The scant items, pictures, books and other things that rest upon our shelves may not represent the important stories in our lives. Most of us try to gift those to family in a benign hope that they will value them as we had done. In truth, those with no true monetary value soon find their way to the local op shop. On the side table next to Jana's bed was a picture of a young Jana in uniform. He had a beautiful woman upon his arm. There were no pictures of children or grandchildren and only a few decorative trinkets neatly sat upon the shelves. Two small paintings adorned the walls and on the writing desk, next to a small pile of books, WW2 medals and another picture of the same woman from the bedside table. The room was ordered meticulously, everything placed just so, the same way in which Jana presented himself.

Jana followed my gaze to the medals and photograph.

'Our generation were all touched by war, not necessarily in bad ways, but in aspects we could never imagine. But you know that—a computer with access to the internet is that what you're after?'

'It is but may I ask how you know?'

'I have spent my life observing, listening and learning. This morning I saw you outside of the office and tonight I watched Max. It makes sense that it's not money you were after.'

'And tonight—when you called out my name?'

'Max would have heard me distract Bill and so it was obvious one of you would come and see me. The rest was a 50—50 chance. While I've been waiting for you, I've come up with a way you can obtain access to a PC.

'Tomorrow is Wednesday. As you know, after dinner, Max, Lilly, Pan Rose and I will play cards until about 10.00pm. In his room, Pan Rose has a computer with an internet connection and he has no password. Wait until we start the game and come back to the card table when you are done.'

'Thank you,' I said and, finishing the last sip of tea, I rose to go.

'When do you leave?

A raised eyebrow acknowledged my surprise but I said only, 'Sunday. Goodnight Jana.'

At breakfast, ever mindful of flapping ears, I suggested to Max that, when he had finished reading the paper, we should sit outside and enjoy what may be the last of the warm days of autumn. No one else had chosen to go outside this morning so we settled, in private, on a bench overlooking a nicely maintained garden bed.

'Well, how was Jana?' asked Max.

'Surprisingly, he was expecting me,' I said, to which Max replied with a grunt. 'And he has guessed we are going to break out of here.'

'Are we that obvious?'

'Who would know? To Jana perhaps.' I then detailed Jana's plan for tonight.

Unlike Max, I find plenty of activities and people to share my day. Today was no different. In the later part of the afternoon, I kept to my ritual of reading and doing crosswords with Max. The day passed quickly, which was surprising, as I was waiting for the card game to begin.

I delayed twenty minutes before excusing myself from watching the game. After making my way to Pan Rose's room I found the door unlocked which was a bonus, though picking it would have taken a matter of seconds. When I entered I saw that the room was identical to all of the other residents' chambers, with the only difference being a few personal effects and ornaments. The rooms even smelt the same, the distinctive aroma of old people, described by some as the sacred scent of *stale urine*.

On the writing desk sat a computer and, as Jana had said, Windows opened with no need for a password. My night's task was simple; all that was required was to book two airline tickets to the UK and two nights' accommodation at Heathrow. I observed that Pan Rose had no printer, but it would be a simple matter of using our Gmail address for the bookings and then accessing and printing the tickets once in Melbourne.

After I typed 'Flights to the United Kingdom' and pressed the enter key, Google returned numerous hits. Choosing the first hit, Virgin Airlines, returned, to my disbelief, what were neither virgins nor airlines.

From the computer screen, images of ladies of an Asian persuasion appeared. Some were wearing airhostess uniforms with no accompanying knickers. They all had bulging pert breasts which their scanty tops were unable to contain. *Interesting. Men never grow up,* I said to myself, now typing the words *Flight Centre*.

This time the search was not hijacked and the web page appeared on the monitor. Using the search menu, I quickly entered—Flights to London between 4th and 11th April- and pushed the enter key.

To my dismay, pop up ads for all sorts of pornographic sites accompanied the results. Most of the ads were not raunchy or erotic but hard core; no uniforms this time. *'Malware, the computer is infected with Malware. Our Mr Pan Rose is a dirty old depraved man,'* I said aloud, but in a whispered voice.

Clicking the back button only spawned another pornography site. I discovered a long time ago that my definition of sexual liberty differs from others. While I support freedom from guilt for consenting adults, what I saw on the screen was exploitation.

Max and I had once touched the seedy world of sex slavery and human trafficking when gathering intelligence on Russian Mafia gangs suspected of illegal arms sales in the Middle East. That trail took another unexpected turn and we entered the underworld of child pornography. What started as a gun sales enquiry ended with a two year search assisting child exploitation units from around the world to find the girl in a picture. A worldly person, I was still unprepared for the graphic imagery depraved people wanted to see, or the scale, debauchery and viciousness of the exploitation. The image of that one twelve year old girl still, at its choosing, chills my dreams. She came to represent the unprincipled evil of crime gangs that had no moral boundaries and were motivated only by greed. We found her, the girl in the picture, and along the way rescued a hundred other children. In those quiet moments when the girl in the picture stares back at me, I would like to think we saved the children but, in my heart, I know it was too late. The deep lingering psychological damage was done. I felt the anger slowly rise as Pan Rose's images evoked the past. It was unlikely that any of the young women on his computer screen participated freely in the acts they displayed. Bondage, drugs, threats or forced prostitution were a sad reality for many who appeared on the internet. Through aggressive policing, things had improved marginally in Europe since we investigated the Russian Mafia but, as Pan Rose's computer revealed, any success only moved the crime syndicates to new battlegrounds.

If I wanted to use this tainted computer I would have to remove the Malware. Fortunately, some thirty minutes after starting the clean-up, I was safely back at the Flight Centre web page; this time unaccompanied by pop up boobs and bums.

Two business class tickets to London on Wednesday 30th March 2011, leaving Melbourne airport at 5.00pm via Dubai. It was quite a long process entering dates of birth, addresses, passport numbers etc., but finally I was taken to the payment page -Enter credit card details—choose—Visa, American Express or MasterCard.

Checking the Visa Card box, I progressed to input the credit card details, all the while feeling strangely uncomfortable.

Perhaps it has been the unsavoury journey into the world of dirty old men that caused this momentary unsettledness. Pausing, my finger rested on the mouse button; a simple click and the airline tickets would be purchased. *There it is, MasterCard* which should be spelt MasterCard. I had no doubt that this was a fake website ready to steal our identity and money. *No virus protection is a bad choice at any time, let alone for a person who surfs the sleazy world of pornography,* I thought. I found once again the anger at Pan Rose rising within me. What to do before I left? Make it so that when he logs into his computer a message appears on the screen saying, 'Dirty old man?' To do so was terribly tempting but silly, I concluded. Staring at the screen, I decided to disable his computer; forever. *He will just think it's broken,* I said to myself.

After leaving Pan Rose's room I made my way back to the card game. In one way I was no more successful than Max had been yesterday but, in another, I triumphed. One thing was for sure, however; escaping was proving a greater challenge that I had anticipated.

'Good evening gentlemen and ladies, how goes the high rollers?'

'Max has won almost all of the matches,' said Jana.

'Pure skill,' said Max.

'I've come to bid you all a good night. Max, I will see you at breakfast,' I said, giving him a peck on the lips before heading for my room.

***

Max

After cards I was feeling more weary than usual, which is difficult even for me to believe. For a second night, I didn't go to Olivia but, instead, returned to my room and went straight to bed. Looking at the clock I saw that it was 11.00pm. With some annoyance at being unable to sleep, I opened my eyes to study the time. To my surprise it was already 7.00am; the night had vanished in an instant. I could count on the one hand the times I had experienced that sensation; the total surrendering of time. Bad dreams had become my constant companion of the night over the last few years. *A real night's sleep*, I thought rolling tentatively out of bed, now late for my morning paper and coffee.

I was always the first for breakfast but this morning, to my surprise, Olivia was already seated at my table.

'Good morning Olivia,' I said as I plonked myself down next to her. Then speaking, not in a whisper that would arouse suspicion, but in a low voice unlikely to be overheard, I said, 'Did you book the tickets?'

'Not exactly!'

It was unlike Olivia to play coy but I couldn't resist playing along. 'What does "not exactly" mean?'

'Unfortunately it means NO, but it was an educational experience nonetheless.'

Olivia then proceeded to give a censored, but detailed, account of our fellow inmate's viewing habits and his lack of any cyber security. By the time she finished her report, we were no longer the only people at breakfast; Alcatraz was waking to another day. Before too many other people arrived and our privacy became compromised, I said, using my most official, but satirical, voice, 'Operation report for Thursday 24 March 2011.

> *'No airline tickets,*
>
> *'No hotels booked,*
>
> *'Taxi for Sunday not ordered,*
>
> *'No train tickets,*
>
> *'UK car not booked,*

'Situation normal m'lady.'

'Good morning Max and Olivia; we received a letter from your daughter-in-law Jane saying you're going home with them on Sunday for a month's stay.'

We hadn't seen Nurse Sian approach and were startled when she spoke. Quickly regaining composure and hoping she had not overheard my disheartening operational overview, I took a sip from my coffee before saying, 'Good morning Nurse. Olivia and I planned that stay during their last visit but we thought it best to wait until you received the letter before talking to you.'

'I hope that was the right thing to do,' Olivia added.

'Yes, we do hope we have done the right thing?'

That's quite all right Max and Olivia. I'll arrange for our pharmacist to make up your medications for the next four weeks and have them put into dosette boxes. Oh and don't forget, your family will have to sign the "Residents' Outing Register". If you think of anything else you need, please let me know.'

Smiling, Sian left our table and swept through the room nodding and greeting other residents before vanishing as quickly as she had appeared. I imagined, after my antics on Monday, that she was secretly pleased to see me gone and wondered if she thought that, somehow, I was behind the CEO office break-in. Since the scooter theft, the atmosphere at the home was, in some way, different. An atmosphere of expectancy, a buzz, could be felt in the dining room. We were trying to be sly in our escape preparations but there was without doubt a *disturbance in the force.*'

'Max, Max. Planet Earth to Major Tom. Jana just said good morning to you.'

'Sorry Olivia. Good morning Jana, I was off with the fairies.'

'That's a dangerous place to be around here,' said Jana, smiling and giving an enthusiastic chuckle.

'Please join us, Jana,' said Olivia while pointing to the vacant breakfast setting on our table.

Without hesitating, Olivia leaned across the table and, in a whispered voice, said to Jana, 'Pan Rose was a good plan but his viewing habits, let's say, have rendered his computer inoperable.'

'I see.'

'Most things we can take care of when we get to Melbourne but it's imperative that we book a taxi for Sunday. Any ideas?'

A short period of silence followed and I became aware of the other conversations which now filled the room—each indistinguishable from the other, unless you focused in on one in particular, then the air of jumbled words suddenly took form and, with it, meaning.

'I have a simple plan,' said Jana. 'Max, you steal a mobile phone, use it to book the taxi and then return it before anyone notices it missing.'

'Excellent, but it's not the planning that's been causing the grief, it's the execution,' Olivia said, while looking directly at me.

'Olivia, that's a little unfair. You did no better than me breaking into a computer.'

'Max, let me count the ways. Let me see, getting Jane to send us home, your driving test, stealing Aunty Vera's Scooter… shall I continue!'

'You can be a harsh woman sometimes,' I said in a jovial tone while casting cute puppy eyes in her direction.

'Max, Olivia, no fighting now. I have a plan. See the mobile phone on Maureen's table? Olivia, you distract Maureen,

I nick the phone and give it to Max who will be waiting in the corridor. When you're finished with it, Max, just drop it and walk away. Whoever finds the phone will take it to the front desk and, when Maureen notices it's gone, it will be returned by staff who will assume she dropped it. What could possibly go wrong? QED, as they say.'

For once the execution went like clockwork, I ordered a taxi for Sunday at 5.30pm and it was to meet us outside number 35. As Jane and Gordon always left at 5.00pm sharp, a thirty minute window was available if anything went wrong.

Checking for watching eyes, it was bombs away as the phone fell to the ground. A quick kick with the left boot moved the phone closer to the wall. Hurriedly I moved away, one stick after the other.

From behind, and in an accusatory tone, a voice called to me, 'Max! Did you drop something?'

My blood pressure and heart rate jumped in unison. Turning slowly revealed only Jana, grinning like a Cheshire cat.

'I'll come over and hit you with my sticks, both of them.' I said, lifting one stick and then the other.

Sunday was soon upon us and, with it, Jane and Gordon's visit.

'What were you thinking; stealing a motor scooter?' These were the first words spoken by Jane as she entered Olivia's room where we were, in trepidation, waiting to meet them.

'Good afternoon to you as well Jane, how nice it is to see you,' I said.

'Don't be sarcastic with me Max! You're both lucky you weren't kicked out,'

'Olivia, if only I had known! I would have stolen a scooter years ago.'

Trying to defuse the situation, Gordon added, 'What's done is done, let's enjoy the visit.'

'Sorry Max,' said Jane. 'Sometime you just exasperate me... enough said.' But then unable to resist, she added, 'You're like a child.'

I bit my tongue, deciding against a comeback line.

The visit was surprisingly enjoyable, most likely aided by the knowledge we were leaving. In all likelihood, this might be the last time we would ever see them. Despite all that had happened, you can't help but feel some affection for your family. I was surprised, as we said goodbye, when a sudden desire to tell them what we were doing crept over me. Fortunately, the feeling passed as quickly as it had arisen.

Using one walking stick, and with Olivia carrying her knitting bag to conceal our medications, we accompanied Gordon and Jane towards their car. On reaching the front foyer, we found Jana, and, after a brief introduction, we continued on our way and exited the building. Meanwhile, Jana slipped into the administration office and signed us out using Gordon's signature; a signature given to him by Olivia and practised over the last couple of nights.

Waving goodbye, Jane and Gordon drove away leaving us standing in the car park.

I looked over to Olivia. 'Are you ready?'

She didn't reply and so we made our way to stand in front of number 35 and await the taxi.

'This is it Olivia, no turning back!'

V-line ran reduced rail service on Sunday, so it was over an hour before we caught a train to Melbourne and we didn't arrive into Flinders Street Station until 8.15pm. After finding a taxi we made our way to the Grand Melbourne Hotel and the reception desk.

'Good evening sir and madam. Do you have a reservation?'

'Good evening, my name is Max Breeze and this is my wife Olivia. This is an unplanned visit and, I'm sorry, but we don't have a reservation. Would one of your suites be available?'

'Certainly sir, the Presidential Suite is vacant. How long will you be staying?'

'We are not sure; our flight is delayed and we will be making alternative arrangements in the morning. Perhaps we should initially book for a couple of nights.'

'Certainly sir. Can I have someone help you with your luggage?'

'Ah. Because of our age, you understand, we experience difficulties carrying luggage and it was sent on before us. Unfortunately it's already left on a plane. It's, um, gone without us.'

'Most inconvenient, sir.'

'Yes it certainly is. Would it be possible for the concierge to purchase a few of the necessities, perhaps a change of clothes and a couple of pairs of smalls for each of us?'

'It would be our pleasure sir and madam. I will have someone sent up to your suite to take your measurements.'

The Presidential Suite had a separate living and dining area, marble bathroom and a magnificent master bedroom. It would have a beautiful view overlooking the Yarra River and the Melbourne skyline during the day. For us the city lights delivered a spectacular vista. A bottle of chilled Champagne, two glasses and some chocolates were waiting for us by the time we reached the room. The long day had taken its toll with exhaustion and the thought of sleep was more enticing than Champagne. We opened the bottle regardless and sipping the sparkles, waited for the concierge to arrive.

Olivia's measurements were dutifully recorded: Height 173cm, Bust 86cm, Waist 73cm Hips 97cm. A dress in preference to slacks was Olivia's wish.

Buying for men is considerably easier than for women just; Height 179cm and build medium. Measurements taken, we asked for clothes that were a little younger, a bit trendy.

'No beige cardigans,' I said.

We also requested two small travel suitcases, on wheels, in which to carry the new belongings.

The concierge assured us that he understood our instructions and would leave precise instructions for Meredith who would be seeing to our request in the morning. He would, he said, be returning to his office and would dutifully record our wishes and measurements in the hand-over book.

Next morning we woke early having slept together, in a double bed, for the first time in two years, made all the more memorable because of the fine Egyptian cotton sheets, which were in stark contrast to our normal hospital grade sheets. Breakfast was served in our bedroom, a treat you can experience at Bellbird Village only when sick.

After breakfast we took a taxi to the State Library of Victoria, situated at the top of Swanston Street, which had free internet access. This time our quest for airline flights did not lead to a collage of pornography sites. Over breakfast Olivia and I had decided we would seek and take the earliest possible flights. Our search revealed that two business class seats were available leaving Tullamarine at 3.00 pm today for London.

'What do you think Olivia, 3.00pm today? We will need to be at the airport by 1.00.' Checking my watch I saw it was 11.00am.

'Now or never Max.'

I pushed the booking confirmation button on the website. 'Let's go, we have only four hours before the plane leaves.' We made our way back out onto the street.

'Max, we should ring Penny.'

'We can ring her from the airport,' I said while hailing a cab.

Back at the Grand Hotel Melbourne, the concierge had left our new clothing neatly packed into our travel bags at reception. Having retrieved our drugs from the suite, we returned to reception to settle the account. Luggage in tow, it was outside to the waiting taxi, the one we had taken from the library and then asked to wait for us, for the drive to the airport. Climbing in the back of the cab and checking my watch again, I saw there was three hours and fifteen minutes remaining. Plenty of time.

A trip to the airport ordinarily takes about thirty minutes but, as we swung off City Link and crossed the Bolte Bridge to join the Tullamarine motorway, the traffic came to a complete standstill. None of the lanes was moving. Nervously I looked at my watch. Three hours remaining. Tick, tick, tick, I could almost hear the minutes slipping by. We waited uneasily in the back of the taxi. After what seemed an eternity I checked my watch once more. Two hours forty-five minutes before the flight left. I looked through the windscreen and still the traffic was stationary.

'What do we do Olivia, wait or get out of the taxi and try and get off the freeway and find another way to the airport?'

'How can we get off the motorway? Nothing's moving.'

'The other side of the road is.'

'You mean to cross the median strip and then all the lanes of traffic. On a motorway.'

'Yes, unless you have a better plan?'

'There's nothing for it Max, let's go.'

To the protests of our driver and after paying him $100, we left the taxi. After we gave him another $100, he reluctantly took our luggage out of the boot and placed it on the ground. Walking stick in one hand and pulling our luggage with the other, we hobbled off toward the median strip which separated the north/south lanes of the motorway. The lanes travelling in the opposite direction, unlike our side of the motorway, were moving and, as we traversed the median strip, I was taken aback by how exceptionally busy the lanes were, with fast moving vehicles and lots of trucks (big trucks; B-Doubles).

Standing at the precipice, Olivia looked to me. 'Now what Max?'

'We have to cross all four lanes, get to the emergency lane and then hitch hike.'

Melbourne has the dubious honour of having one of the only International Airports in the world with no rail link. To travel to Tullamarine airport you go either by car, taxi or bus; all using the roads.

'It's a plan if we live! But let me tell you, I will be most annoyed if you get us killed.'

'I know; you won't ever speak to me again.'

Walking stick held out in front and waving it towards the mechanical monsters, Olivia stepped onto the freeway taking one shuffle at a time and then pausing to jerk the luggage closer with her free hand, before shuffling forward once more. The sound of chaos was deafening. Tyres screeched and horns rang out as the first truck narrowly missed her. The next vehicle swerved and the smell of burning rubber filled the air. The first lane was now at a standstill and, with me walking in her wake, we approached the second lane. Looking only at the ground, too frightened to see what was going to hit us, we stepped off into the second and third lanes.

'One to go,' I called.

The inside lane was still moving as, together, we stepped out from in front of a now stationary truck, which had just managed to come to a complete halt in the nick of time. Traffic in the inside lane had slowed considerably, with the other lanes now stopped, but still the first vehicle was blindsided as we appeared from in front of the truck. I didn't want to look up but found myself staring at the bonnet of a car under full brakes appearing as if it would never stop until it had killed us both. When it came to a halt, it was resting against my stick. Looking back to Olivia I saw that she was quietly moving towards the emergency lane. Looking back, I saw that the freeway was at a complete standstill with people looking in utter disbelief.

'What are you doing?' called the man, in a distressed but concerned tone, from the vehicle that almost collected me.

Turning and walking up to the now open passenger window, all the while thinking of what lie to tell, I said. 'Our son in England is dying; he has twenty-four hours to live. We have to be on a plane in one hour's time or we won't be able to say goodbye. Our side of the motorway, the one going to the airport, has come to a complete standstill. We couldn't think of any other way of getting to the airport other than getting off the motorway.'

As I finished speaking, I turned and pointed to where we had come from. To my dismay, traffic was now moving.

'Get in,' the man said.

With the freeway still at a complete standstill and under the amazed gaze of those who could see, we got into the car with an unknown man and moved off. Two hours, five minutes to go.

The trip to the airport was slow but luckily traffic kept moving. As we pulled up at a drop off spot in front of the international terminal, I glanced once more at my watch; one hour to go.

'Good luck,' were the parting words from our driver as we made all haste into the airport.

Having checked in our luggage we made our way to the departure area which seemed an incredible distance away.

'Final call for passengers Max and Olivia Breeze travelling on Qantas Flight QF 172 to London,' was the plea that came over the PA system. We were stuck in a long snaking queue at passport control.

'Excuse me, Excuse me—that's us; can we get through please,' I said, now queue jumping as quickly as possible. Our frenzied actions were fortunately seen by the immigration officials, helped, I think, by our frantic waving of our walking sticks in their direction. We also hit people standing too near to us. Within a matter of minutes, we were through passport control and seated on an electric transport vehicle, requested by the customs offices, speeding off towards the departure lounge. After arriving at the gate, I looked up at one of the TV screens which was running a breaking new story with the caption:

"Pensioners close the Tullamarine Motorway".

'A multi car pile-up on the Melbourne-inbound lanes of the Tullamarine Motorway has caused traffic chaos with all lanes still closed,' said the news reporter.

'Authorities are looking for two pensioners who allegedly tried to cross the motorway near the Bolte Bridge. This triggered the multi-car pile-up some two kilometres further back. There are no reports of serious injuries. Anyone with any information is asked to contact Crime Stoppers on 1800 333 000.'

Olivia and I handed over our boarding passes and made our way down the gangway and on to the plane for the twenty-three hour flight to London. It wasn't until the wheels finally left the ground that we allowed ourselves to relax, amazed to be on the flight and too weary to bid Melbourne and Australia farewell.

I was still haunted by the memories of our last international flight, returning from Britain after the accident. But this trip was different; no sooner had I settled into my seat than sleep greeted me. The trip passed quickly and was not the nightmare I recalled from our last flight. Before I knew it, we had landed at Heathrow Airport.

'You have to ring Penny and let her know we have arrived safely!'

'I know, Olivia, as soon as we disembark and before we pass through Customs.'

One of the many joys of travelling business class is that you're first off and having, during the flight, requested assistance leaving the airplane we enjoyed a ride on another electric chariot before leaving our transport in the baggage collection area. Looking around, it did not take long to locate a phone.

'Hello, Penny this is Max.'

'Pops, where are you?'

But before I could answer, she added, 'They know you're missing.'

'What's happened?' I said, pretending we had not seen the news bulletin as we were readying to catch the flight.

'I don't know how they found out but the news report said the police are searching for two elderly people reported missing from Bellbird Village. They also said that they suspected you were the people who yesterday caused chaos on the Tullamarine Motorway. Was that you and where are you?

'It's okay Penny, we are safe and sound in London. We wanted to call because we didn't get a chance to say goodbye and to let you know we are safe and well. Olivia wants to know if the news said anything about us going to the airport?'

'No, and they haven't released your names yet. But when they do, it will be only a matter of time before someone links you, the motorbike accident in Europe and the car crash in Moonee Ponds.'

'There is no need to worry Penny, everything is going perfectly. It's been great talking with you; we had better go and make our way through Customs. One final question though. Since we have made the news, has anyone spoken to you about us?

'No, not yet.'

I explained to Olivia what Penny had said as we asked a kind young gentleman to lift our luggage from the carousel. We then proceeded to Customs, hoping to be waved straight through, but unfortunately we were not.

'Madam, did you pack these bags yourself?'

'Yes,' said Olivia.

'And sir?'

'Of course,' I said, feeling slightly annoyed.

A Customs officer, somewhere in her thirties and very polite and friendly, then proceeded to unzip Olivia's suitcase and held up a monthly dosette box containing five pills per day.

'Are these yours Olivia? Is it okay to call you Olivia or would you prefer Mrs Breeze?'

'Yes, call me Olivia and yes they are mine. It's prescription medication.'

'No problems, Olivia. Do you have either a letter from your doctor or a copy of your prescription?'

'No.'

'Are you sure these are your prescription drugs?'

'Of course.'

'And this is your suitcase?'

'Yes,' Olivia said, now sounding impatient.

The young Customs officer then proceeded to take from the suitcase, and hold up so Olivia could see, a G-string.

'And these; are they yours Madam?'

Before Olivia could answer, she took a lace bra from the luggage and again holding it up so Olivia could see, said, 'And this!'

'No,' said Olivia, 'they are not mine.'

'But Madam, you said that you packed this bag?'

I looked on in bewilderment before realising the message to the morning concierge had been muddled up. Rather than buying for eighty-somethings and making the clothing more trendy, the message for trendy must have been given without reference to our age.

'There has been a mistake,' I said. 'That's my suitcase.'

The Customs officer was not amused by my humour, saying, '*importing prescription drugs into the UK is a serious offence.*' She held up the dosette box from my suitcase and a pair of silk boxer shorts. 'Can you tell me the names of these prescription drugs?'

'Olivia knows better than me but it's something like Zoloft, Prednisolone, Coversyl, Panadol, Furosemide and,' I added, breaking into a singing voice, '*a partridge in a pear treeeeee.*'

'Max,' Olivia reprimanded me.

'I don't think you appreciate the seriousness of this sir. I will need to talk with my supervisor and it's quite possible that you won't be granted entry into the UK.'

Thirty minutes seemed like three hours before she returned and said, 'You are free to go and welcome to the United Kingdom. Please enjoy your stay.'

After repacking our cases, we passed through Customs and into the arrival area. Even when you know there is no one waiting for you, it's an impulse to look around. Perhaps somewhere there's a sign being held with your name on it. But there was not. For us, it was outside and a wait for the free bus ride to the hotel and I had the uncomfortable feeling of being watched.

'Olivia, I think we are being followed.'

'I consider you're a little paranoid; besides there are hundreds of people about, so if we were, you couldn't tell.'

Olivia was probably right, but I remained uneasy waiting the ten minutes for the bus to arrive.

Stepping off the bus and looking at the hotel, I was overwhelmed by fatigue but also exhilaration. We had made it to Britain and, with it, part one of our journey was over. Now the dangerous part would begin.

Taking Olivia's hand, just for a second, I said, 'Are you ready?'

'To book in to the hotel or for bed?' Olivia smiled at her own answer and then strode off towards the front entrance of the hotel. I followed and thought to myself, *bed*.

Chapter 6
Kate and Edward

'An eighty-seven-year-old couple from Australia, who ran away from their nursing home, caused a multi car pileup in Melbourne on Monday when they walked, with outstretched walking sticks, across a four lane motorway. The couple are believed to be the same people who in 2008 captured the imagination and hearts of the public when, aged 85, they were involved in a serious road accident in Poland while riding a vintage motorbike and sidecar across the Britain and Europe. Police are following reports that they were heading to Melbourne International Airport hoping to fly to Britain. Authorities have grave fears for their safety. According to their nursing home both Max and Olivia have major health issues. A spokesperson from the home said, "They are quite possibly showing the signs of dementia and had mentally slipping back into the past, trying to reach Britain, where they grew up."

'If you are coming to Britain I hope you make it,' concluded the news reader, before moving on to the next item.

'Olivia,' I called.

'What is it Max?'

'We are on the news. It may be time to consider leaving the hotel.'

'Do they know we are in Britain?'

'It's not been reported but that doesn't mean the authorities don't know.'

'Max, we can't, the letter from Penny hasn't arrived. We have to wait, just one or two more days.'

Olivia was right as always; we just needed to be patient. It would not take long for us to be traced to the UK but, until they released our pictures and the surnames we were travelling under, we should remain safe at the Hotel Renaissance. Anyway, it was highly unlikely that the authorities would devote any serious resources to tracking us down. Who would really care about two old farts from Australia? The more I thought about it, the more I thought we should be safe for at least another day or two but then it would be wise to move, with or without Penny's letter. We could make other arrangements to obtain the letter from the hotel when it arrived.

I spent the early part of the morning, our second full day in Britain, continuing my search for cars on car sales internet sites. Our plan, before leaving Australia was to hire a vehicle, but my current thinking was that it would be safer to buy a car privately. 'Purchasing a classic car, would in my opinion, appear less suspicious to the seller,' I told Olivia, who just rolled her eyes.

'And that's your story and you're sticking to it!' she said, before adding, 'I expect a leather interior. Red.'

Searching the web, I looked for a Jaguar. A beautiful British racing green Jaguar, 1960s Mark 2, with the 3.8 litre motor and 5 speed gear box, was my preference. I found one in Oxford, only seventy-seven kms away and easy to reach from Heathrow. Making a phone call and then chatting with the owner, I concluded that he was a true car enthusiast. We agreed on an inspection time of 2.00pm the following day with a cash drive away purchase, if I liked the car. It was fortuitous that I had taken a £20,000 cash advance on the Visa card the previous day which did raise some eyebrows at the bank.

The rest of the morning passed quickly. As on the other two days, other than going to the bank and searching for a car, we had done little and mostly remained in our room. We hadn't even been clothes shopping because the effects of jet lag hung like a heavy fog and refused to lift. Olivia and I were in the midst of discussing a light lunch in the hotel dining room when the phone rang.

'Mr Breeze, good afternoon sir. This is Reception, we have a priority package from Australia for you.'

'Excellent. I will be down shortly. We will be checking out tomorrow morning.'

'Certainty sir.'

After lunch and having securely attached the recently arrived post office box key to my key ring, we passed the afternoon with another extended nap. We both woke shortly before 5.00pm. Ordinarily I would have spent time packing for the trip to Oxford the following day, but, with our luggage still only consisting of toiletries and silky and skimpy things, pre-dinner drinks at the bar seemed a more fulfilling way to spend the next hour or so. Besides, 5:00 to 6:00 pm was Happy Hour.

The bar was busy with people dotted throughout the room. After ordering glasses of chardonnay, we found comfortable chairs with a view of one of the large TV screens which lined a number of the walls of the bar.

'Olivia, I have an uncomfortable feeling we are being watched.'

'Max you're getting more and more paranoid.'

I gave a despondent sigh and took a sip of wine, which I swilled in my mouth, savouring the flavour before swallowing. As I leaned back into the chair a feeling of dread swept across me as the teletext which scrolls across the bottom of the TV screen announcing news highlights read, '*Special report in the 6.00pm News on the missing Australian nursing home residents who are on the run in the UK.*'

'Excuse me, Olivia and Max.'

Olivia and I looked up to see a smartly dressed young man, aged somewhere in his early thirties.

'My name is Edward Phoenix; I am the afternoon manager of the hotel.'

He paused but we said nothing.

'I followed your story after the motorbike accident in 2008. I remember wanting to be like you when I was your age.'

'I am terribly sorry Edward, we know of the story of course and Olivia and I do share the same Christian names, but we are not those people. Unfortunately you are mistaken.'

'That may be so sir but you may want to know that we have just received a call from the police asking if Olivia and Max Breeze are guests at our hotel. They know you are travelling under false names, as do we all; it was on the news earlier. The police are on their way here; now! If you wish to leave, my wife Kate, who also works here, is waiting for you at the rear.'

'Young man, we have changed our minds; you clearly have a very good memory, unlike my husband who can't even remember who we are. Lead the way,' said Olivia, grabbing our walking sticks and thrusting mine into my hand. I needed it to help me stand.

Edward started towards the front reception but stopped abruptly and turned before saying, 'This way.'

As we pushed through the swing doors leading to the kitchen, I looked back over my shoulder to see a uniformed and, in all likelihood, plain clothes police officers walking towards the reception desk. I also noticed the man, whom I thought had been watching us, leave the bar.

'See that door at the far end of the kitchen? Go through and follow the corridor to the end. It will lead you to the delivery area. Kate will be waiting for you there. I must return to my office so nothing looks suspicious,' said Edward. 'I will see you later tonight.'

I raised an eyebrow and looked back at Edward.

'You will be staying with us tonight. Unless you have a better plan?' he added in an enquiring tone. He did not wait for a reply before hurrying away.

We made our way down the corridor and into the loading and staff parking area. Waiting for us was a young woman in her early thirties. She was tall and slender with magnificent jet black hair and a calming smile.

'Hello Olivia and Max, I'm Kate. I've been so looking forward to meeting you. This way.'

Without speaking further, Kate led us to her SUV, which was a blessing. SUVs are easy to get in and out of with seats at bum height. Oldies like us can just swing in. I sat in the front and Olivia in the rear.

Traffic was heavy as we swung left onto Bath Road, then north on the M25 and then the M40 heading towards Oxford.

None of us spoke as we drove. After fifteen, or maybe twenty minutes, I broke the silence and said, 'Kate, It's quite possible we will be followed.'

'I thought we might be. I am planning to make a detour by swinging onto some country lanes. That will tell us if somebody is following.'

Kate turned left off the M40 and on to the A40 and then left past a pub with a sign saying the "Cricketers Arms".

'Is there anybody following us?' I asked.

'Not as far as I can tell,' replied Kate.

She made a series of turns before crossing the A40 again and then joined Bayswater Road. We were all, once again, silent until I said, 'Kate, don't get me wrong, we are very grateful of your help, but why are you helping us? And you said, in the car park, "*I've been so looking forward to meeting you.*" It sounded as if you know us.'

'I feel as if I do. I will tell you our story over dinner, when Edward arrives home.'

A feeling of panic swelled in my stomach. Had we left the post office box key back in our room? Anxiously, I grabbed for my pocket. My keys were there and with them the post office box key.

Kate looked across and said, 'Are you okay Max?'

'Yes, everything is fine.'

Kate told us that Edward and she lived in Horton-cum-Studley, a country hamlet about 10 km north east of Oxford. Horton-cum-Studley was a quaint English village consisting of a parish church, St Barnabas and a pub. Arriving, I took careful note of the directions, watching the street names as we turned into Oakley Road and then swung into the driveway to a house completely obscured from the road by trees.

The guest room of their house was spacious, for an English residence, most of which are considerably smaller than what we are accustomed to in Australia. Kate kindly lent us a change of clothes. Edward's shirts and pants fitted me surprisingly well as did Kate's for Olivia. Buying a new wardrobe was on the list of to do for Friday, after we picked up the Jag. We washed and changed and went downstairs, carefully holding onto the banister. It was 9.00pm before Edward arrived home and, by that time, we were feeling rather peckish. As we were gathering around the table for dinner the phone rang. Kate left the table to answer the phone, which was within hearing distance.

'Hi Dad,' said Kate, 'it's really great to hear from you but we have some friends over for dinner; can I call you back tomorrow?'

We couldn't hear his response but gathered from Kate's conversation that he was intending to visit.

'I see.' Then came another lengthy pause as Kate listened before saying, 'No Dad, I understand; we saw the story about them on the news as well.' Another pause. 'You know you are always welcome. When do you hope to be here? Saturday! That will be fantastic, see you then.'

Kate hung up the phone and returned to the table.

'That was my father. He lives in Lyon in France and is coming over to the UK on Saturday to look for you two,' said Kate looking at first to Olivia and then at me.

There was a moment of silence, as if Kate was waiting for us to say something. When Olivia and I both kept quiet she continued, 'I didn't tell him you were here.'

'Why is your father interested in us?' asked Olivia.

'He drove past you in Poland, when you had the motorbike accident. When he heard the accident reported in the news, he thought it sounded suspicious. Sorry; I neglected to say, he works for Interpol. Anyway, because he works for Interpol, he was able to make some inquiries about your accident. He didn't know it when he began, but his investigation crossed paths with his father; my grandfather, Jean Axel.'

'What do you mean?' I said.

'Jean, Pop, is no longer with us; he passed away some years ago now. He escaped from France during the war and came to Britain in 1940. He joined the Royal Navy and served in Coastal Forces, or so we believed.'

I looked at Olivia, and our eyes met, but I remained silent and waited for Kate to continue.

'My mum died when I was quite young and, with Dad a policeman, I spent a lot of time with my grandparents and in particular with Pop. Towards the end of his life, after Gran died, he started recalling stories from the war. He talked to both Dad and me about going to Brittany on MTB or in vessels disguised as fishing trawlers. He said he would sometimes go ashore staying in Brittany to help organise escaped prisoners, airmen or important people, to come and go from Britain. I remember thinking that they were truly amazing tales. Once, he even told a story of having to travel to Paris on reconnaissance, hiding from the Gestapo to bring information back to Britain. I still struggled to believe what he and people like him did during the war. I don't think I would have been that brave.

'As I got older, I realised what he had to say and what he did, is an important part of his story. It's also our family history.' Kate had to pause and I could hear the lump in the throat, as her voice was on the verge of tears. She gave a slight cough before going on.

'I'm sorry,' she said. 'But like all too many families, it wasn't until after his death that we decided to write his story. When we started to research his stories, we couldn't find any mention of him being involved in any secret trips to Brittany. We got a copy of his Military Service records and it recorded him as an ordinary sailor in the Coastal Forces. The boats on which he served may have crossed the channel, but none was recorded as a clandestine vessel. You start having doubts—we wondered for a long time if he had made up the stories, although we could see no reason for him doing so. We were left with all of these questions we wished we had asked while he was alive.

'One night, when Dad was here and we were talking about Pop, we remembered a name of a person Pop said he used to meet in Brittany, Pierre Gicquel. Dad decided to see if Pierre was still alive and found he was living in Lannili. In 2005, he went to visit Pierre Gicquel with the hope that he may remember Pop. He did. It was through him that we came to understand Pop's real story and his contribution to the war. I also went to visit him and he was kind and welcoming… and patient, as my French was not as good as it once was.'

'I see,' I said, still not wanting to give any information away and how do you think this relates to us?'

'Dad believes you went to see Pierre Gicquel just before he died. He thought your trip across Europe in 2008 was in some way connected with the Second World War and perhaps his father, my grandfather. If not his father, then what his father believed in. He also thinks, or so he said on the phone, that your escape from the nursing home in Australia to come to the UK, is in some way related. He said you are likely to be in grave danger and he wants to find you.'

Kate stopped speaking and there followed an uncomfortable silence which we did not fill. We waited for her to speak again.

'Is this about the war?' she asked, but then said, 'I'm sorry, I shouldn't ask. Would you like some more gravy?' And then hastily she added, 'we will help you regardless, won't we Edward?'

Olivia gave me *the look* which said we had lived our lives too long in secrets.

I looked at Kate and saw in her our Penny, but I was not sure what or how much I should say. In the end I decided on a simple explanation. 'We knew Pierre Gicquel. He was a special friend and we were deeply saddened when we learned of his death.'

'I knew it,' said Kate excitedly. 'Dad was right. Did you know Pop?'

I looked over to Oliva again and after a short pause said, 'Perhaps Olivia and I can take a short stroll in your garden. I know it's late but I need a little air.'

In truth I wanted time to think and to ask Olivia what she thought. How much should we share? We needed help on this quest and, perhaps, Kate and Edward would be the answer to our prayers.

Edward, like Olivia, looked quite surprised by my statement.

'Let me get you some coats,' he offered.

It was dark and cold as we made our way carefully up the garden path and away from the house.

'What's on your mind Max?' said Olivia.

'Maybe this is the most amazing coincidence, in which case we have been exceedingly lucky, and they happen to be the loveliest couple you could hope to meet. God knows we need help.' I paused. 'Or maybe we are being a set up and it's time to leave. Like right now!'

'Max, my sense is they are genuine but what's bothering you?'

'It's Penny.' I looked to Olivia expecting her to be surprised but instead she nodded before I continued.

'She reminds me so much of Penny that I want to believe her but I think that might be the trap. Would it be possible to set this and us up so quickly, though?'

'She reminds me of Penny too and I feel drawn to her and Edward. Our agents at Cliff told us about Inspector Axel, so we know he investigated us. I say let's go along with them, for now, but cautiously. Tomorrow we can do some snooping and check them out. If she really is the daughter of Inspector Axel then we know what she is saying is true.'

'Yes, but what do we do about Axel, now we know Interpol is looking for us?'

Having reached the end of the garden, we turned to start the walk back. The house shone like a picture from a sales magazine, its lights penetrating the darkness, silhouetting the house against the black of the night. Then it was gone. Not one light at a time but instantaneously as all of the lights went out. A power outage, I thought, but then, through the dining room window, we saw a flash of light and then another. There was no sound.

Gunfire.

Olivia and I lowered ourselves to the ground and crawled into the garden shrubbery. Finding cover, we watched the house and waited. Every now and then, through the windows, we saw flashes of red as the laser sights scanned and searched the house. We knew Kate and Edward were probably dead and, but for fate, us with them.

With no lights emanating from the house we didn't see the back door open and two figures emerge into the garden. The first sign was the faintest sound of footsteps, barely audible even in the still night, and then red dots hitting one tree and then darting to another in a systematic arc as the assailants moved closer to our hiding place. I had little doubt that they would be wearing night vision goggles. Our best chance of survival was to remain perfectly still, not moving and hardly daring to breathe. A leaf crunched only inches from my nose and even in the dark, lit only by the overcast night sky, a pair of shoes was clearly visible. The assailant remained motionless for what seemed an eternity, listening for any sign of our presence. Then the toes of the shoes turned and moved slowly and methodically on. I gasped for air, realising that I had been holding my breath. The shoes briefly reappeared before vanishing back into the still of the night.

As we lie, waiting for a safety only time could now deliver, I could see in my mind as clearly as if it were true— Penny, our Penny, dying from a gunshot in the house. I knew then the pain, the agony, Kate's father would feel when he heard the news. We had killed them as surely as if we had pulled the trigger ourselves and we had been willing to put Penny in danger before embarking on this trip. I prayed for Penny's safety and then felt guilty for thinking of Penny instead of Edward and Kate.

I reached for Olivia's hand and the only words I could manage to say in a soft whisper were, 'I'm sorry.'

Perhaps an hour had passed before we thought it safe to leave our hiding place.

'Let's go,' I whispered to Olivia.

Boom! The night sky lit up with a red and yellow hue as flames leapt out from where the windows had once been. The explosion was deafening and, if we were not still prostrate on the ground, perhaps that too would have been the end of us.

Olivia called into my ringing ears, 'Gas! They're covering their tracks.'

We could hear neighbours emerging from their houses shouting in voices of anguish and urgency. I signalled to Olivia and we slowly stood and made our way farther up the garden until the dark of night once again gave concealment.

Chapter 7

Jaguar

Stealing a car took longer than we both hoped. The explosion had woken the slumbering village and it wasn't until the early hours of Friday morning that we could finally flee to Oxford. We thought it too late to book into a hotel without arousing suspicion, so we looked for a B&B with a car park in which we could hide and sleep until daylight. Driving down Banbury Road, Olivia noticed the Parkland B&B which appeared to have a nice sized car park. After pulling in we settled, the best we could, for the remainder of the night.

Despite being seated, or leaning back in the seats, sleep came easily for both of us. It was about 6.00am when night began to fade.

'The sun will be up in about thirty minutes,' said Olivia. 'What's our plan for the day?'

Twenty years ago we would have abandoned the car at the B&B and walked into Oxford. Now, with walking any significant distance a challenge, we decided on dumping the car at the railway station, even though there would be CCTV.

To minimize the risk of being recognised, we had resolved to split up for the day. I left Olivia at the Oxford Railway Station, she having decided to take the 7.09am train to Manchester and a return train in the afternoon. Her idea was quite clever, to catch up on sleep where she would be totally inconspicuous, sitting and dozing on a warm intercity train. Her day would pass in relative comfort, I surmised.

My plan was that, having bought the Jaguar, I would pick Olivia up from in front of the Eagle and Child hotel, at about 3.00pm. From there, we would drive toward Exeter in Devon and the post office drop box, staying overnight en-route. With that in mind, I walked what was for me a considerable distance, from the station and up the high street, resting along the way, until I came across a quaint café, the Queen's Lane Coffee House. Both the name and the building facade were appealing but I think it was the sign that claimed that they were the longest established coffee house in Europe that won me. Undoubtedly they were proud of their age, which I interpreted as a good hint that they appreciated older things and, with me being old, I thought I would be welcome inside. Casting one final critical eye over the premises, looking for what I don't know, I entered intent on breakfast, a hot coffee and reading the newspaper, my normal morning ritual restored.

The Queen's Lane Coffee House would be my hideout for the next few hours, or until the library opened. That is where I planned to conceal myself for the rest of the day until catching a taxi to purchase the car.

I ordered from the menu the scrambled eggs on toast but looked, in envy, at the Full English Breakfast, 'eggs on toast, sausages, bacon, baked beans, tomato and mushrooms'. The gentlemen seated opposite had ordered it. The smell was mouth-watering but, unfortunately, two bits of toast is a big breakfast for me nowadays, and I had to be content in indulging my senses by savouring the aroma.

The waitress, probably a student at one of the colleges nearby, brought the newspaper with my coffee and I settled in for a quiet read while breakfast was cooking. The radio played a local station in the background and, as with many morning programs, was more talking than music. Glancing at my watch, I saw it had just turned 8.00am and with it the morning news came on.

'This is the Heart of Oxfordshire News. Leading our bulletin this morning, police are investigating a house explosion late yesterday evening at Horton-cum-Studley, a small village east of Oxford. Two people are reported as missing. Police are

not saying if they are treating the explosion as suspicious. The names of the missing people have not been released.'

Remembering Kate and Edward sent the radio broadcast drifting from my consciousness until being snapped back into the present with the mention our names.

'Olivia and Max, our Bonnie and Clyde nursing home escapees from Australia, narrowly avoided capture by police yesterday. Eye witness accounts say Max and Olivia, who entered Britain on false passports, avoided police by leaving through the kitchen of the Renaissance Hotel as authorities were coming through the front entrance. A spokesperson for the police say there are concerns for the health of Max and Olivia as they fled in such a hurry that all of their medications were left behind. It is believed that they are heading to Oxford. Police are seeking the assistance of the public for any information.

'Listeners may remember Olivia and Max, who became famous following a motorbike and sidecar accident back in 2008, while riding across Britain and Europe at the young age of eighty-five. The major papers have reported that, tomorrow, they will be running editorials on Olivia and Max, along with speculations as to why they have returned to Britain.

'If you see Max or Olivia, you are asked to contact your local police station.'

Our photographs had already appeared on TV but, once we made the major newspapers, anonymity would become increasingly difficult. Things would become even more complicated if we were linked to Edward and Kate and the house explosion. The current casual police interest could quickly turn into a serious investigation, making evasion far more difficult.

I looked up, feeling the eyes of all the customers within the café staring at me, only to find that nobody was paying any attention to me at all. I must have then drifted off and become deep within my own thoughts, being brought back to the present by the sound of the waitress's voice.

'Are you all right? Sir, are you all right?'

'Yes, yes I'm fine. Thank you,' I replied.

The waitress smiled and, indicating with her eyes, drew my attention to my hands, where I had inadvertently allowed the coffee cup to slip in my fingers thus dispensing what was left in the cup over the table and newspaper.

'Let me clean that up for you sir,' she said.

Using paper napkins, she methodically worked around the table soaking up the spilt coffee. When she had finished, she removed the sodden newspaper and returned a minute or two later with a new unsodden version.

'Can I get you another coffee?' she asked in a kindly tone, as if nothing had happened.

'That would be nice, thank you,' I said, secretly grateful that I had not been dribbling.

The rest of the morning and early afternoon passed uneventfully. I even had a nice snooze, along with some other venerable men at the library. Shortly before 2.00pm, I took a taxi to where the Jaguar was housed. I intended to purchase the car regardless of its condition but, to my great pleasure, it was as described; immaculate. I bought it without moment's hesitation.

With the cash transaction completed, I slid into the driver's seat of my new chariot, ever mindful that, aside from yesterday's dash in the stolen car, I had not driven since the crash in Moonee Ponds. The old custodian watched, perhaps with apprehension, as I put the keys into the ignition of his once beautiful mistress and brought the Jaguar to life. A couple of kangaroo hops later and I was on my way to the Eagle and Child, the pickup point for Olivia.

'Gee some of these laneways are narrow,' I said to myself, as I swung left into a cobbled road which I hoped would cut across town. I waved back to some pedestrians who were clearly delighted to see a beautiful classic British car prowling the equally elegant streets of Oxford.

The road was empty in front and behind, which was fortunate for I couldn't see how oncoming traffic could be passed. There must have been a traffic light somewhere up ahead for, all of a sudden, I was facing a stream of traffic with no place to go. Bringing the Jaguar to a halt, I heard a knock on the driver's window. I wound it down, and a man in his thirties smiled back sympathetically and in a kindly voice said, as only the English could, 'This is a one way street and, I hate to be the bearer of bad news, but you are going the wrong way.'

The first of the approaching cars was now stopped just a few feet from my bonnet emblem but not a car horn sounded. Hastily, I tried to make a three, then four, then seven point turn. Each time I ended up with the front wedged across the footpath and the back blocking the road. With great effort, I managed to drive the car back to where I had started, facing the stationary oncoming car.

To my dismay, I noticed what appeared to be a policeman, but could quite easily have been a parking officer, walking slowly up the lane.

'Shit, police,' I said loudly enough to be heard through the open window by the man who had alerted me to the one way nature of the street.

'Would you like me to turn the car around for you?' the window knocker said.

'That would be most generous of you. I've only just picked her up and find that I'm struggling a little without the aid of power steering!'

Having finished the sentence, which was obviously a lie, I alighted from the car faster than I had moved in the last two years and was in the passenger seat before he knew what was happening.

'If you could turn her around and put her out of sight,' I said, speaking in a mocking tone, as if giving instructions to a chauffeur, to which he laughed aloud before asking, 'Are you on the run?'

He didn't wait or seem to expect an answer but manoeuvred and turned the car around with three sweeping motions, before driving it back to the main road and away from my chaos.

'You're not from Oxford?'

'No. Does it show?'

He laughed again before saying, 'Oxford is a maze of one-way streets, so even the locals struggle. If you like, I can drive you to where you want to go in Oxford. By the way, I am Zarheer,' he said, holding out his hand.

Without thinking I automatically replied 'Max,' and while regretting my lapse, I reached across to shake his hand.

'Where to Max?'

'The Eagle and Child.'

'Good choice. Did you know Tolkien and C.S. Lewis used to meet there?'

We made our way across Oxford and didn't speak again until pulling up outside the Eagle and Child.

'Thank you Zarheer.'

'I hope you don't scare Olivia too much with your driving skills. You take care Max and good luck.'

'Are we that obvious?' I said to Zarheer, as he left the car, and handed me the keys.

His only reply was a warm smile accompanied by a departing nod of the head as he strode away from the Jaguar and back from where we had come.

***

Inspector Axel

It had been another long week at Interpol and I was looking forward to the weekend and flying to the UK to stay with my daughter and her husband. The sound of the phone ringing brought me back into the now.

'Inspector Axel, this is Detective Lynda Wells,' said the voice at the other end of the phone and added, 'of Scotland Yard.'

'Good afternoon, Detective Wells, it's been quite a while. How can I be of assistance to the Yard?'

'I wish that chatting to you again could have been under better circumstances. I have some difficult news. There's been an explosion at your daughter Kate's home in Horton-cum-Studley. I'm afraid that we are really concerned for the safety of Kate and Edward. It's too early be a hundred percent certain, but there are two bodies at the scene. As you would appreciate with an explosion and fire it will take a little time to make a positive identification.'

Disbelief, grief and panic in a melange of emotions overwhelmed the moment. Tears welled and dripped down my cheeks depositing their salty sorrow upon my lips.

'Are you still there Inspector?'

'Yes, yes, I'm sorry.

'I understand that this is difficult.'

Choking back the tears, I asked in a voice that quivered, 'Do you know what caused the explosion? Is it suspicious?'

Detective Wells outlined what she knew and told of the CCTV footage showing Max and Olivia leaving the Hotel Renaissance with Kate.

Curiosity fused with grief; through our family connection, it was not surprising that Kate would help Max and Olivia if given the opportunity. My immediate thought was whether I should share this link with Detective Wells? I chose to remain silent.

'Detective Wells, if you remember the last time we spoke, I was investigating Max and Olivia, following their motorbike and sidecar accident in Poland. That must have been sometime back in 2008. Is it possible the bodies are of Max and Olivia and not Kate and Edward?'

'Possible, although we have received some unconfirmed reports that Max and Olivia have been seen in Oxford. We are still looking into the sightings. As I have said, we don't know with certainty whose the bodies are.'

'Do you know, I was convinced back in 2008 that someone was trying to kill those two. I am willing to bet my career that whoever caused that explosion was after those wily old buggers and not my daughter.'

'Our authorities agree with you; they think there is something else going on here which is why Scotland Yard has been asked to take over the investigation of both the explosion and of finding Max and Olivia, if they are still alive. Because of your previous investigation, I am authorised to invite you to join us in the UK and assist in finding Max and Olivia. For obvious reasons, you can't be part of the investigation into the explosion; you will have to leave that one to us. As part of our team you will know exactly what's going on.'

'Thank you Detective. I was planning a visit to the UK this weekend, to see Kate, so I already have a flight booked for Saturday morning.'

For the second time in a couple of minutes I decided against telling Detective Wells the whole truth. I neglected to say that the real reason for my visit was to unofficially look for Max and Olivia.

'I will see if I can get an earlier flight and leave tonight instead. I would suggest that we don't fuel public interest in Max and Olivia. If we can, we should try and keep them out of the media, at least until we know what's going on.'

Detective Wells agreed.

On hanging up the phone my body felt numb but, when I closed my eyes, I was touched by the certainty that Kate was still alive. *A father would know. A father would feel it if she was gone, or am I just kidding myself?* As quickly as that sense of knowing came, it was replaced by uncertainty and then the inevitable acceptance of forfeiture. Fatigue overcame me and all of the energy drained from my body. In despair, I sank deeper into the office chair. I had lost my wife and then, during her formative years, through necessity, Kate was raised more by my parents than me. *I've been a neglectful father. If only I had spent more time with her.*

Despite this I recalled a good relationship; she never complained of the hours I worked, the school concerts I missed or the birthdays I forgot. Closing my eyes once more, I could see Kate staring back at me. Her eyes sparkled with love and compassion. *When was the last time I told her that I love her?* With that thought I let the tide of sorrow and regret take me and I wept silently, alone.

***

Max

I found Olivia seated at the back of the Eagle and Child drinking a class of white wine. She had given up waiting outside but showed no concern with me arriving thirty minutes late.

'Did you get it Max?'

'Yep.'

'Is it any good?'

'Gorgeous, absolutely stunning.'

'Can you drive it?'

'Nope.'

'Nothing's changed then. I picked up a road atlas while I was in Manchester.'

'Can you read it?'

'Nope.'

'Nothing's changed then.'

'Touché,' said Olivia. 'Are you ready? Let's do it. Let's get out of here before it gets dark and you have a real excuse for your bad driving.'

'You can be cruel sometimes,' I said in a loving tone, lifting one eyebrow.

I barely negotiated a roundabout the size of a US Aircraft Carrier and with more lanes and exits than the tentacles on an octopus. The beeping and gesturing from our fellow road users were ignored while I randomly changed lanes mid roundabout and we found ourselves on the A40 rather than the A42, our planned route.

'Whose mistake was that?' I said to my navigator, Olivia.

'Whose do you think?' came a barbed reply.

Checking the map, Olivia concluded that the error didn't matter as we were travelling generally in the right direction, towards where we wanted to go.

'I think we should keep off the major M roads,' said Olivia. 'At Burford I want you to turn left onto the A361. Our new route is through Swindon and if you want, you can skirt the centre of town. Then I want you to take the A4361 to Devizes, after which you turn right onto the A361 to Frome and then the A359 down to Bruton.' After pausing for a breath, she continued, 'Then drive to Yeovil and finally take the A30 to Crewkerne to join the A35 for the run into Honiton. Once there, I expect you will remember the way to the Five Bells Inn where we are planning to have dinner. Did you get all that?'

'I did. The roundabout was my mistake. Turn left at Burford?'

After the roundabout the traffic thinned. The countryside was stunning and the Jaguar purred like the cat she was, eating up the miles with ease.

It was a tad over three hours later that I brought the Jag to rest in the car park of the Five Bells Inn. This had been one of our favourite pubs from earlier visits. Coincidently, it was hidden down one of those narrow country lanes that only the Brits could love.

The pub building was as I remembered it and must have dated back to the 1500s. From memory, it had been a pub for over 150 years and made a perfect dinner setting for a Jaguar and its two weary occupants. We were both stiff and tired after what was a long, but pleasant, afternoon's drive. Holding on to the door handle, I pulled myself from the driver's seat and then stretched before walking around to Olivia's side of the car. She was already out of the car and waiting to go in.

The dining area was quite large but tonight was a quiet affair, with only a handful of other guests. We were seated in the corner, near a distinguished silver haired lady, who appeared to be eating on her own. She looked to be in her sixties, although I guessed she was really in her late seventies and weathering well. She was one of those ladies that you couldn't resist looking at, wearing a presence that emanated a vibrant, alert and at-one-with-the-world persona.

'Max, it seems such a long time ago that we were last here. It's so nice to be back.' Olivia's voice drew my attention away from the lady with the distinguished appearance.

'Sorry Olivia, what was it you said?' I thought I might have missed some earlier observation.

'I said, it's nice to be back.'

We talked quietly, rekindling the memories of the war and the secret liaisons we had in the gardens that surround the pub. We talked of the many times, in the decades which followed, that we returned to this special place. This had been one of the locations we'd intended to visit on our last motorbike trip but we never made it. There's something magical when location, or perhaps a piece of music, can transport you back to an earlier time and the events and emotions which accompanied it.

'We need to find somewhere to stay overnight,' I said to Olivia. 'Perhaps we could ask the bar attendant if she knows of anywhere close by?'

'Excuse me,' said the elegant woman sitting opposite. 'I don't wish to appear nosy but I couldn't help overhearing that you are looking for somewhere to stay. I have a B&B not far from here, just round the corner in a little village called Clyst Hydon. You might know it? I'm sorry, again I am being rude. I heard you say that you used to come here quite regularly once.'

'That quite all right,' said Olivia. 'We welcome your offer of a place to stay; it's been a long day. Max, I'm sure we went to church once in Clyst Hydon?'

'St Andrews,' said the distinguished looking lady. 'We still have services there. Oh please excuse me again, I neglected to introduce myself, I'm Elinor Grange.'

Not having anticipated an introduction, I quickly searched my memory, trying to remember if we had called each other by our real names while at the table. After an uncomfortable silence of perhaps five seconds, which is a long time when a person is waiting for a reply, I decided upon the truth. 'Max and Olivia; how pleased we are to meet you.' I couldn't tell if she thought I was lying but, nonetheless, stood and walked to where she was seated, and shook her hand. Olivia remained at our table and simply waved her greeting before adding, 'Elinor, Max has a wonderful memory, perhaps with the exception of his own name.' She sent an annoyed glance in my direction. 'Who was the minister when we last went to St Andrews?'

'Reverend Charles Sherwin was there from 1899 to 1930 after which there was a succession of vicars from neighbouring parishes until 1940 when the Reverend W.H Blight arrived. He was taking services when we went there in 1944. He was followed by the Reverend Richard James Attfield from 1948 to 1960.'

'He has a good memory when he tries,' said Olivia, causing Elinor to laugh.

The uncomfortable silence was forgotten. I could tell that Olivia and Elinor were going to be good friends.

After dinner, it was a short drive to Clyst Hydon and to our host's home, Grange Cottage. I decided it was undoubtedly named after her family who, in all likelihood, had lived here for generations.

I switched off the engine and Olivia looked across to me and said, 'We have no luggage. Not even a toothbrush this time.'

A disgruntled shrug of my shoulders was the best and only response I could come up with before I said, 'I thought you were going to buy something on your trip to Manchester?'

'And I thought you would have got something in Oxford.'

'We both just forgot. It would help, Olivia, if people weren't trying to blow us up or if we weren't having to flee hotels. Underpants will become the most expensive item of this trip if this continues. First thing tomorrow, when we go to

Exeter, we go shopping. In the meantime, what are we going to say to Elinor, if she asks?'

'I doubt she will even notice but, if she does, we tell her that we went for a drive, it got late and you were too tired to drive back to Oxford.'

Grange Cottage was a white detached home neighbouring the church. It was fairly spacious with four bedrooms, a formal dining room, a living room and a reading-room-cum-library. Shortly after entering the front foyer, I couldn't help imagining the online B&B advertisement for this place. *Delightful B&B* (code for: In need of renovation) *with country charm* (lucky to have running hot water) *set in idyllic location* (narrow country lane with no amenities nearby). It was difficult to envisage Grange Cottage as a B&B. There was no feeling of other guests having been here; in fact, there was no sense of anyone other than Elinor having been here in a very long time. The house appeared closed to the world, smelling airless and dusty. What once must have been white sheets covered much of the furniture and the house, and perhaps Elinor, seemed to be caught in their own time warp.

Our bedroom was little different from the remainder of the home. The grand double bed, being the centre piece of the room, was not, however, covered by dust sheets though slapping my hand on the bed covers caused a fog of dust to be illuminated in the light.

'I think we will be sharing the bed with more than one another,' I said.

'Max, a bed mite or two won't hurt you. Elinor is waiting for us in the reading room for a night cap, so stop your moaning and come on.'

'We have survived how many attempts on our lives? We've come all of this way only to be killed; poisoned by an eccentric old biddy serving 150 year old off port.'

'I like her and so did you at the pub. I saw you looking at her. Anyway, you never know; she might serve you a bottle of 1811, Château d'Yquem. That would keep you quiet.'

Elinor was waiting for us when we made our way down the stairs to join her in the library. There were no sheets covering the furniture but we could see them unceremoniously thrown in the corner. The room was dimly lit but had a romantic charm, added to by the warmth and glow emanating from the fireplace. A bottle of wine, already breathing, and three glasses, waited in anticipation of our presence. I couldn't resist picking up the bottle, inspecting the label, and dreaming of the Château d'Yquem.

'Would you pour?' Elinor said.

Her words were followed by a silence, filled only by the crackling of the fire and then the unmistakable sound of wine leaving its vessel and settling in crystal. Having filled the glasses, I handed one to Elinor and then to Olivia. Holding my glass towards the fireplace, I could see the colour of a big red.

Sipping it and then allowing the wine to swirl in my mouth before swallowing, I found the taste to be sensational. I could see Olivia was annoyed at my act of snobbery. Fortunately, when I glanced at Elinor, she was looking into the fire and appeared lost in thought.

'I don't have many visitors,' Elinor said.

Olivia and I looked at her but remained silent, waiting for her to continue.

'This is not really a B&B. It could be with a little work. I don't really know why I invited you back. I've kept to myself since my husband died.' She paused, then continued. 'More than fifteen years ago now. I still like to get dressed up and go out for dinner but I rarely talk to anyone and never have anybody here.

'I think it was the way in which you spoke to one another. It brought back fond memories of Henry and me. When I overheard you say that you were looking for somewhere to stay, on an impulse, I made up the B&B story and so here you are!'

'It's a lovely home,' said Olivia. 'We are both pleased you chose to invite us. You must miss your husband very much?'

'We did so much together and had some grand adventures. When he died, a part of me died as well. I think I've been wallowing in my own self-pity and guilt ever since.'

Elinor, over the duration of the bottle and aided admirably by the second bottle, told of her life with Henry, who was in the Foreign Service. Stories of living in Africa, India and even Papua New Guinea poured forth. She spoke of meeting and entertaining world leaders and celebrities. With his retirement, they returned to the ancestral home, here in Clyst Hydon. With contacts all over the world, Elinor told of the dreams they had of travelling and visiting the many and varied friends they had made, but neither had counted on the 'Big C'; cancer.

'It came without warning and ate away at him until he was almost unrecognisable. It took his body and spirit,' said Elinor.

Elinor told of how she had nursed Henry day and night for two years, as he became increasingly dependent. She confessed that, in the final year, she secretly wished he would die, so she could be free. When his time did come, rather than being free, she found herself becoming more and more reclusive. Even facing the everyday challenges became difficult. She said that she still harboured the dream of travel and of meeting old friends but the dreams had faded with time and she became increasingly accustomed, or is it safe, in her own company. Once a week she still dressed up and went out for dinner, which is how she met us.

Elinor seemed content on filling the evening with her story. We said little in reply but listened; *really* listened. It grew late and with the wine gone and the fire dying away, we stood up, bade Elinor good night and left the room.

'Breakfast is at 9.00,' called Elinor as we tackled the stairs.

CHAPTER 8

Post Office Box

Next morning we were greeted by the alluring aroma of bacon and eggs complemented by fresh brewed coffee percolating gently on the combustion cooker. Entering the kitchen we could see the table was laid in preparation of breakfast and Elinor was busying herself in readiness for us, her guests. The TV was playing in the background, unwatched but likely providing company in what normally would be an empty house.

'Good morning; I hope you're hungry, as we have quite a feast. Coffee?' said Elinor.

'That would be sensational,' I said with Olivia nodding her agreement.

'Did you both sleep well?'

'We did,' replied Olivia.

I looked up at Elinor, to see if she too was listening to the TV, and the breakfast talk show segment about us. She seemed completely oblivious to the report, so I guessed the voices to her were just a reassuring sound, filling the void of her daily routine.

***

Inspector Axel

'*What are the police doing? Giving out those details on Max and Olivia to the media will only fuel the public interest,*' I said aloud. Picking up the phone and trying to control my anger, I rang Scotland Yard and asked to be put through to Detective Wells.

'Detective Wells, this is Inspector Axel. Have you seen the news report linking Max and Olivia to the house explosion? I thought we discussed keeping the public interest in those two to a minimum. Last time, after the motorbike accident, there were a hundred Facebook posts of people who said they had seen them; the last thing we want now is people reporting on social media of their sighting and movements. If someone is after them, they may be dead before we find them.'

'I agree Inspector. The information didn't come from us. I received your text last night saying you had arrived in the UK. Why not come into the office, then we can go over what we know and with luck they will pop up somewhere today.'

***

Max

After breakfast, Olivia and I began to make our plans to retrieve the clue from the post office box in Exeter.

'I can drive you into Exeter,' said Elinor, who had obviously overheard our kitchen table conversation while clearing away the dishes.

'That would be very nice of you,' said Olivia. 'I would say Max could drive us all, but I like you way too much to inflict that upon you.'

I raised my gaze from the table and made a face in the pretence of being hurt. The girls just laughed.

I guess Olivia was thinking exactly the same as I was; people were expecting to see two of us, an old man and woman, and not three people. In addition to providing cover, we could split up. Olivia and Elinor together would garner no attention and neither would I alone. It would make retrieving the clue far less hazardous.

Elinor's fifteen-year-old C43 AMG Mercedes was in immaculate condition, the bone coloured leather as fresh as the day it was made. The V8 motor, unlike the Jaguar's that purred, growled into life when she turned the key. We moved off through the narrow lane and I was about to say, *you mustn't take the Mercedes out very often because it's in such good condition*, but all of a sudden, I struggled to find my voice as she accelerated the Mercedes to over 60MPH, flinging the car from blind corner to blind corner on the narrow lanes as though she was on the Nuremburg ring. The hedges brushed past, occasionally scraping the driver and then the passenger side mirrors. Elinor seemed totally relaxed chatting away to Olivia, so I closed my eyes and prayed that nobody was coming the other way. I opened my eyes just in time to see a huge tractor wheel inches from the front bonnet, and panic radiated throughout my whole body. With impact imminent, the Mercedes veered to the left, and the tractor to the right. Elinor waved, totally unfazed by the experience, to a tractor driver sitting too high to be seen by me. She flew around the next bend. Minutes later, we popped out from the narrow country lane surrounded by its beautiful green countryside, onto a main road with cars whistling by. We were just outside the City of Exeter; from one world to another in the blink of an eye. It could only be Britain.

We parked quite near the Exeter Cathedral in the Guildhall Central Car Park, undercover and out of sight. Before leaving Clyst Hydon we had confided in Elinor that we needed to make a secretive pick up from the post office; secretive in that we wanted to go in and out without attracting attention to ourselves. It was Elinor who suggested that they, the girls, should go to the post office and then do a little shopping. Olivia and I agreed with the plan, as it would also allow me time to find a menswear shop. Our agreed meeting point was to be the Ships Inn for lunch and a nice unhealthy burger and chips.

One of my biggest dislikes was shopping for clothes, but when needs must, needs must. Having left the car park and the girls, I meandered around the streets looking for a store, which I hoped would be staffed by someone old enough not to have acne. *'Whatever happened to the old men's tailors,'* I mumbled to myself. *'Nowadays all these shops that appear to be boutique businesses are really just part of a larger chain brand.'* Feeling old and grumpy, not aided by Elinor's driving, I decided that, as I pounded the pavement, I could wallow in my own self-pity, and bemoan the loss of the good old days; at least until lunch time when it would no longer be safe to do so.

I paused briefly at the first couple of menswear shops that I came to and ruminated as to whether or not I should go in, before moving slowly on. *'You're procrastinating,'* I said to myself. *'The next one you come to… in you go.'*

'Good morning; may I be of assistance?' said the middle aged woman serving behind the counter.

'I'm in Exeter for a wedding and it's this afternoon.' I paused trying to feign embarrassment before continuing, 'It's my granddaughter and, in a senior moment, I left behind my bag with my suit, socks and shoes, basically everything. I travelled down on my own and my wife is already here, staying with our daughter before the wedding. She is none too pleased as I am sure you can understand. So here I am and, yes, I am hoping you can be of great assistance.'

'That's quite all right sir, it happens all of the time. I am certain we can kit you out and organise the other things you need.'

Over the next hour the makeover took place and I changed into the new outfit in the shop. I also I purchased a week's supply of smalls, shirts and a second set of trousers. The attendant made good on her word and a selection of shoes was brought up for me from a shop two doors down.

'I am confident your wife will be pleased,' said the shop assistant, while standing back and admiring her creation.

'I am worried that I may get cold during the evening. Do you have a nice coat?' I asked.

'How about this double breasted wool cashmere full length coat?' she said, laying it across the counter. 'It is expensive but exceptional quality and right on trend. Could I also suggest, perhaps a nice hat and scarf to finish off with? Oh, sorry, perhaps one final thing. We have some lovely canes; they would really complement the outfit and, excuse me for saying so sir, in preference to that old walking stick you have. And which I see sir, you don't rely on.'

I left the shop unrecognisable from the person who walked in; a new man. Rounding the corner and seeing a rubbish bin, I deposited my old clothes inside, the ones lent to me by Edward, and continued on to our agreed meeting place.

****

Olivia

'The post office is this way,' Elinor said to me, while taking my arm and gently guiding me around the corner.

On reaching the post office I fumbled in my pocket for the box key. Max and I had agreed that it was essential that I maintain momentum, approaching and then opening the box with confidence. We believed this would draw the least attention to me. While fumbling for the key, I couldn't help myself from stopping and surveying the surroundings.

'Olivia, are you all right?' asked Elinor.

'Quick, take my arm. Look as though you are helping me.'

Elinor placed her hand under my elbow and together we went inside to where the post office box was waiting. Upon opening the box I was surprised to see three envelopes, which I quickly removed, and slipped into my pocket.

161

'Let's go,' I said.

We left the Post Office making our way for a little girls' shopping expedition before heading to the rendezvous point.

***

Max

'I see you have been shopping as well,' I called to Olivia as she and Elinor entered the Ships Inn.

'My goodness, I hardly recognised you Max. You don't scrub up half too bad,' said Olivia.

'You don't look half bad yourself in that charcoal suit. You sexy thing you.' Then, deciding to not worry about Elinor or even try to hide what we were doing, I said, 'Did you get it?'

Olivia placed three envelopes on the table and I added, 'Did anybody see you?'

'I'm not sure.'

'What did you see?'

'Excuse me,' said the waitress. 'Are you ready to order?'

After making our selections from the Menu, Olivia continued with her account. 'I thought two people were watching from across the lane. I did glance at them as we were leaving but they didn't seem to be paying us any attention. If it was us they were waiting for, I don't think they were expecting two women.'

Having finished her account, Olivia opened the first envelope. It contained two credit cards; one in the name of Max

Williams and the other, Olivia Williams. The second contained £2,000 in cash. Picking up the last envelope, Olivia looked over to me and I nodded. She opened the envelope to reveal its secret; the missing piece of information, a clue, for us to find and recover Janus. In her hand she held a single piece of paper.

'What does it say?' I said.

'It's a two line message.'

'Can you read it aloud?'

'The first line says, *Sacred pop group and pale fellow confused in duke's country*. The second line is, *Angry chiseller operated at ground level*. It makes make no sense to me. What do you think?'

Olivia pushed the paper over toward me. Taking it and surveying the writing, I said, 'Obviously it's some kind of clue but it's not the code we were expecting; there are no numbers.'

'Do you mind if I look?' asked Elinor.

I passed the paper across the table. Elinor picked it up and studied it intensely with a frown of concentration appearing on her forehead. I could see her mouthing the words silently to herself, which she did a couple of times before saying, 'Yes. Yes, I see it now. It's simple. It's a cryptic crossword clue. I am sure of it.'

'I hate cryptic crosswords, so can you unravel it?' I said.

Elinor hesitated and I could tell she was thinking hard. 'If I tell you, will you take me with you?'

'Now that's not what I thought she was going to say,' said Olivia. 'What do you think?'

'Elinor, can Olivia and I talk in private, just for a minute?'

Elinor rose from her chair and saying, 'I need to powder my nose,' she left us alone.

'Max, I can't stop thinking of what happened to Kate and Edward. If Elinor comes with us she might not come back but I also know we need her help. The three of us travelling together are much less conspicuous and we are unlikely to be recognised.'

'I feel the same; we do need her but, at the same time, I don't want to exploit her by putting her in danger.'

'Let Elinor decide… but I already know what she will say.'

'I agree, but I suggest we don't mention Janus by name.'

Olivia was right; despite our telling Elinor that her life may be in danger and telling her of Kate and Edward and the explosion, she wanted to come anyway. We said we were trying to recover an item which people were willing to kill for. We also said that, right now, it would be best if she did not know what the item was. Elinor seemed contented and didn't ask any questions.

'Welcome to our team,' I said to Elinor.

'Thank you,' she replied.

Our attention was drawn to a couple who were seated at the table right next to us. Rather than moving so that we could continue our conversation, we decided to wait for our lunch to arrive; a choice I had been much anticipating. From the menu I had not been able to resist the chips. Unhealthy salt and fat are on the banned list at homes for those trying to extend their final day of reckoning by a few meagre minutes or perhaps an hour.

When lunch was served, a bowl of hot steaming golden hued chips was placed in front of me. One at a time, I lifted each chip and dipped it into tomato sauce before surveying its golden brown surface, to ensure it was covered by the white crystals of salt. Finally, as if sipping a glass of fine wine, I slowly raised the chip to my mouth and enjoyed the explosion of flavours of a forbidden fruit.

'That was a really nice lunch,' I said when I'd finished and, checking no one was still in ear shot, continued. 'Elinor, you said you could solve the clue. Can you tell us where are we going?'

'A church in Mawnan, Cornwall and you are looking for a stone cross which is lying on the ground.'

I looked at Olivia, instantly knowing the church, the one overlooking the River Helford. The river was where many of the SOE operations were staged during the war.

'How can you get that from that?' I asked, pointing to the clue on the page.

'It's quite easy when you do these things every day. Sacred pop group refers to "The Church", "pale fellow" can become "wan man" which is an anagram for "Mawnan". The word "confused" points to it being an anagram. And "duke's country" refers to the Duchy of Cornwall.'

'And the next line?'

'"Angry" becomes "cross". "Chiseller" becomes, "stonemason" and "ground level" becomes, "fallen".'

'You must be kidding,' I said.

Leaving the Ships Inn, we made our way back to the car for the journey to Elinor's home and then to Cornwall. Within minutes of exiting the car park we were speeding along Stoke Hill Road, out of the city and surrounded by beautiful fields. I am not sure if Elinor was in less of a hurry, or I was becoming accustomed to her driving, but I felt far more relaxed on the return journey. We passed through a little hamlet and then veered right, on to a road signposted *Danes Hill Road.*

'That's strange; don't look, but I think we are being followed,' said Elinor glancing again in the mirror. 'Maybe I became a little paranoid after your warnings. Just to be on the safe side, I'm going to turn right up ahead and go through a place called Poltimore. We can get back on this road from there, but it's a detour no one would ordinarily take.'

Elinor slowed the Mercedes, indicating a right turn towards Poltimore. Ignoring Elinor's instruction I looked out the back window to see the following red SUV. As we turned so did it.

'Elinor, I think you are right, they may be following. Why don't you put a bit of distance between them and us. That should tell us once and for all,' I called from the back seat.

Olivia and I were thrown sideways in our seats as Elinor floored the Mercedes, taking the first left hand sweeping corner at a speed I found unbelievable. Either the car's handling was outstanding or Elinor could *really* drive. In what seemed just seconds, we entered Poltimore approaching a T intersection which looked more like a triangle. The tyres screeched as she wrenched the steering wheel to the left and, using the whole road to take the corner, we rocked off in a new direction.

'They are still with me,' Elinor called in a voice which could not hide the stress of the car chase.

Looking out through the front windscreen I saw the corners unfold in a blur. A tight left was followed, almost immediately, by a sweeping right before opening onto a small straight.

Crunch.

The sound was of the SUV smashing into the rear of our car, knocking me forward in my seat. Moments later we were rammed again and sent spinning out of control up the road. I braced myself for an impact which never came as rather than crashing, we spun into an intersection. Elinor floored the Mercedes and we rocketed past a farm, before braking severely for a T intersection which I could see fast approaching.

Somehow Elinor executed a left turn on to a road leading us back towards Poltimore. I looked behind to see what has become of our pursuers. The SUV clipped the bank as it attempted to negotiate the intersection and maintain its pursuit. Once again we entered Poltimore and the triangle which, only moments earlier, we had negotiated. This time we swung right heading down the wrong side of the road, narrowly missing the tree growing in the middle of the triangle.

'Max!' called Elinor. 'Are they still with us?'

Looking back I saw nothing and momentarily felt relieved. But, before I could report, the SUV came into view.

'They're still with us and gaining at an amazing rate of knots.'

The SUV caught us just as we approached the intersection with Danes Hill road. A violent shudder and the sound of smashing panels rocked the car and sent us screeching through the intersection and, following a small excursion, we found ourselves in a farmyard.

Elinor launched the Mercedes into the field and followed the road heading back towards Exeter but on the other side of the fence I saw a closed farm gate approaching. Rather than braking, Elinor smashed the Mercedes straight through it.

A driveway on the other side led us onto Stoke Hill where, unfortunately, the SUV was waiting for us and narrowly missed our rear quarter panel.

'I should be able to outrun them on the straighter bits of road heading back into Exeter,' Elinor said, her voice almost drowned out by the howl of the V8.

In an instant, the car was travelling at over 100mph, braking and squealing as it negotiated the sweeping curves and not slowing as we came back to the built-up area on the outskirts of Exeter and where we had to negotiate traffic. Although we seemed to have the right of way, we approached and then passed through the first busy intersection at such a speed that the other vehicles using the intersection had no chance of seeing us coming. Looking back, I saw two cars stopped in the intersection and another car smashing into the stationary cars having swerved to avoid the speeding SUV.

Looking back out of the front windscreen, I saw cars parked on the left hand side of the road meaning we shared the equivalent of one lane with oncoming traffic. I could see Elinor repeatedly pulling the dip switch, flashing the headlights at oncoming vehicles, telling then we had no intention of giving way. We parted the oncoming cars as Moses parted the Red Sea. Our speed was way too hot as we approached a roundabout and, despite heavy braking, we launched across the middle of the roundabout, narrowly missing a tree obviously strategically placed to cause havoc in case of a car chase.

Looking back, I saw the SUV follow our flight path. We both landed on the wrong side of the road with parked cars to our right. Elinor swerved back into our lane but only for the briefest of moments before she swerved right again, weaving in and out of slower cars that blocked our progress.

Approaching the next roundabout, it was obvious that Elinor was not going to make any attempt to keep to our lane. She went straight ahead and we narrowly avoided cars as they traversed the roundabout. A light truck swerved in front and toppled onto its side, as if in slow motion. I saw the SUV skidding sideways and coming to a complete halt to avoid the truck, before continuing the chase. Again we were on the wrong side of the road. I could see an exit but it was blocked by vehicles preparing to enter the roundabout.

Elinor veered the Mercedes to the left and we headed the wrong way around the roundabout. Smoke was pouring from the tyres as we slid sideways with the nose pointing into the roundabout and the back pointing out. A flick of oversteer and she had us heading back down the road from whence we came, but only briefly. I was swung violently to the right, held in place only by my seatbelt, as Elinor threw the car left. For a brief second I saw the name *St James Road* as we accelerated up this new highway.

We were fast approaching a T intersection and I watched as Elinor unsettled the car with a flick of the steering wheel to the left. At that very moment, I felt the SUV clip us from behind and for the second time we were sent spinning through an intersection. The rear of the car slammed into a white house on the other side of the junction. Looking forward again, I saw the red SUV which was now stopped in the middle of the road, blocking our escape. The driver's and passenger's doors opened and the occupants, apparently unconcerned at being seen by the onlookers, exited. The Mercedes was stalled. Elinor tried the key and the engine turned over, but did not start. The two men watched from beside their car. Elinor tried the car again. Nothing happened.

'It won't start,' she called in panic.

'You have done well Elinor, really well. Count to three and then try again,' I said.

It seemed like a long three seconds before Elinor turned the key. The car fired back into life and the V8 screamed its vengeance. Elinor, obviously seeing an opportunity for escape, released the brake and the car accelerated, pointed straight for the SUV's driver. He had just enough time to dive back inside the car as we struck the open door which went flying from its hinges.

'We will have to take another way home,' said Elinor now in a calm and controlled voice.

Without slowing the pace, we raced back the way we came, turning right then right, then left and right and left onto a more major road. Here she slowed and then drove as if nothing had happened. We made our way back towards Clyst Hydon but the car did not sound well. If we did make it back, I thought, the car was finished.

'Fine driving Elinor,' complimented Olivia. 'Max, they must have been watching the drop point.'

'My thoughts exactly. It's likely, during the chase, that they have taken the car's registration and have the means of tracing it. When we get back Clyst Hydon we can risk only five minutes before we flee. Elinor, don't pack, just grab some essentials. If you have a mobile phone or any other electronic devices, leave them behind. They will track your phone if you take it. Five minutes, not a second more.'

'What about clothes and money?' Elinor asked with some concern in her voice.

'Bring nothing, Max and I will take care of everything.'

'Last night, when you arrived… Is this why you had no luggage?'

'Unfortunately, yes,' said Olivia.

Steam was billowing from the Mercedes' radiator as we pulled up in front of Grange Cottage. Elinor leapt from the car and ran into the house while Olivia and I carried our new belongings around the back to the Jaguar. With the car loaded, I drove around to the front to where Elinor was already waiting. It was as if we were professionals; four minutes after arriving we were underway. Speeding away, I looked back to Grange Cottage through the mirror and prayed that Elinor would return soon.

'I'm so sorry Elinor, we both are,' said Olivia. 'Max and I didn't mean for you to become embroiled in our misadventure.'

'It's okay, you did warn me. To tell you the truth, I didn't think anything would actually happen. I mean, really happen. I'm not sure if I am petrified or excited. What happens now?'

'Max, what do you think?'

'I think we should go somewhere safe for the night and take stock. Somewhere we can plan our next move. Elinor, do you have any ideas of where we could go and hide?'

My question was followed by a few seconds' silence. Looking in the mirror to see if she had heard the question, I could tell that Elinor was thinking.

'Dartmoor National Park is not far from here and I doubt any one will expect us to go up there. I know a nice old pub in Postbridge, the East Dart Hotel; we should be able to stay there.'

The drive to Postbridge took only an hour and the scenery along the way, the wildness of the downs, was stunning but eerie. Watching the wind rip across the barren, rocky and desolate landscape with the haunting grey and overcast sky above, had given life to the moors, which at times closed in around the car. Any moment you expected to see the hounds of the Baskervilles or a deranged murderer jump out in front of the car. Then the moors had given way to beautiful wetlands with running streams. They were places of life but also peace. This was a place of contradictions. We had seen few cars and none had followed us. Bringing the Jaguar to rest beside the East Dart Hotel, I knew the moors would give us sanctuary for the night

With the exception of not having a thatched roof, the East Dart Hotel looked like your quintessentially English pub. It was a white two storey building that looked old and loved. Wagon wheels hung on its exterior.

Upon entering the pub, we were greeted warmly by the landlady who introduced herself as Rosie. She told us that they had only nine letting rooms but, fortunately, two were vacant for tonight. After booking in, we headed upstairs for a nanna nap and agreed to meet in the lounge in an hour's time.

'Max, after we have been to the church cemetery, what are we going to say to Elinor? Are we going to take her to wherever it is we are sent?' asked Olivia. 'And what about Cliff?'

'This feels like déjà vu; didn't we have this same conversation just before Kate and Edward were killed?'

'We can't let that happen to Elinor. We've already turned her life upside down; who knows when she will be able to go home.'

'Olivia, I agree, it will be safest for Elinor to stay with us until the end and we need to tell her that she can't go home. We hide nothing from her but let her ask the questions.'

'Right. On a purely selfish note, she will make it far more challenging for people to recognise us.'

Having woken from our nap, Olivia and I made our way down to the lounge and waited for Elinor, who arrived minutes later. With the exception of us and the barman, whose name we didn't know, the lounge was empty.

'What ale do you serve?' I asked the barman.

'Our most regular ale is the Jail Ale, brewed at Dartmoor Brewery in Princetown. We also have Devon Dew from Summerskills Brewery in Plymton and Honey Bunny from Hunter's Brewery in Ipplepen.'

'Being that there are three of us and you have three on tap, we shall have one of each. Three pints, if you please.'

'I can't believe how tired I feel,' said Elinor.

'That's not surprising, seeing everything that has happened today,' I said.

Sipping the ale, I glanced to check if the barman was still with us, while not making it look obvious. We were alone, so I continued, 'Elinor, you do realise you can't go home.'

'Yes.'

'I'm so sorry we got you into this.'

'I haven't felt so alive for years. What do we do now?'

'The way I see it,' said Olivia, 'we have two choices. We either all go to Mawnan or we split up. Elinor and I could go to Scotland and you go to Mawnan. Once you have found the clue from the cross, you ring us and we will recover Janus. It would save a lot of time and catapult us in front of those people trailing us. Elinor and I would make our way back to England, we'd meet up and together go to Cliff.'

'We don't know for sure that Janus is in Scotland.'

'Max we both know it's hidden somewhere in Scotland.'

'Scotland's a long way to go if you are wrong but, if you are right, it would be playing to our strengths… I could become a decoy.'

'Another pint?' came Rosie's cheerful voice from the bar. 'Will you be eating in the lounge or restaurant tonight?'

'What do you think, ladies?' I said, trying to hide any hint of surprise in my voice, hoping none of our conversation had been overheard.

'I would like to eat in the lounge and perhaps have a glass of white— anything you have that's out of a bottle,' said Olivia.

'Make that two,' said Elinor.

'Looks like it's the lounge and I will have another pint of the Jail Ale please.'

The conversation at our table went oddly silent. Our attempts at small talk, from my perspective, made it more obvious that we were trying to hide something.

'Are you on holiday?' asked Rosie while bringing the drinks to our table.

'We are,' replied Olivia. 'We are on our way to Plymouth. We were in Exeter today and rather than driving straight to Plymouth we thought it would be a nice drive to go via the moors. We are really pleased we did. It was a lovely drive and your pub is really nice.'

'Have you been here before?'

'No, this is our first time,' said Olivia.

'I don't mean to be nosy; it's just that you seem familiar, as if I've seen you before.' When none of us spoke, she continued. 'Oh well, enjoy your stay and I will bring menus a little later on.'

When Rosie had left the room Olivia said 'What a charming lady?

I replied. 'And I thought all landladies were brash, brassy and leopard-print wearing!!!'

Half an hour later we were no longer alone in the lounge. The pub was coming alive with people. Our meeting place was transforming into what it is that makes a traditional English pub. From those from other countries and particularly our experiences in Australia, English pubs are different. There is something magical about a night in the British boozer, they ooze a spirit that welcomes men and women alike. At home we would never dream of going down to the pub, but here it's the social gathering place and I was looking forward to the evening.

'Staying together or splitting up; that is the question.' Reaching into my coat pocket I removed a coin and showed it to Olivia. I said, 'Heads Scotland and tails we stay together.'

With a flip of the finger, the coin launched towards the ceiling, catching the light as it spun, before falling back to earth and being caught in my hand.

Chapter 9

Lostwithiel

Inspector Axel

I dialled Scotland Yard on my mobile phone and asked to be put through to Detective Wells.

'It's Inspector Axel,' I said.

'Hi,' came the reply. 'Did you have a good drive down to Exeter?'

'Yes, it's an easy and quick run from London.'

'And they were expecting you at the police station?'

'Yes, thank you. They were most helpful. I'm at Elinor Grange's house now. The Mercedes is here but it's pretty well smashed up. I'm surprised they made it back. The house looks empty and the back door is wide open. Either they made a very hurried exit or someone else has been here.'

'Have you had a chance to have a look around?' asked Detective Wells.

'No, I haven't gone in yet but, as soon as I've searched the house, I will call you back, say in thirty minutes.' Before hanging up I added, 'Have there been any new sightings of them?'

'No,' was the response, to which I replied, 'Okay, I'm sure they will turn up soon; they seem incapable of going anywhere without leaving a trail of destruction in their wake.'

'Be careful,' were the final words from Detective Wells before hanging up.

The back door was slightly ajar and, pushing it a little wider, I entered and sought the light switch.

The kitchen was tidy and showed no signs of a hurried exit, although some of the drawers and cupboards were open. Nothing looked obviously out of place but it was almost as if someone had been looking through them. *It is possible that whoever was chasing them in Exeter has also been here,* I thought. Detective Wells may have been right when she had told me to *be careful.*

The sitting room, like the kitchen, gave just the slightest hints of things having been disturbed. I stood noiselessly in the room and allowed my eyes to scan the surroundings. *Was that a creak from upstairs?* I looked up while remaining completely still and listened. A touch of apprehension swept over me. *No footsteps but definitely a creaking.* All houses make sounds; the expanding and contracting caused by heating and cooling and movement due to the wind. Staying very still, I waited, but no further noises were forthcoming and I tentatively dismissed the idea of the presence of another person.

I moved methodically upstairs observing as I went. Opening what appeared to be the master bedroom, I peered inside; the bed was made and there was no sign of a hurried leaving. I stepped cautiously inside and unexpectedly felt the point of a gun being pushed firmly into the small of my back.

'I wouldn't move if I were you,' came a voice from behind.

As I stood absolutely motionless, the available options flashed through my mind. I could swing quickly and try and disarm whoever was behind, or do exactly as I was told, at least for the time being.

'Well Inspector, it looks like we are searching for the same people.'

Despite trying to remain relaxed, I felt my muscles tighten, to which the man behind responded, 'Don't make any sudden moves; it would be most annoying if I had to kill you.'

'You may do it anyway!'

'Now, now Inspector, that's a very negative attitude. It will all depend on how well we get on. And I have a feeling we are going to be the best of friends. Now, can you spread your legs? Nice and wide for me please. A little wider. That's very good. And your hands, if you would please place them behind your back, I would be most grateful.'

With my legs spreading to the point of almost losing my balance, I placed my hands behind my back and I felt a single cable tie being used to secure them together.

'You can straighten up now. Do you see the chair next to the bed? Move towards it and take a seat.'

While making my way to the chair, my heart was heavy with dread for my impending demise. To seat myself in the chair I would have to look upon my assailant. If I saw his face it would mean certain death. I turned slowly to lower myself into the chair. He was wearing a balaclava and pointing his silenced pistol directly at me.

'Sit, sit,' he said, motioning with the pistol. 'Please Inspector, make yourself comfortable. Please also excuse the disguise, most annoying and itchy, but as you understand, very necessary.'

Feeling I had little to lose and stalling for time in the hope that Detective Wells would ring and then be concerned enough to send help when I didn't answer, I asked, 'Who are you?'

'Let's just say I am someone like you who is interested in Max and Olivia.'

'Did you set the explosion in Horton-cum-Studley?'

'Your daughter's house? Very sad, sad indeed. No, that was not me; far too crude. I haven't been sent to kill you, Inspector. As I said, if we get along, you will be safe. I want us to have an open and frank conversation about Max and Olivia. You need to keep nothing from me and don't tell me something

I already know. If you lie to me, I will be really annoyed because then I will have to shoot you. I don't want to do that and I'm sure you don't want that to happen either. Do you think we can be friends?'

'The best of friends! I am having a party next week; would you like to come?'

'Bravo Inspector, we are going to get on famously. Now tell me something about Max and Olivia that I don't already know, like where are they?'

'I'm sorry, I have no idea, that's why I am here, looking for clues.'

'Good, I believe you. See, that was very easy. Now Inspector, I want you to think very carefully before answering. What else can you tell me?'

I hesitated, taking the time to collect my thoughts. What was it that he wanted? Where did I begin?

'In 2008, when they were riding across Europe, I believe they were searching for something. Whoever tried to kill them in Walbrzych must have thought they had it.'

'Very good Inspector, go on.'

'Max and Olivia, being back in the UK, must, in some way, be related to that trip in 2008. I also believe that this involves something that happened during World War Two.'

'What makes you think that?' said my assailant, while keeping his gun pointing at me.

'Max and Olivia knew a man called Pierre Gicquel. In 2008, they visited him just before he died. Pierre was in the French Resistance, risking his life on clandestine operations, helping allied service personnel escape from Brittany to England from the beaches nearby. I believe Pierre was murdered shortly after Max and Olivia went to see him.

'My father, who escaped from France in 1940 and came to England, worked for the SOE or some similar secret agency. He also knew Pierre Gicquel. I believe therefore that Max and Olivia knew my father, or at least that they worked for the same people.

'My best guess is that this involves some operation from WW2 and the people they worked with and for. As to what, I have no idea. Really that's as much as I know.'

'Excellent, Inspector! That was not too difficult. I do apologise for leaving you here and I'm afraid I will need to tie you to the chair before I go. I'm sure you understand. I can't have you finding your freedom before I've had the opportunity to disappear

'Now Inspector, can you please hook your feet behind the legs of the chair while I tie you up?'

I followed his instructions.

'Excellent.'

This six foot man of a slender build, wearing a grey pinstriped suit, red tie, light brown gloves with meticulously polished black shoes and speaking with a beautiful English voice took from his pocket a roll of cloth tape and proceeded to tape my body to the chair, making four or five passes.

'Farewell Inspector and be careful. I am not sure you understand what you have got yourself involved in. Unfortunately, as you have discovered from what happened at your daughter's house, people are willing to kill for Janus.'

With those words, he slipped quietly from the room. I didn't hear him descend the stairs, leave the house or even start a car, but I was in no doubt he was gone.

Not long after I was left alone, perhaps twenty minutes or so, the phone rang. It was in my right hand trouser pocket and out of reach. Ten minutes later it rang again. Tied to the chair and with no choice but to be patient, I waited in my confinement. How long I remained in the chair is difficult to estimate; the sense of time alters when restrained with nothing to do but wait. Eventually, there was the distinctive sound of a car slowing and stopping. Shortly after came the noise made by two car doors being closed and, at last, voices.

'It's the police,' I heard called from downstairs. 'Inspector Axel, are you here?'

'Upstairs,' I called back. 'I'm tied up but otherwise okay.'

***

185

Max

'Tails, we stay together,' I said, looking to Olivia and Elinor who nodded in agreement, before Olivia added, 'Two out of three.'

'Are you trying to get away from me?' I asked. At this, the girls laughed.

After dinner we remained in the lounge enjoying its energy and atmosphere. Its smells, the ale, food, fire and people were so different from that of our nursing home which had its own distinctive aroma and a sound of silence. This stillness was broken only by what little energy the dining guests of the evening had in reserve. Every day that energy was eaten away, little by little, until it was all gone and you visited no more.

Here the room was alive, sharing its vigour and vitality with whoever entered.

Despite our fatigue, we remained at our table until it was gone ten and then, bidding each other good night, we made our way upstairs and to our respective rooms. We agreed to meet again at eight in the morning for breakfast.

I awoke to a gentle knocking and, from my bed in the dim light of morning, I saw a piece of paper being slid under the door. Olivia had stirred to the sound as well.

'What time is it?' she said.

The bedside table clock informed me it was five past seven.

I swung my legs from the bed and placed my feet on the floor. Like a new born butterfly rising from its cocoon, I waited, stretching my wings as the blood pumped through before attempting flight. With care I rose from the bed and moved across, or perhaps shuffled is a more accurate description, to where the paper lay on the floor.

'What does it say?' called Olivia in a voice still mixed with sleep.

I picked up the paper and fumbled to find the light switch and the page, which just seconds ago was a blur of indistinguishable lines, came into focus.

You're on the morning news and Facebook staying here

I read aloud the words from the scrap of paper, adding an interesting observation, 'The handwriting doesn't appear to be in adult script. It looks like a child's writing.'

'Do you think the Facebook post is on the news or they are two separate things?' asked Olivia.

'I don't know but let's not wait around to find out. I'll wake Elinor while you get dressed.'

Within ten minutes Elinor had joined Olivia and me in our room. After showing Elinor the note I said, 'We need to slip out separately and meet at the car. I'll go first and start the engine, then Elinor, you come next and then Olivia. A minute apart, perhaps two, but no more. We can't risk waiting around!'

Leaving £200 on the bed to cover what we owed, one by one we left as planned. Having all made it safely and unseen to the car, I pulled out of the pub and accelerated towards Two Bridges.

'If questioned, the owners think we are going to Plymouth. I reckon we should keep a healthy distance from Plymouth and try and stay on B roads. Any suggestions Elinor?'

Elinor thought for a few seconds and then said, 'When you get to Two Bridges, rather than continuing down towards Yelverton, we could turn right to Tavistock and then go through Gulworthy to Gunnislake. The problem is we end up on the A390 which takes us to St Ives, Lostwithiel, then all the way to Truro. To get us from Truro to Mawnan I would need a map.'

From within the mirror I saw Olivia reach over and pass forward to Elinor the map we had purchased in Oxford. At almost the same moment we arrived at Two Bridges and I almost missed the right turn to Tavistock, having to brake heavily to make the turn.

'Hang on, I'm going to put some distance between us and Postbridge.'

The Jaguar unleashed her six cylinders in a distinctive low growl. She sprinted to full speed and the road unfolded as sweeping curves flowing left then right, the bends only serving to encourage the Jaguar's pedigreed speed. No one spoke while I wrestled the big cat along the unveiling bitumen. Seven minutes later, by my watch, we arrived in Tavistock.

'Gee I enjoyed that,' I said. 'That's a real motor car! The best of British.'

Choosing to ignore my driving exploits and comments, Olivia said, 'We need to stop for breakfast and plan our assault on Mawnan.'

'I was thinking of Lostwithiel,' I replied.

'Is that wise, stopping so close to Cliff?'

'Do you think it matters?'

'No, I suppose not, it's as good a place as any.'

'I do feel left out sometimes,' said Elinor from beside me. Her voice however was warm and displayed neither sarcasm nor antagonism.

The drive to Lostwithiel, once back on the A roads, was spirited but, not wanting to attract unwanted attention, I did not make it racy. Arrival at the historic town of Lostwithiel brought back fond and challenging memories. From Olivia came silence but I imagined she was having similar thoughts.

Swinging left at the Kings Arms Hotel, I remembered its annoying narrow one way street. We crawled down the road and past what looked like, on the right, a coffee shop. By the time I had recognised it as such, I had missed the parking opportunities which were on the left side of the road. I turned at the first intersection, Church Street, and was greeted by a large red sign with a horizontal white line running through it.

'That would be a one way street,' instructed Elinor. 'And not our way.'

Grunting my displeasure, I reversed back into the road from where we had come and continued down the lane, until finally I could turn left and then another left which brought me back on to the A390.

'Take two,' I said. 'But this time, as soon as I turn left past the Kings Arms, we will park.'

The second attempt to stop for breakfast was done with perfect execution. We pulled up and parked in front of a newsagents, with the coffee shop just a few metres down the road on our right.

'My treat, everyone.'

'I would hope so,' replied Elinor in a jovial voice. 'You won't let me use my credit card or go to the bank and I have no money with me. I expect to be treated like royalty.'

'Max will treat you like royalty!' Olivia teased. 'The moths flutter from his wallet when he opens it.'

'Harsh ladies, very harsh,' I replied in good humour.

Despite the fear that the police and whoever else was after us had by now seen the Facebook post, we enjoyed a relaxed breakfast while planning our route to Mawnan. The discussion ranged to hiring a boat and coming in by river, but the long climb up the hill put paid to that idea. We moved on to waiting for midnight and sneaking around the graveyard under the cover of darkness. In the end we settled on the frontal assault.

'Let's do it,' said Olivia, getting to her feet. She moved towards the front door.

Elinor and I joined her and we made our way back to the Jaguar. Out of habit, I glanced up and down the street, but all was quiet on this slow Sunday morning. Olivia and Elinor swapped seats so now Olivia sat opposite me. I put the key in the ignition and the engine turned over but did not fire. I tried again but nothing. And then again, still nothing.

'It's the electrics,' I said.

'British motoring at its best,' came a voice from the back seat.

I tried to start the car a few more times but to no avail; the mighty Jag was going nowhere.

'Now what?' Said Olivia.

'We will need to find somewhere to stay and wait until a garage opens on Monday. It's unlikely, I guess, that we will find a workshop open today. Alternatively we dump the Jag, steal a car and keep going.'

These were the only options I could think of.

Olivia considered my response before saying, 'Regardless, we can't leave the Jag out on the street. Let's call a tow truck and have it taken to a garage. With luck the garage can repair it in the morning. If we can't have it repaired tomorrow, then we leave it.'

We agreed on Olivia's plan knowing that, to stay in Lostwithiel, would bring our pursuers one step closer.

While Olivia went to find a phone booth and call a tow truck, Elinor and I walked up to the Kings Arms Hotel to secure a couple of rooms for the night. Olivia was to stay with the car until the tow truck arrived and then meet us at the hotel. It took a couple of hours before the tow truck finally came and Olivia joined us.

***

Inspector Axel

Having been released from my bonds and spent the night at a very pleasant hotel, I was surprised to find Detective Wells waiting for me at Exeter Police Station.

'Good morning Inspector Axel. I hope you slept well considering your ordeal.'

'Thank you Detective, I didn't expect to see you here on a Sunday morning.'

'Please call me Lynda. I drove down from London early this morning. We are going to set up a temporary operations centre here.

'After we spoke last night, three things kept going around and around in my mind. The first, there must have been something in what you told your assailant. Something he thought was important. We need to work out what it was. Second, what the hell is Janus? And finally, why give us the name Janus anyway?'

'I agree, but I have a confession and an apology to make. There is something I haven't told you and it is something that I shared with my assailant last night.'

192

Detective Wells folded her arms and I could tell that she was none too pleased that I had been keeping secrets. She said nothing but waited for me to continue.

'My father knew Pierre Gicquel, the man who died in Lannilis shortly after being visited by Max and Olivia when they were in Europe in 2005. I believe it's possible that my father also knew Max and Olivia and that they, most likely, worked for the same organisation during the war. This all has something to do with that time.'

'It was 2008, Inspector, when they were in Europe but I agree with you, this has something to do with the war. I have thought so from the moment this enquiry came across my table. I remember our chats in 2008 and your theory then that the trip to Europe stemmed from clandestine missions to France during the war. Please, remind me again, who was Pierre Gicquel?'

I quickly but methodically told what I knew from my first investigation and then what I had surmised. Detective Wells sat patiently asking no questions until I had finished.

'When you first investigated Max and Olivia, did you know then that they may have known your father?'

'Not to start with; not until Pierre Gicquel came up during my enquiries. Even then I couldn't prove Max and Olivia went to see him just before his death Because of my connection to Pierre, whom I met in 2005, I thought people might consider that the meeting may have clouded my analysis. I thought it best to keep quiet.'

'If we are to work together, it's important that we trust one another.' She paused before continuing, 'Do you know what Janus is?'

'No and I promise the connection to my father is the only thing I haven't told you.'

'Okay, let's agree to work together from now on. The other reason I drove down, other than so we could talk, is that I thought we might need the help of a war historian, if we are to ever understand what is going on here. I know a professor, a lady called Lacy Drew at Exeter University. She's part of the History faculty and has written extensively on the clandestine naval operation to France. I rang her last night after speaking to you. When I mentioned the name "Janus", she appeared to be taken aback but then agreed to meet us at the university tomorrow morning at nine.'

'You couldn't arrange to see her today?'

'I tried but, unfortunately, she was away and isn't back until late tonight. Tomorrow was the best I could do.'

I felt a little impatient at having to wait until tomorrow but tried not to show any frustration. I returned to the observations of the previous evening. 'The other interesting thing the assailant said was that he was not responsible for the explosion at Kate's house. I took that to mean there must be at least three groups, including us, looking for Max and Olivia.'

'I thought about that comment too. I think he was right when he said that we don't understand what we have got ourselves into!'

'Oh, what I haven't told you is that, while I was driving down, I received a call from the Yard. They had picked up a Facebook post of a sighting of Max and Olivia in Postbridge which is in the Dartmoor National Park. I imagined they would be long gone by now. I thought, seeing we can't see the professor until tomorrow, we should take a run up there. You never know, they may have said something to someone that may be of use. I also thought we could sit and watch and see who comes and goes. You would think the post might also attract the attention of those others looking for them. You might even recognise your assailant!'

It was a pleasant drive from Exeter to the Dartmoor National Park. It did not take long and, perhaps forty-five minutes later, we were pulling into the car park of the East Dart Hotel. The hotel manager, Rosie, remembered Max and Olivia, identifying them from the photographs we showed them. Looking at a photograph of Elinor, which I had taken from her house, she confirmed that Elinor was travelling with them. We also learned that they were driving a green Jaguar. An old one, Rosie said. Using my phone and by searching the internet of images of old Jaguars, we learned that they were driving a 1960s Mark 1 or Mark 11 Jaguar.

Before we left, I handed a business card to Rosie, and asked her to ring if anyone else came asking questions about Max and Olivia.

Back at Exeter and before calling it a day, Detective Wells put an APB for stations in the Devon and Cornwall areas to be on the lookout for Max, Olivia, Elinor and the green 1960s Jaguar. The alert also advised officers not to use the police radio if they had a potential sighting as she feared the police frequencies might be scanned for information.

My first impression of Professor Lacy Drew's office was that it was cluttered with books and papers. Some were in piles, where there was semblance of order, but mostly they were scattered, apparently at random, to all corners of the room. Next to the desk, her feet swam in a sea of paper to which she appeared oblivious.

'Detective Wells, nice to see you again,' said Professor Drew in a tone which hid all emotions.

I wasn't sure if we were welcome guests or an annoyance.

'Professor, this is my colleague Inspector Axel of Interpol.'

I extended my hand to which Professor Drew reciprocated.

'Sit down. How may I help you?'

We stepped over the books and made ourselves comfortable in the only other chairs in the room which were in front of a table.

'As I mentioned on the phone,' started Inspector Wells, 'we would like your help. We are hoping you may be able to tell us what someone may have learned from the conversation Inspector Axel had with his assailant. If you can, we are hoping that you may assist us in locating the two people we are seeking.'

The professor nodded. 'Go ahead.'

'I mentioned the word "Janus" on the phone to you. We are wondering if you know who or what it is?'

Looking at me the professor said, 'Perhaps you can go over again what it is you said to your assailant. Detective Wells did tell me, but it is best if I can hear it from you.'

I took a breath and relayed the events of Saturday night and my conversation as well as my recollection would allow. As I spoke Professor Drew jotted notes on scraps of paper which she placed, in no apparent order, on her desk.

When I finished, the professor made noises as though she was speaking to herself, putting forward ideas and then dismissing them. After several repetitions of, *No it won't be that,* she said, 'Yes, I think I know where they are going!

'If what you said is true and Max and Olivia worked with Pierre Gicquel, most likely they are going to either the River Helford or Falmouth. Most of the clandestine sea operations to Brittany during the war were mounted from these two places.'

'Why?' I said aloud without thinking.

'Inspector, I just told you what the facts say. Why is up to you,' she said in a most dismissive tone.

Detective Wells drummed her fingers on the table before saying, 'And Janus?'

There was a pause after Detective Wells question - before Professor Drew started her explanation in a monotone voice. 'I had given up my search for Janus long ago. Of those who have heard of the Janus Project, most believe it never existed. To tell you the truth, over my lifetime of work, researching this period, I have never found a single document that mentions Janus. A lot of what I am about to tell you is true, but whether Janus played a part in it or not I cannot say. Whether the reality of Janus is true or not, I cannot say.

'No war before had such a profound effect on the advancements of science. You can point to any number of inventions and advancements that emerged during the war, particularly from the Nazis. The jet engine, v rockets, ballistic missiles and even computers came from that time. The war also saw incredible advancements in medicine—the mass production of penicillin and blood transfusions, for example. But much of the science drive was to develop weapons of mass destruction and concentration camp prisoners made ideal guinea pigs.

'In 1942, intelligence from the Polish Resistance movement reported that the Nazis were conducting human experiments at a concentration camp called Majdanek. Majdanek, unlike other concentration camps, was not located in a remote rural location away from population centres, but had been established on the outskirts of the city of Lublin during the

German occupation of Poland in 1941. Its location meant that the intelligence from Majdanek was considered reliable. Majdanek was killing people on an industrial scale, but reports also talked of a new super biological weapon being developed by a man called Dr Von Erick Brack. He came to Majdanek from the Nazis' bio-weapons facility on Riems Island. The new weapon was alleged to be a convergence of chemistry, biology and genetic science.

'Towards the end of the war, with the Red Army advancing from the east, it is alleged that UK intelligence became determined to stop the weapon from falling into Stalin's hands. Stalin had a reputation as a brutal butcher with little or no moral conscience. Churchill and other allied commanders feared that, once the conflict with Germany was won, the war with Russia would begin, a far bloodier war, fuelled by the new and developing technologies captured from the Germans; jet fighters, missiles, chemical and biological weapons etc.'

With my interest in WW2 history, in part because of my father, I sat spellbound despite the dry style in which she relayed the information. I found myself distracted for a moment, pitying her students sitting through one of her history lectures. The pity was not because she was boring, but because, in all likelihood, they would fall asleep and miss the wealth of knowledge and wisdom this woman held. I drew my focus back to her words.

'Working with the Polish Resistance movement, a number of covert operations were planned to penetrate the camp, kill Dr

Von Erick Brack and either retrieve or destroy the weapon, but none was successfully carried out. So concerning was the intelligence coming out of Lublin that Operation Pluto—a plan to bomb the camp, to obliterate, everything and everybody—was considered but dismissed. Not on humanitarian grounds, but because, militarily, it was unlikely to succeed.

'As the Red Army advanced, eastern concentration camps were evacuated. Majdanek became the first concentration camp discovered by allied forces because it was captured nearly intact. The Nazis had succeeded in partially destroying the incriminating evidence but infrastructure remained mainly intact along with administrative records of war crimes. That is, with the exception of the biological weapons facility. Intelligence concluded the program, Dr Von Erick Brack, and his research had moved to another concentration camp; one called Bergen-Belsen.

'In mid-April 1945, the 11th Armoured Division of the British Forces liberated the Bergen-Belsen concentration camp, south-west of the town Bergen near Celle. They discovered some sixty-thousand prisoners and thirteen-thousand corpses. History recalls how the overcrowding of the camp led to a vast increase in deaths from typhus, typhoid fever, tuberculosis and other diseases. The conspiracy theorists believe this is only partially true. They believe the Nazis, through their Majdanek program, had weaponised these and other diseases and had discovered how to make and attach diseases and viruses to individual immune cells through the use of a special plant's DNA. The plant itself, it is said, had no immune system. The discovery had the potential for great good but also for unparalleled evil, worse than the atomic bomb. Whereas the atomic bomb kills indiscriminately, this weapon could be tailored for specific people, races, or even hair colour; whatever you wanted. If used for good, the technology would allow the targeted treatment of almost any illness. It could have revolutionised medicine as we know it. Even more importantly for arms, it could potentially render all biological weapons useless.

'The story goes that Dr Von Erick Brack had encrypted the secrets of the weapon into a machine, codenamed "Janus", for which he made two identical keys, the "Janus Keys". How can I explain this? The machine is a little like an early pocket computer, or perhaps more like a variation on the Enigma Machine, the German cipher machine from the war. The Janus Key was a three-dimensional rotor, which looked more like an ancient artefact from *Raiders of the Lost Ark* than a key. When inserted into the machine, the Janus Key enabled the decoding of endless combinations of chemical symbols and genetic codes. What is said of Janus is that it tells how to create and target bacteria and viruses. Neither the machine nor the Janus Key is of any use without the other bit.

'As best as I have determined from the stories, with the Red Army only a few days away from Majdanek, Dr Von Erick Brack was instructed to blow up the bio-warfare research facility at the camp. He left one of the Janus Keys behind to be destroyed by the explosion and took the Janus Machine and the other Key with him to Bergen-Belsen.

'Operatives within the Polish Resistance entered the evacuated camp in search of the machine just hours before the Red Army and found in the rubble the Janus Key. It was still intact and they believed it was still working. It is said that the Soviets also knew of the bio-weapons program, the Janus Project, at the camp. Some believed they had an informer inside the Resistance. What allegedly ensued was an epic cat-and-mouse struggle between the GUGB, the predecessor of the KGB, and Polish operatives as the Janus Key was smuggled 2,600 km from Lublin to Murmansk. Six operatives, it is said, were dead by the time the key reached Murmansk where it then journeyed to the UK on a return Russian convoy. It was delivered into the hands of a secret agency the name for which I have not discovered. I will just call it the Agency.

'Dr Von Erick Brack destroyed the second Janus Key shortly before Bergen-Belsen was liberated and, thinking the Janus Machine now useless and both keys destroyed, he fled, leaving the machine behind. In possession of the first Janus Key and with the discovery of the machine at Bergen-Belsen, the Agency, as you could imagine, was in a dilemma; should they keep or destroy the weapon? The Agency decided it was not time for the world to have such knowledge. Rather than destroying either the Key or Janus they were hidden separately, just before the end of hostilities in Europe. Nothing of this story was committed to paper and the hiding places were entrusted in parts to a few people who are either now very old or dead. Or so the story goes.

'But there is another story. A third Janus Key was made and is in the hands of those who may seek to exploit the technology, if, that is, the Janus Machine ever resurfaced.

'If your Max and Olivia are indeed trying to retrieve Janus, then a battle of epic proportions will follow.

'As I said, this is just a story and you must believe what you will.'

Professor Drew finished telling her story and Detective Wells and I looked at one another.

'Do you believe the Janus Project stories?' asked Detective Wells.

'Do you believe in the Holy Grail?' retorted Professor Drew. 'It matters not if the Grail exists; it has touched man and history throughout the ages regardless. So beware of Janus.' With that remark she stood, making it obvious that our time with her had come to an end.

With the meeting over, we walked outside and back towards the car.

'Do you get the feeling she knows more than she's saying?' I asked.

'Inspector, I think everybody knows more than they say. An occupational hazard.'

Returning to the police station, we were greeted by the news that a green 1960 Jaguar had been sighted by a patrol yesterday. It was apparently broken down in Lostwithiel. A few phone calls later to the local car repair garages confirmed that we had the car and that the owner was picking it up in an hour's time, at 11.30am.

It took only another thirty minutes for our team to ring accommodation places near to where the car had been sighted. The enquiries revealed that three older people, a man and two women, had booked into the Kings Arms Hotel, initially for one night, but had then extended their stay to two nights.

'What do you think Detective?' I said. 'Do we wait until they pick up the car and follow them to where they are going, or do we go in now?'

'I have just got off the phone from the Yard. It seems the Spooks and Europol have taken an interest in our Max and Olivia and we are to use all resources to apprehend them. It's just after 11.00 now; there's no way we can get there or organise any special units in time. We will have to rely on the local police intercepting them when they pick up the car. I also think we should raid the Kings Arms Hotel, at the same time. The best we can do is to coordinate the operations from here.'

'I agree, but we will have to lift the ban on radio communication. With luck the police presence will be a sufficient deterrent for whoever else is seeking them.'

The unexpected interest of Europol and the British spy agencies gave weight, in my mind, to Professor Lacy Drew's Janus story. A mixture of concern and dread for Max and Olivia swept over me. 'Did you tell them, the spooks, that we think we know where they are heading?'

'No.'

Detective Wells and I were seated in our newly appointed offices at the police station looking up at the speaker which would broadcast the police radio channel to be used in the operation.

With only twenty minutes to set up the operation and with limited resources, the local police had decided to monitor the garage from outside. They hoped to intercept Max and Olivia as they arrived to pick up the car. At worst, they would intercept the car as it left the garage. The hotel team was to raid the hotel the moment the car team moved and intercept either the Jaguar or the people.

'Jag one in position,' hissed the radio, followed by, 'Hotel one in position.' Then silence.

Detective Wells and I could do nothing but sit in nervous anticipation. Like the radio we too were silent.

'Green Jaguar leaving workshop.' The radio went silent.

'Go, go, go!' came the voice of the local operational commander. 'Intercept the car!'

Detective Wells looked over towards me. 'We've got them.'

'In pursuit,' came the radio.

'Not yet,' I said.

'It's 80mph on South on Castle Hill Road.' In the background could be heard the sound of the police siren as the pursuit car driver spoke.

'You have authority to continue with the pursuit,' came the commander's voice.

Silence and a long silence.

The radio abruptly came back to life at first with the sound of the siren. Then, perhaps a second or two passed before a voice said, 'We have come to grief. We are okay but have crashed into a cemetery. The Jaguar is continuing south on Castle Hill Road.'

More silence.

'Pursuit two we have a visual on them, south on Castle Hill Road.'

The commander voice said, 'Speed?'

'It's 75MPH—it's a narrow country lane.'

'You are to terminate the pursuit and follow at a safe distance. We are blocking the B3269 North West of the Castle Hill Road intersection and we have another vehicle coming in from Tywardreath to block the B3269 south of the intersection.'

The silence seemed to last an eternity before; 'Tywardreath road block in place.' Next came, 'B3269 North road closure in place.'

Again we waited.

'Pursuit two we are at the B3269 intersection and heading south towards the Tywardreath road block.'

'This is the Air Support Unit,' crackled the radio. We are tracking south above the B3269 and have pursuit two in view.'

Silence.

'This is Tywardreath road block. The Jaguar has stopped 50 metres from us.'

'Hold your position. Do not engage,' came the local commander's voice. 'You are to wait for pursuit two and Air Support.'

'This is Air Support; we have a visual. The vehicle is stationary. Pursuit two is a couple of minutes away.'

Detective Wells and I looked at one another but said nothing. It was a long two minutes.

'Pursuit two. We have the Jaguar, one female occupant.'

Detective Wells reached over to the radio microphone and, in a voice that displayed some urgency, said, 'Can you identify the occupant?'

'Elinor Grange,' came the reply.

'Can we have an update on the Kings Arms Hotel?'

'No sightings ma'am,' came the unwelcome response.

'What now?' I said to Detective Wells, all the while harbouring a little admiration for the tenacity of Max and Olivia, which was perhaps betrayed by the slightest of smiles as I spoke.

'We close down everything; everything coming and going from Falmouth and the Helford River. I want it more secure than

Fort Knox. We know that they don't use mobile phones so we check all the phone booths nearby and the pub to see if we can work out where they have gone. They must have rung someone for help.'

'They could be hiding at Lostwithiel?'

'True, but I doubt it. I'll have Elinor brought here. Let's find out what she knows!'

'In the helicopter?' I said.

'No, they're still down there somewhere. Once we know what we are looking for I want Air Support on hand.'

Chapter 10

The Grave

Max

'**M**ax, this place hasn't changed in seventy years. The view of the river and the sea is still as beautiful and unspoilt as when we first came here during the war.'

'I remember, Olivia. It is truly wonderful,' I said, looking out over Helford Passage on what was a vividly clear day. 'Do you recall lying on the grass gazing out over the river and looking down on all of the ships and landing craft in the build-up to D-Day?'

'I do, Max.' Olivia took hold of my hand and gave it an affectionate but sombre squeeze.

'I sometimes long for those days. The time when we were still young and our whole lives stretched before us.' Feeling a little melancholy, I added, 'We've had a good life, you and I. Have I been a good husband? Has life, you and I together, been what you hoped for?'

'Max, Max,' said Olivia in soft and tender voice. 'It was here that we first made love, the night before another one of those suicide missions which were guaranteed to shorten the war, this time to the Bay of Biscay. You were going close to the U-boat pens at La Rochelle. I didn't think you would come back and made a promise to God, if you lived, I would love you to the end of my dying days. I've kept that promise and you have been the bravest, kindest and most loving man I have ever known.' Taking a breath, Olivia continued in her mellow tone, 'I don't want to go back, Max. We can't go back, not now. I want— I want us to die together, while we are still free.' Turning to look deep into my eyes and taking hold of my hand again she said, 'Promise me you won't let them take us back.'

'I thought you were happy at the home?'

'I can't forget the terrible, lingering way in which some of our close friends died. I don't want a death that someone else determines for me. I want to choose my own passing. I want to choose what happens at the end of my life. I'm frightened we may experience the unbearable suffering of a terminal disease and that no one will assist us to die if that happens. It's more than a fear of being chronically and terminally ill.

'We survive in the home, but that's not the same as living. Tell me how we added value or made a contribution. When did we do anything constructive other than go through the routines that sustained the meagre biological life we had left? The conversations and the stories we tell are the same day in day out.

There are no new experiences to share. If it were not for you, there would be no love. We are cared for but not loved and without love there is no life.

'Death is the last intimate thing we do and, when the time comes, I want to share it with you. I can't go back now, knowing what we know. We've had a good life and should leave on our terms. Thelma and Louise driving over the cliff, exiting in style.' She paused, then added, 'Are you ashamed of me?'

'No, I'm not ashamed. I envy your courage and surety. Not Thelma and Louise, a bored waitress and a disillusioned housewife. That's not our story, but I love the imagery.' The injection of a little humour broke the sombre moment and, in silence, we stood, looking out across the passage.

'We should walk back to the church and see if we can find the gravestone,' I said.

It took a few minutes to make our way along the coast track and return to the entrance of the church yard. Hesitating at the gate, I looked up and read to myself the Cornish inscription which hung above the church lynch gate. **"It is good for me to draw nigh unto God"**. *I promise Olivia; I won't let them take us back,* I thought. 'Are you ready?' Taking Olivia by the hand I walked through the gate and entered the church grounds and cemetery.

On a cold dreary day, the old stone building, seemingly unchanged since the twelve hundreds, could have been eerily detached if not spooky. The graveyard, with its weathered, unloved and forgotten gravestones, could have been a bitter place of indifference. Today, overlooking the mouth of the Helford River, it was a splendour to behold, an ancient wonder, a custodian of time and history, offering sanctuary to those interred within. Almost immediately I understood the clue, seeing a stone headstone fallen on a grave. Approaching the site I was disturbed to see numerous graves with toppled stones. 'This is going to be more difficult than I thought.'

'We are looking for a toppled stone cross,' Olivia reminded me.

Surveying the surroundings, we saw only one choice, but first we were drawn to walk the uneven ground among the forgotten, stopping to read the gravestones and pondering the lives of the people who, in their absence, still brought life to this most remarkable of places.

Our survey over and, looking one final time out over the river, we turned towards the church and the toppled cross which beckoned. With each step toward the cross, back up the uneven hallowed ground, hope, eagerness and apprehension held our thoughts. Was this the clue? How would we know if it was and would we understand it?

Reaching the cross we realized, with all certainty, that this was the clue we sought for, written on it, worn but visible, was our code word, *"Claude DUVAL"*.

Died 1723

Secret Kingdom of Fife

*__"If you knew the gift of God and who it is that asks you
for a drink, you would have asked him and he would
have given you living water."__*

'Do you know what it means?'

'I'm not sure Olivia, it's probably another one of those bloody cryptic clues. Where's Elinor when you need her?' At least, being a vicar, I know where the passage comes from; it's John 4:10. And the Kingdom of Fife is easy.'

'Scotland, as we thought,' interrupted Olivia.

'More precisely, the tunnels outside of Anstruther,' I replied. 'The ones we sometimes used during the war. What's Elinor to tell the police if she is caught collecting the Jaguar?'

Exactly what we discussed, Max. As much of the truth as she can with the exception of the cryptic clue and Cliff.'

'Do you remember if we said Janus was in Scotland?'

'We did Max; remember when you tossed the coin?'

'I did. That doesn't seem like such a good idea now. With luck, if all's gone well, she will be waiting for us with the car at the Kings Arms and her knowing about Scotland won't be a problem. Let's copy every detail from the cross just in case the clue is more than the words. Then I think we should get out of here.'

Both Olivia and I copied what we saw so as we could compare later, minimizing the chance of one of us missing some important detail. Then we headed back around to the front of the church. As we rounded the building we were stopped in our tracks. The police were talking with our ride. Quietly backtracking and keeping out of sight, we remained hidden but could just overhear the conversation.

'We are setting up a road block just down the road from here but, before we do that, we are just checking that the people we are looking for are not here. Have any of you seen cars or other visitors since you have been here?' said the police officer.

Olivia and I held our breaths and waited for the answer.

'No, just our group,' came an unresponsive and uninterested reply from one of our guides, who with his leather jacket off, revealed huge biceps tattooed with skull and crossbones… an intimidating sight.

'Okay, have a nice ride.' With that, the police officer returned to her car and drove off down the road, I assumed to set up the road block.

'Elinor must have been caught. How else would they have known to come here?'

Olivia nodded.

With the police car gone, we casually walked out of the gate, pretending we had not seen or heard the police. Approaching the motorbike riders and speaking to none of them in particular I said, 'It hasn't changed at all,' turning back to look at the church. 'This is a fantastic tour; thank you for agreeing to bring us here.' Then, in a raised jubilant voice I called aloud,

'Let's ride Olivia,' while throwing her a leather jacket from the back of the Harley Davidson she was pillion riding.

Putting on the helmets of our respective Harley Davidsons, we mounted pillion. The black leathers, insignia and helmets of our riders made them look menacing, as did the sound of five Harleys barking into life, intruding on the serenity of the picturesque setting. Within seconds we roared down the road and gave the slightest sign of acknowledgment as we passed through the police checkpoint before rumbling into Mawnan Smith.

***

Inspector Axel

We were no longer alone. Our makeshift control room at Exeter Police Station was abuzz with people: officers following the various leads that might divulge how Max and Olivia had left Lostwithiel.

'Ma'am,' I heard a young police detective call, a person whose name I had not yet learnt; 'I think I have something. Last night a call was made from a public pay phone on the corner of Cutt Road and the A390 in Lostwithiel. This was the first time the phone had been used in three months. The call was to Cornwall Harley Davidson Pillion Rides. They have confirmed a booking to pick up two people from the Kings Arms Hotel this morning, for a full day ride in Cornwall. They were also joined

215

by three other Harleys, friends so the business owner said, riding because it was such a nice day to be on the road.'

'They certainly like to stand out,' I said to Detective Wells who nodded in agreement before adding, 'At least they won't be difficult to find; five Harley Davidsons.

'All right team,' she said in an excited voice. 'Let's put it out there, tell all our patrols to be on the lookout for any person riding a Harley Davidson, but in particular any with pillion passengers and riding in a group.'

'All we have to do now, Inspector Axel,' she said, turning towards me, 'is wait. I can't imagine this taking long.'

'Ma'am,' said the man whose name I did not know, 'Our people at the Mawnan road block spoke to a group of Harley Davidson riders at the Mawnan Church earlier today. They didn't see Max or Olivia, but admit to not checking the church grounds. They later waved the bikes through the road block thinking they had already been checked.'

In a voice that betrayed her annoyance, Detective Wells responded, 'How long ago?'

'Twenty minutes, ma'am.'

Looking at a map of Cornwall flattened on the desk, Detective Wells muttered to herself, 'How far can you go in twenty minutes?' Then she said aloud, 'Stop everything coming and going from Cornwall. I want Air Support to sweep west from Truro. If they had gone towards Falmouth we should have had a report. I don't care if it's a hippy wagon, I want it stopped and searched. Two octogenarians can't be that hard to find. Do I make myself clear?'

A united '*ma'am*' came from those gathered in the control room.

'And now we sit tight,' I said to Detective Wells, in a voice that was both cheeky and thoughtful.

'Let's get a coffee while we wait. Contact me if there's any news,' she called as we moved towards the door.

Walking together in silent contemplation, it was refreshing to leave the building and feel the warmth of the sunny day. Not five minutes had passed before Detective Wells' phone rang.

'Yes?' she said and then fell silent, listening to whoever had called. Hanging up the phone she turned to me and said. 'The helicopter has five motorbikes in sight, so we should get back.'

For the second time that day, we sat watching the radio speaker, listening for the interception to transpire

'Air support— we still have the five motorbikes in sight, heading west from Truro on the A390.'

'Are there pillion passengers?' I said aloud. It was almost as if the helicopter heard my question.

'We can see two pillion passengers.' followed by silence until a minute later. 'The bikes are turning right of the A390 at Penstraze.' More silence, then, 'They have taken another right towards Tregavethan.'

More silence. I looked to Detective Wells. 'Where are the road units? They should have them by now.'

She looked at me and said nothing then moved her gaze back towards the radio speaker.

'Air support —Tango one two has them.'

The next two minutes felt like an eternity. I stood and paced the room while Detective Wells remained motionless in her chair. I took my seat once more as the radio voice filled the room.

'Tango one two—No pillion passengers, repeat no pillion passengers. Riders report they were dropped off in Truro. We can confirm the passengers were Max and Olivia. Air Support must have seen the spare pillion helmets and jackets on the passenger backrest.'

Detective Wells put her head in her hands and said, in a subdued tone, 'What now?'

No one answered her rhetorical question and she added, 'I want to know of any cars stolen in or around Truro.'

The instructions given to her team, she returned her attention to me.

'I am guessing they have whatever it was they were after. We have road closures and the railway stations being monitored, so all we can do is wait. To tell you the truth, I think they will make it out of Cornwall, if that's what they are trying to do. Perhaps we are not given them the respect they deserve. They are either incredibly lucky, stupid or very good. One thing is for sure, they will pop up somewhere.' She placed her hands over her face, briefly hiding it from view before slowly drawing her hands down to reveal her face once more and continuing the conversation.

'Okay, once we have interviewed Elinor, there's no point in staying here. We should take a ride to Mawnan and look at this church and perhaps we can work out what they were doing there. I also think we should go public. Put their faces on the front page of every newspaper, try and break any public support the romance their story is creating by linking them to the house fire that killed your daughter.'

'Detective Wells— Lynda,' I interrupted. 'You know we can't do that, even though it would help us find them. It would also help other people to find then. It would put Max and Olivia in untold danger and, with them, Janus.

'I suggest we take Elinor with us to the church. We act as if we know what it was Max and Olivia were going there for. With luck, this will encourage Elinor into revealing what she knows, if anything. If the church divulges nothing, then we wait and, as you say, they will most certainly pop up again.'

Detective Wells thought for a moment before nodding her head in agreement adding, 'Coffee while we wait for Elinor to arrive?'

For the second time that morning we left the station and made our way to the coffee shop. This time we were not called back before our arrival.

It was difficult to guess Detective Wells' age; somewhere in her fifties I surmised. She was a heavy set woman but not in an unattractive way. Her clothes were slightly jumbled, dishevelled without being untidy. She wore no wedding ring and other than inviting me to call her by her first name, she revealed nothing of her personal life. Not rude but, like me, private. Our conversation stayed centred on the case and, even when it turned to the house fire, there was not a word of acknowledgement that I was the father of the lady who died. Yet, her tone and manner was such that I knew she cared.

We had just finished our coffees when her phone rang. The conversation lasted less than thirty seconds before Detective Wells hung up and said, 'Elinor is at the police station. Time for the drive to Mawnan.'

Even when living in England, I rarely visited Cornwall. Arriving at the Mawnan Church and looking out over the fields, river and Helford Passage, I regretted this lack for there is no doubt that this is one of the most beautiful places in the world.

The drive down had been purposely quiet and our ploy had worked almost immediately. When Elinor asked, 'Where are you taking me?' I had simply replied, 'We thought you'd like to see what brought Max and Olivia to Mawnan Church.'

'You know about the church and the fallen stone cross?' Elinor had said, with emphasise on the word *cross*, making it more of a statement than question. To this I simply nodded yes and said nothing. After perhaps thirty seconds, Elinor felt compelled to fill the silence.

'It was me who solved the cryptic clue. Mawnan was the difficult part, the fallen stone cross the easy bit.'

'It's quite an art, solving cryptic crosswords,' I said. 'It's good that you have come with us, just in case the fallen cross proves to be another puzzle.'

'Thank you,' Detective Wells also added.

Standing in front of the fallen cross, Detective Wells read aloud the words that were written.

'What do you make of it?' I said to no one in particular.

'Yes, what do you make of it?' came a voice from behind; a voice I recognised as my assailant from the night before.

'Don't be alarmed,' continued the voice. 'Inspector Axel understands the rules; do nothing silly and all will be well.'

I turned slowly, bringing the assailant into view. As before, he was wearing a balaclava. With one hand he waved a greeting while the other hand remained in his coat pocket. Moving his head, he motioned down to the coat pocket where I could see the outline of a gun moving against the material.

Elinor started to move but, quickly, I held her arm. 'It's okay Elinor. Everything will be all right.'

My assailant casually moved and stood beside Elinor to look at the stone cross. The sound of the helicopter distracted us from the assailant's presence. It appeared from below the sloping land leading down towards the river. After rising into view, it settled on the grass field outside of the boundary of the churchyard.

Taken by surprise we did nothing but watch the three people alight from the helicopter and, before we had a chance to register the danger, two men were pointing assault rifles directly at us. They advanced while a tall, slim, blonde haired woman, probably in her thirties, following closely. She was dressed in a full body suit of tight blue leather. Looking to her feet I expected to see high heels, but she wore more practical flat soled shoes which looked out of place with the suit. Lifting my gaze, I saw the body suit accentuated the pertness of her breasts and was unzipped, revealing cleavage.

'Hello sweeties,' she said. 'What have you found?' To this, no one responded.

'That was a question,' she said and, pointing to Elinor, she continued, 'You, sweetie, tell me what you know.' As she spoke, one of the men holding an assault rifle levelled it at Elinor.

Elinor stammered at first but quickly regained her composure. 'All I know is the gravestone cross is meant to be a clue to the location of something which is hidden. They, Max and Olivia, did mention the name of the thing but honestly I can't remember.'

'Thank you sweetie; did they say where they thought this thing might be hidden?'

'No,' replied Elinor.

The lady in blue took a few steps closer to the gravestone and, using her mobile phone, took a picture. Without saying a word she turned and started walking back towards the helicopter and the whooshing of the props, which disturbed the serenity of the location.

The men with the assault rifles also withdrew. The red dots emanating from the laser sights bounced from us to the ground as they walked carefully backwards until they had cleared the churchyard and were once again in the field. They jumped back into the helicopter, which lifted slowly off from the ground.

'One of yours?' I asked my assailant.

'Russian Mafia. I hear there's a syndicate looking for Janus.'

'Do you know her?'

'No, not my type.'

The helicopter hovered above the field just outside of the churchyard.

'Move, take cover!' shouted my assailant, shoving Elinor to the ground.

Turning, I saw a red dot flicker on the stone cross and flung myself down and then rolled a couple of times, finding temporary cover behind a grave. I heard nothing other than the rotor blades slicing the air not far away but saw puffs of dirt and mud as bullets landed where I had been.

The sound of gunshots only metres from my ears was deafening. Bang, bang. Bang, bang; two rapid shots followed by another two rapid shots. Looking over, I saw my assailant lying with his back to the ground, two hands steadying the gun aimed at the helicopter. The response was immediate; the helicopter swung away and dipped below the hill and was gone.

Detective Wells and Elinor lay motionless on the ground. I rushed to Elinor's side and knelt. I placed my hand under her head and lifted it gently. Her eyes were open but stared vacantly back. She was dead.

'Help me,' I cried out in anguish but all was silent. Looking about, I saw my assailant was gone, vanished back into the world from which he came. I stood up and looked towards Detective Wells who had not moved. Fearing the worst but in hope of the best, I moved to where she lay.

'Lynda, Lynda,' I cried. 'Can you hear me?' My calling was in vain; she was voiceless and only the hallowed ground whispered with the breeze, *Princes or thieves, believers and non-believers—all are welcome. Sanctuary and peace are to be found in my ground*, as its parched soil drank the blood that trickled from the lifeless souls.

Chapter 11

Windermere

Max

'Oh Max, I do wish you would steal a less conspicuous car; the police are everywhere and perhaps it's best we blend in.' This was spoken in a tone reminiscent of Lady Penelope from *Thunderbirds*, a game of ours from a bygone era.

To it I replied, 'Yes m'lady, unfortunately m'lady, it seems the older type automobile is more accommodating to the senior touch.'

'Oh Parker; well done. Have you prepared the Rolls Royce? Is it ready to run?'

'Oh yes, m'lady? Quite ready. Everything's been done. I've lubricated all of the cannons and I've polished up the gun.'

'Very well Parker. I think I'd like to take a little ride. And Parker…'

'Yes, m'lady.'

'Somewhere just around the countryside.'

'Land's End Airport m'lady.

'Very well Parker.'

The drive to Land's End, which was just over an hour away, was uneventful. Leaving Olivia at the airport, I drove to Penzance to dump the car, vowing, along the way, to buy an old Roller as our next get-about. Having disposed of the car and leaving a hundred pounds in the glove compartment, I acquired the services of a taxi to whisk me back to the airport and Olivia.

I didn't ask what lie, in the guise of a story, Olivia had told for our charter to Bristol. Having told so many lies over our lifetime, they were for us, if only for a short time, the truth. Once in Bristol we decided on staying at least for a couple of days. Olivia and I were in need of rest and the purchase of another car before any recovery attempt could be made in Scotland.

'Who could imagine fitting so much into a single day?' I said. 'What lie are we going to tell this time for having no luggage and no clean underpants?'

'It's all right for you boys. The same pair of underpants lasts you a week and even then, you just turn them inside out and start again.'

'Tomorrow, "Operation Underpants'," I replied.

'Max, although I don't want to, I think we should find separate hotels. At least until the heat settles.'

I reluctantly agreed and, before parting said, 'Let's meet back here at nine o'clock, outside this café. It looks a reasonable place for breakfast. Afterwards you can buy the undies and I'll find a new set of wheels.'

Having seen the police at the Mawnan church, we knew it would be only a matter of time before they discovered the fallen cross if they had not done so already. It seemed fair to conclude that our other pursuers already knew we were heading to Scotland.

Much of the next two days was taken up with finalising the plans for the trip. Only in hindsight would we know if the plan had been a success or failure. We discussed all the modes of transport; flying, train, bus and driving. In the end we returned to our initial idea of purchasing another car. Our own wheels gave flexibility.

With transport decided, it was then a matter of working out how to drive north. Travelling together, two old farts, would provoke the attention of anybody pursuing and also those following our story in the media and on Facebook.

'Max, I think two women journeying together would be less obvious. Old ladies always travel together, so they would seem—well, quite natural.'

I agreed but pointed out that Elinor was no longer with us.

'I'm not thinking of Elinor,' came the reply.

'You're not suggesting what I think you are suggesting?' I said—and was right; Olivia's scheme was for me to travel in drag.

With me having grudgingly agreed to the cover of two women travelling together, we fixed on adding as many elements and layers to our deception as possible. Every possibility, no matter how ridiculous, had been put on the table for discussion. In the end we settled on having two young people drive us. To do this we visited a local backpackers' hostel and offered a free ride for two people wishing to travel to Scotland on Thursday 7th. All they needed was a current driver's licence. The advertisement was placed on the backpackers' noticeboard on Tuesday afternoon and, by Wednesday morning, we had our chauffeurs. The next element of our plan was to use the old Visa card, the one in the name of Max Breeze, which was undoubtedly monitored, to book two nights' accommodation in London.

All that was needed now was the purchase of the car, another British classic. I started my search first thing Tuesday morning, in between shopping for our new wardrobe and visiting the Backpackers' hostel. Luckily Olivia did, in addition to my disguise, purchase some man's things for when we arrived in Scotland.

Unsurprisingly, my search for a Rolls Royce Silver Spur, similar to the one I had borrowed from Truro, was not successful in or near Bristol. To my dismay, other than MGs and Austin Healy Sprites, all of which were too small and far too difficult for us to get in or out of at our age, the choice of British classics on offer was pitiful. That's not entirely true though. There was a magnificent brown 1970s Aston Martin V8 Vantage, one of my dream cars. Looking at it on the internet, I could imagine Max and Olivia Bond flying up the motorway towards Scotland, but in our reality it was outside of any reasonable cash advance I could secure without rousing suspicion. In the end, my British classic dream came down to a Russian 1956 GAZ-M20, left hand drive. On Wednesday night and £12,000 later, the M20 was mine. I drove back to Olivia's hotel and showed her our relic from the cold war days. She could not control her laughter, knowing my passion for British cars.

'Now I know why you said it would be a surprise,' she joked.

Before leaving Olivia for the night, I had asked what time our backpackers, Jess and David, were meeting us tomorrow.

'At about eight,' said Olivia. 'At my hotel, not yours.'

'I sure hope one of them can drive a left hand drive car; it handles like a battleship,' I said before giving Olivia the mandatory farewell kiss and driving away.

Next morning, the new wardrobe was lying in wait in Olivia's room. She took great pleasure assisting me in dressing and then applying lavish amounts of excessive makeup. It was shortly before 8.30 in the morning when the two old ladies left the hotel.

'Good morning David and Jess, this is Maxine,' said Olivia, pointing to me. 'And I'm Olivia. Oh, we are both so much looking forward to your company on our run up to Scotland today. Aren't we Maxine?' To this I nodded. 'If you don't mind, Maxine and I prefer to sit in the back. You don't mind driving do you?' Olivia said to neither of them in particular.

'What a magnificent looking car. What is it?' asked David, although I detected an air of sarcasm in his voice.

Trying for a more feminine voice, in keeping with my disguise, I replied, 'I have absolutely no idea, love. It was my husband's. He's dead now—rest his soul. Had it for years, he did. Not the easiest thing to drive, but very comfortable and lots of room in the back. Oh, and love,' I continued, 'Can you take us up via Liverpool? We would like to make a detour into the Lake District. Perhaps we can have lunch there; it will be our treat. Are you ready, Olivia love?'

'Ready for what, dear?'

'To leave. For Scotland.'

'Oh, of course, dear.'

The M20 car was surprisingly better from the back seat, both roomy and comfortable. I gazed across to Olivia who was wearing a ridiculous red wide brimmed fedora hat, brown pinstriped jacket and matching skirt. She seemed something of a cross between Mata Hari and Hilda Pierce from *Foyle's War*, one of my favourite TV series. From the charity shop, Olivia had chosen for me a wool cloche bucket hat, a cream shirt with frills, an extra-large dark green cardigan and a dark cream scarf adorned with red flowers. She did allow me the dignity of a long black skirt—I had refused a short skirt which would have necessitated stockings to hide my sexy legs. To complete my shame, I wore ostentatious pearls, clip-on earrings and bright red lipstick.

The first half an hour of the journey was completed in relative silence, with David and Jess talking quietly between themselves, accompanied by the drumming of the car as we sped up the motorway.

'Love, where are you from?' I called from the back seat to neither one of them in particular.

'We are both from a town called Warragul. In Australia,' answered Jess.

'Australia! Olivia, isn't that exciting? They have come all the way from Australia.' After a short pause I added, 'What are you doing in the UK?'

'We are on our honeymoon and have just finished a Contiki tour of Europe and are now having a few weeks in Britain before heading home.'

'A honeymoon! Congratulations. Aren't they a lovely couple Olivia?' Before Olivia had a chance to answer, I continued, 'Are you going to Scotland sightseeing?'

'Yes and no. David's grandparents came from Scotland— Glasgow. His grandfather, Jim, worked at the John Brown shipyards, after the war. By all accounts life was hard. They emigrated to Australia from Britain as ten pound poms in the late 50s when the shipyard was struggling to compete with Korea and Japan. In the stories Jim tells, he could see no future for their family in Scotland. Despite needing to leave, he still lamented the sheer beauty of Scotland; not only the countryside but the beauty within the bleakness of working class slums. For us, it's hard to understand how, despite loving a place, you can pack up everything and leave for a foreign land—forever. We want to visit where Jim came from, to help us understand his story, which is part of David's story.'

'What a wonderful thing to do,' put in Olivia. 'I'm sure, when you return, Jim will love hearing of your adventure. I bet he will be touched that you took time to learn of his journey.' The hum of the road filled the car before Olivia added. 'A lovely young couple don't you think Maxine?'

'Oh yes Olivia; a lovely young couple.'

Over the next while we became quite fond of our backpacker chauffeurs and conversation flowed easily as the miles sailed by, before I said, 'I am afraid, Loves, I need to powder my nose. Can you pull into one of the motorway places?'

David answered with a simple, 'Yep.'

We were, by now, past Birmingham as the M20 glided to a halt in a motorway service centre. Reaching over into the front of the car, I handed David a £100 note with instructions to fill the car with fuel and then meet us for coffee.

Once inside the service centre I looked about for the conveniences. It felt strange walking into the ladies' toilet with Olivia, but nice to have a privacy not found in the men's. The separate cubicles were far better than standing shoulder to shoulder at a urinal, where despite busting to go, often nothing happens. The more you try, the more nature refuses. You find yourself glancing side to side thinking the world is laughing at your *stage fright*. Worse, for us private Englishmen, is when travelling on the continent. In Italy, stern-faced Italian women manage the men's toilets and seem quite content to clean the urinal, right next to you, as you stand with your pecker hanging out. Once, I even experienced the embarrassment of one of these big Italian mammas looking directly at me, as I stood astride the urinal, and saying in her heavy Italian accent, 'Are you having problems going, dear?'

When it comes to lavatories, it is the Parisians who openly display a centuries-old contempt for the reserved English gentleman— with public WCs that provide privacy from the knees to the navel only. When the call of nature beckons, one must stand erect, looking out over the passing crowd. An essential travel companion for any older gentleman, but particularly an English gentleman, is a location map of the local McDonalds—the world's WC, with a powder room on every corner.

Olivia was seated at a table in the café area by the time I returned from the ladies'.

'You were a while,' she said with a grin.

'It's these stockings; they are just impossible!' My reply overlooked the fact that I was wearing a long skirt and socks.

Seated at a table in the corner of the café and a good distance from us, was a face I was sure that I recognised. Joking over, I sat down with Olivia at the table, all the while trying not to look in the direction of the man, or give an inkling that I suspected we were being watched. My mind searched its memories, trying to recall the face. *Where had I seen him before*?

I became abruptly aware that Olivia was speaking to me, I looked up. 'Sorry, I didn't hear what you said; my thoughts were elsewhere.'

'I said, we are making good time.'

Ignoring Olivia's statement, I said. 'Don't look up, but there's a man sitting behind you who looks familiar. I'm racking my brain trying to remember where I have seen him before.' Then it came to me. 'The Hotel Renaissance, he was the man I told you about, the one watching us from the bar.'

'Are you sure? It must have been nearly impossible for anyone to follow us here.'

'It's him, I'm sure of it.'

'What now?'

Before I could answer, David and Jess joined us at the table. Dropping any inkling of eccentricity from my voice, no dears or loves, I asked David and Jess to buy the coffees. A look of mild confusion came over their respective faces; an indication that they sensed something was different, although they were not quite sure what it was. By the time David and Jess returned, Olivia and I had settled on a strategy.

'David,' I said, 'try not to look surprised or startled, but just listen. If you're ready, nod once.' Immediately he looked towards Jess, who just shrugged her shoulders, before returning his gaze to me. 'Olivia and I are being followed and we need help—from both of you—to slip our tail. Don't look around but we are being watched. You're in no danger, it's just a game between some harmless old wealthy but bored friends of ours. Olivia used to be an author writing mystery spy novels. We played these games back then with our friends to help write the plot. A couple of years ago Olivia started writing again and this—you—us, is all part of one of those games, right now.'

'So,' said Jess. 'Are you telling us this is part of the book?'

'I hope so,' replied Olivia. 'But not if our escape plan has failed so miserably and so early in the plot. I want my stories to be —well—at least a little believable. So we test them out.'

'I told you the car would be a dead giveaway; you used an old car last year in a book,' I put in. Looking to David and then to Jess I could tell we had them; they were falling for the tale hook line and sinker. *Go on,* I said to myself, *ask some more questions; we almost have you.*

David was thinking, you could tell by the look of concentration on his face and finally he said, 'Did you sell many books?'

Before Olivia could answer I spoke, intent on playing the sympathy card and completing our entrapment. 'Thirty years ago, yes she was a very successful writer but, as you get older, it gets harder. Her heroes aged along with us and, it turned out, that no one was interested in stories about old people. For a long time she stopped writing and, when she did start again… what is it the critics wrote?'

Olivia let her head drop slightly and introduced a subtle change in her tone, one with a hint of melancholy.

'I can still remember the review. *The New York Times—an enthralling read—for those suffering from insomnia.* Imagine suggesting my book would put you to sleep. The cheek of them! Anyway, I'm going to show those critics; I don't care what they say, this one will be a best seller. Oh and there's £500 in it if you help us.'

'What happens in this story?' asked David with a look of bewilderment.

'Well that depends,' I said. 'It depends on whether you help us, or we stay here ourselves. That's the exciting part; the plot will just unfold. Are you willing to play along, to be part of the book, so to speak?'

David gazed to Jess before saying, 'Go on, but it will depend on what it is you want us to do.'

'Oh it's nothing,' said Olivia. 'Just leave us behind, drive the car to Windermere and wait for us to arrive. If we are not there by six o'clock tonight, you can take the car and the £500. Drop the car sometime tomorrow in Edinburgh at the Waverley railway station. Leave the keys in the glove compartment because we have a spare set. You get to keep the £500. Our plan, however, is for our friends to follow you. What you have to do is stop at another service centre, say for at least half an hour somewhere before heading into the Lake District. Our tail will see we have given them the slip and come racing back here, by which time we will have gone. All you then do is drive on to our meeting place in Windermere.'

'Whereabouts in Windermere?'

'The Ferry Pier; you can't miss it. Just park the car and Max…Maxine and I will find you.'

'I need to talk it over with Jess.'

'I'm afraid that's not possible—only because our friends will see something up—they will know we are onto them.'

David and Jess again looked at each other.

'It's either a yes or no,' encouraged Olivia.

'What do you think Jess?' asked David.

'Sounds like some harmless fun and we may even find ourselves in a book. Why not? Let's do it.' Then turning her attention to me, she said, 'You are a man aren't you?'

'Yes; how can you tell?'

'Well besides the bit where Olivia called you Max, it's a pretty good disguise… really good, you had me fooled. You guys must take this game really seriously! What now, do you stay dressed as a woman?'

'I was meant to be a woman for quite a while yet; Olivia thought it was one of her more brilliant plans and would make for an entertaining read. I think the game's well and truly up. So, no.'

'Go on with you,' said Olivia in a light-hearted manner. 'Who was it that refused the good old fashioned bloomers, and demanded knickers instead?'

'Now you're scaring them,' I retorted.

To maintain a calm and unhurried appearance, we slowly drank our coffees and then had Jess purchase some nibbles for what would appear to be the next part of the road trip. We made our way back to the car and David opened the boot to remove a small plastic bag containing my men's clothing, including a warm jacket—packed in case of an emergency. The bag accompanied Olivia and me into the back seat. The M20 rumbled back to life and moved effortlessly through the car park toward the exit, stopping for the briefest of moments between two parked trucks. We slipped out of the car, leaving our hats and, in my case, a wig, behind, and concealed ourselves beside one of the trucks. From our hiding place we watched as the M20 disappeared off into the distance. If it was followed, it was difficult to tell, as a constant stream of traffic was coming and going from the service centre.

From our hiding place next to the truck we moved stealthily between the parked cars, trying to keep our bodies low, hidden and concealed by the vehicles. Being crouched over was no mean feat for eighty-somethings and God only knew if we were going to be able to straighten up again.

Split up, believing one person alone was more easily concealed, we agreed to stay hidden for another few minutes, after which we would simply stand up and separately walk back into the service centre café. If our tail was still there and had not fallen for the bait, another plan would be devised from our table inside.

I was the first one of us to make it inside and was relieved to see our shadow was no longer there. Olivia came in a short time later and, again, we found ourselves seated at a table sipping coffee.

'What now Olivia?'

'As cute as you are in that dress, I'm not sure the bald head is that becoming and may actually clash with your lipstick. Perhaps a change is in order?'

'Sometimes you can be so demanding,' I said, giving my eyelashes a flutter.

I made my way, this time, to the men's toilets and joined a constant stream of other men using the wash room. In one of the small toilet cubicles, I tried to slip out of my dress and put on trousers. In the cramped surroundings, changing my clothes proved more than a little challenging. In the end, I found sitting on the toilet the best way to pull on my trousers. Having transformed, I went to the basins and washed the makeup from my face. No one paid me any attention until I was preparing to leave, when a burly man, probably a truckie, said, 'Ha, excuse me buddy, you've left the earrings on.'

'Ah, thanks,' I replied reaching up and pulling the clip-ons free of my ears before depositing then into the plastic bag containing the discarded clothes, which I then put in the bin on the way out of the toilet.

'That's a better look,' greeted Olivia upon my return.

'We won't have long,' I said. 'Once Jess and David stop, they will see we have given them the slip and come racing back. If we are going to leave, we need to make it soon. Any ideas?'

'Yes, I think I do. Just play along with me—And Max, look old.'

That won't be hard, I thought.

Olivia smiled, before changing her expression to one of anxiety. Then she stood and in a loud distressed voice cried out, 'Oh no Mac, the bus has gone without us. What are we going to do?' Starting to cry she added, 'how are we going to get to Windermere, oh Mac the tour has gone and left us behind!'

Her sobbing intensified and, with it, the café fell into a hush. I stood, feigning to almost fall, and comforted Olivia. 'It will be all right dear, I'm sure it will be all right. Sit down now, don't distress yourself so.' Gingerly and with great care I helped Olivia to retake her seat. As if on cue, a man and women in their fifties, perhaps early sixties, came over to the table.

'Hi, my name is Gwen and this is my husband Ari. We are on our way to the Lake District and staying in Windermere. You would be more than welcome to join us—until you find your tour.'

'That would be awfully kind of you,' I said. 'Please excuse our little show of distress, it was bit of a shock when we realised we had been left behind.'

'I understand,' said Gwen. 'Would you like me to ring someone, to let them know you are okay? Do you have the number of your tour leader?'

'Oh, yes dear, that's such a good idea.'

I looked to Olivia as she spoke, wondering how she would lie her way out of this one. 'Mac go over there,' she said, pointing to a pay phone in the corner, 'and give them a call. Do you know, Ari and Gwen, I totally forgot. They will be so worried when they realise they have left us behind.'

'Would you like to use my mobile, or I could call for you,' said Gwen.

'Oh no dear, you have already offered too much, Mac is quite capable of making a phone call. Go on Mac, off you go.'

Taking my name as the cue, I left and headed towards the pay phone. As I moved away, but was still in earshot, I heard Olivia introducing us to Gwen and Ari. 'I'm Lilly and that over there is my husband Mac.' Remembering our new names, I was determined to call Olivia Lilly upon my return, thus cementing our deception.

The drive to the Lake District was uneventful and we made good time. Because we didn't stop en route, we assumed we would arrive before the M20.

Gwen and Ari proved to be delightful company and chatted away freely. When we said we were residents in a retirement home, Gwen began sharing her mother's situation, as a resident in a home in London.

'We've stopped trying to take her out; she virtually refuses to leave the building. We really thought she would enjoy having lunch, or sitting on the beach watching the waves but, the last time we persuaded her to leave, we had to hop from one toilet stop to another. Sometimes she would stay in there for an hour and half—an hour and half at a time. She was distressed and we were distressed. It was no fun for any of us. When we visit now, we don't even suggest going out. The problem is, she's desperately lonely but, when we do go, there's nothing to talk about. We just go over the same old stuff while secretly wishing we could leave. We don't like going and sometimes don't but then we feel racked with guilt for not spending more time with her. I wish she was more like you two! And now I feel really bad for saying that.'

It was difficult, if not impossible, to respond to Gwen in any way that could ease her guilt or make the dwindling time she had left with her mother more rewarding or meaningful for either of them.

'The best I can do,' I said, 'is to tell you how we sometimes feel, but this may not be the same as your mother—you understand that?'

She nodded in agreement and Ari shifted his head slightly, focussing his hearing towards our conversation, in expectation, perhaps, of some pearl of wisdom. But, no insight was forthcoming and, for a moment we all sat in total silence, until "Lilly" interjected, 'As we get older we find we have less and less control over our lives. It's not that people want to take away our control, it's often just driven by necessity. That's particularly so when you live in institutions, which, no matter how hard the nursing homes try, in Australia at least, they are. As the control increases and our ability to make decision falls away, our confidence goes with it. Sometimes our confidence and our dignity are inextricably linked. With little else under our command, the loss of control over the water works and bowel movements is the final indignity. To be out and feel the shame and humiliation of soiling oneself becomes an insurmountable fear. What little self-reliance we have left comes only from being within the surroundings where we feel safe from shame. If you want to expand your mother's boundaries of security, start close to the home and in places that have the facilities she needs to avoid her shame. Or take her out for very short periods. Let her confidence build.' "Lilly" paused as if expecting Gwen to respond, but there was nothing forthcoming.

'Mac and I are in a home together but we know that they can be lonely places, even when surrounded by caring staff. Loneliness is self-perpetuating. When Mac is having a down day or two, he often behaves in ways that cause other people, particularly staff, to avoid him. I could tell you some stories and you would get a real giggle out of them. Some of the things he has done and said are outrageous—in hindsight, hilarious, but not at the time for those around.'

I found myself unable to control the urge for a jovial interlude and, despite the genuineness of the discussion, interrupted Olivia's flow with, 'Lilly, I've told you a million times, a million times not to exaggerate.' But she ignored me, and after taking a slight breath, continued honestly, 'If I was not there, I fear he would fall into depression and, as you have noticed, we are better than most. So try not to feel bad; what you see and experience is the reality of our lives—it's not your fault. Despite the best intentions, we live in institutions, which is both fortuitous and unfortunate. Somehow, in the future, aged care needs, in part, to include the wider world, the sights, sounds and experiences of the outside world and even real people; things that will bring in new experiences and invigorated fresh conversations. There's nothing we oldies like better than complaining about the youth of today but, how can we whinge about their drinking games or how they wear their trousers around their knees and underpants around their necks, if we don't get to see them? For your mum, be relaxed about filling the space with conversation. Try instead to fill it with an activity that she likes or used to like. Perhaps that was reading, cards or board games. Do the activity and the conversation will come and the time will pass. That is the end of my *TED* talk.'

Lilly's' *TED* talk proved to be an absolute conversational stopper. After about sixty seconds, I asked Gwen what she thought. The final miles of the trip then vanished quickly with reflective and thought-provoking conversation. It was this type of conversation that I have so dearly missed. My intellect was alive and when Ari said, 'Whereabouts in Windermere do you want us to drop you?' I felt a tinge of sadness when I said, 'The *Ships Inn*, down near the pier. They are going to meet us there.'

As Olivia and I waved a final farewell to our newfound friends, I glanced at my watch and it was 2.00pm. No wonder I was feeling a little hungry. We waited for the car to vanish around the corner before making our way to where we had a good view over the parking area near the ferry pier. Once secreted in our observation post, Olivia went off, leaving me to keep watch, while she found us a late lunch. Despite it being fairly cold, in my warm jacket and with no wind, the 10 degrees Celsius was not overly uncomfortable.

The Lake District is truly a place of unsurpassed beauty and even more so on a fresh invigorating day such as this. Gazing out over the lake as the light from the sun hypnotically danced with the water, I was lost in the moment, and all expectation of the M20 faded and in its place the inviting prose from Wordsworth described the scene in imagery beyond my words.

Cultured slopes,
Wild tracts of forest-ground, and scattered groves,
And mountain bare—clothed with ancient woods

Surrounded us; and, as we held our way

Along the level of the glassy flood,

They ceased not to surround us; change of place,

From kindred features diversely combined,

Producing change of beauty ever new.

    Ah! That such beauty, varying in the light

Of Living Nature, cannot be portrayed

By words, nor by the pencil's silent skill;

But is the property of Him alone

Who hath beheld it, noted it with care,

And, in his mind, recorded it with love!

Coming back to the present, I smiled at the richness of the words and the sheer beauty of this Earth, only to be overwhelmed by emotion as I said to myself, *'When was the last time you have felt so happy to be alive?* Pondering the past, I recalled, not only the places and people that had been special, but the joy and pleasure found in the daily mundane rituals— *I've had a wonderful life—thank you God. I promise I won't complain ever again.'*

My gaze slowly moved from the lake and the past, to focus back once more upon the car park. It was about half an hour later when Olivia returned and we enjoyed a leisurely lunch expecting the M20 to appear at any moment.

'How long do we wait, Max?'

'I don't know but, if they are not here by six, then it's safe to assume they are not coming. If that happens, we will have to find ourselves somewhere to spend the night.'

'You don't think we have put that nice young couple in danger? Did we do the right thing—using them as a decoy?'

'I reckon they just took the £500 and bolted. It will be a miracle if they leave the car at the Edinburgh railway station. You needn't worry about them, as long as they stopped so that our pursuers could see we had given then the slip, they will be safe. I can guarantee it!'

'For a priest, sometimes you're not very charitable. They haven't done a runner or taken the money. If we do at some time meet them again, I'm sure there will be a simple explanation.'

With the temperature dropping and six o'clock having come and gone, we went into the town, reconciled in the knowledge that the M20 was not coming. Our task now was to find a place to stay for the night and so we perused the abundance of guest houses, most of which were old two storey buildings of some kind or another. The one that caught our fancy was near an intersection; we like intersections as they provide a variety of escape routes, if needed. What clinched the deal, in this case, was what was behind two open heavy black doors, in the garage next to the front entrance of the guest house. It was a beautiful old pastel blue Austin 7.

A man, not too many years younger than me, maybe a decade or so, was hunched over the Austin, obviously tinkering with its engine. I attracted his attention by calling out, 'Is this your place—are you taking guests for the evening?'

He uncurled his back and turned to face us.

'Ah, it is. My wife is inside and you will find yourselves most welcome. It gets a little quiet this time of year.'

'An Austin 7,' I replied. 'She looks absolutely beautiful. Do you mind if we take a look before going in?'

We were invited into the garage and the man introduced himself as George and he seemed genuinely pleased to show us his pride and joy. The car, he told us, was a 1937 Ruby and had been fully mechanically restored, but he had chosen to retain the "used look", to reflect its age. There were a few scratches and bumps here and there. It had a folding top which was down; the seats were not torn but showed the wear and tear of being loved. On the passenger's floor was a huge torch and, although I did not ask, I wondered what he used it for.

Before leaving the garage, I noted a rear entrance which led out into the garden, behind the guest house. Exiting via the front gates and before entering the B&B, we surveyed the road and our surroundings, taking special note of the parked cars, people and options for escape. The surveillance was undertaken with no obvious head movements and without as much as a pause, on our journey to the front door.

On entering the building we were greeted by a lady in her 70s, who introduced herself as Daisy, George's wife. We sought the availability of an upstairs room overlooking the main road.

'The noise of the street helps us sleep,' I said to Daisy.

Having finished the booking, Daisy showed us upstairs and to our room. Before going inside she drew our attention to an alternative set of stairs at the end of the corridor. 'These lead to the kitchen,' she said. 'They are only to be used in case of emergencies, such as a fire, when the main stairs are out of action. Evidently,' she continued, 'these were servants' stairs from a bygone era.'

Our room was tastefully furnished with its main feature being a king-sized bed. A writing desk sat in front of a single window and, from its chair, we had an unhindered view of the street.

We had given our usual excuse for having no luggage; that it had been lost at the airport. Daisy provided directions to where we might avail ourselves of some toiletries and perhaps a change of undergarments—again, although it was a little late for clothes shopping.

As we were the only guests that evening, Daisy invited us to join George and her for dinner, so we quickly slipped out to make our purchases, not wanting to be late for the meal. With our shopping in two plastic bags, we returned to the guest house and made another assessment of the surroundings.

Dinner brought back fond memories from my childhood with *toad in the hole*, a meal I had not experienced in sixty or seventy years. It was absolutely wonderful; just plain old sausages in Yorkshire pudding, served with vegetables and gravy. Lots of gravy.

Over the meal, we learned that Daisy was equally as passionate about the Austin 7 as was George. They belonged to a historical car club and, over the summer months, they would dress in period costume and go on many an outing. They not only went out locally; it was not uncommon for them to travel a hundred miles or more. George proved to be a wonderful storyteller who seemed able to turn a simple tale into an exciting adventure. It had been a long time since I had laughed so much or truly enjoyed sharing another person's passion. After dinner, we thanked them for their wonderful hospitality and then gave our apologies for needing an early night. We left the dining room and made our way up the stairs to our room.

'What do you see?' I asked Olivia who was seated at the desk looking out through the window.

'The blue SUV on the other side of the road is still there. All the other cars have changed.'

'Can you see anyone inside?'

'Not really; it's got those annoying dark tinted windows but there were definitely two people in the front when we came back from the shops.'

'Let's put the lights out, as if we have gone to bed, so they can't see in the window. I think we're going to need to take it in turns and keep watch. It's going to be a long night and I have a sneaking suspicion we will have unwanted company!'

Unusually for once, Olivia agreed with me and, while she watched the SUV from the window, we made our plans of escape for when the attack began. It was my shift when the interior light of the SUV came to life as the doors opened.

Looking to my watch I saw that it was precisely 1.30am. 'Olivia; wake up, it's on, they're coming,' I called in an urgent but measured voice.

The outside street light gave enough glow for me to see Olivia as she stirred. In the early hours of morning, or whenever we seniors first wake up, our bones and muscles object to the disturbance. Quickly but gingerly she put her legs over the side of the bed and, in accordance with our plan, reached for the bedside phone. I watched as she punched in the numbers *-999-* and listened as she spoke decisively but calmly.

'Police please. My name is Olivia Breeze and you are currently looking for me and my husband Max. I am at number 28 Williams Street in Windermere of the Lake District. The guest house is near the intersection of William and Chapel Streets. The people who killed Kate and Edward Phoenix from Horton-cum-Studley on the 31st of March are about to murder George and Daisy Ruskin of this address. You have only a matter of minutes. I suggest you make as much noise as you can on the way here in the hope you can scare them off. I'm afraid you won't make it here in time otherwise. I'm going to leave the phone off the hook. As you will undoubtedly understand, Max and I have to flee. Good luck.'

'Well done Olivia; that's the best we can do for George and Daisy. I can still see them outside; they are not quite at the front door yet.'

Olivia made her way to the bedroom door, and put her hand on the door handle.

I said, 'Wait just little bit longer. Don't open the door until we can be absolutely sure they can't see our window and any light that will flood in from the corridor when you do.'

About twenty seconds later, the two figures walked from my view and were most likely picking the lock of the front door.

'Go,' I whispered. 'I'll meet you at the servants' stairs.'

Olivia slid out through the narrowest of cracks she could make in the door, pulling it closed behind her without fully shutting it. I made my way to the door and did the same but closed and locked it behind me. We went carefully and silently along the corridor before we descended the servants' stairs. On reaching the bottom, I paused. One final step would take us into the kitchen. My heart was racing and, for a few seconds, I stayed frozen. My mind was filled with thoughts and fears—*If we stay very still perhaps the police will come and we will be safe. If I step out, they may be waiting for us, then we will be dead.*

I felt a gentle but purposeful jab in my back. Olivia wanted me to keep moving. '*Keep going,*' she whispered, and I stepped out.

The kitchen was quiet and eerily still; through the dim light we could see the back door and our escape route, only metres away. Now, in full view of anybody looking into the kitchen, we moved on cautiously, to avoid running into or knocking anything over as we made our way to the door. Turning the door handle and giving it a gentle pull I discovered the door was locked. An old fashioned key protruded from its resting place just below the knob.

Clunk! The tumblers of the lock made a deafening racket as they gave way. The door screamed out in deafening agony and defiance as it gave way to my will and opened. We sneaked out through the crack but not before I removed the key from its lock and replaced it on the outside. We fastened the old wooden door behind us, as a temporary barrier if our pursuers were to follow, and made our way to the back entrance of the garage.

Once we were inside, the double fronted garage doors opened more silently and willingly than had the old kitchen door. With Olivia at the wheel I pushed the Austin 7 out into the street before joining her in the car. It rolled soundlessly down the road and around the corner, coming to rest well away and out of sight of the guest house. Swapping seats we noticed, with much relief, that no one had followed us. It took me just seconds to breathe life into the Seven and we chugged away from Windermere without switching on its lights and with an engine so silent that it wouldn't have woken a sleeping baby.

'There are only a few roads out of here,' said Olivia. "I think we should go via Troutbeck and then cut back onto the highway. With any luck the police will pass us while we are on the back road.'

'And our pursuers?' I said.

'With luck they will be forced to go to ground and hide.'

The crispness of the night air was broken by the sound of wailing sirens as we turned right to Troutbeck. The darkness of the night closed in all around us as we left what meagre light the town had offered. I fiddled and searched around the steering wheel and then the dash for the headlight switch. I needn't have bothered. Even when illuminated the Austin 7 lights were in name and for show only; nothing lit the way. If there was light, it fell as a dull cream glow, no more than a few feet in front of us. Remembering the torch, Olivia reached down in between her feet and picked it up. Flicking the switch brought forth a narrow but bright beam of light.

Loud thundering, which trailed off into the distance, shattered what little serenity was left of the night.

'Sounds like rain,' I said before noticing there were no clouds to be seen, but then giving it no further thought.

Standing, Olivia braced herself by holding on to the car with one hand. In her other hand she held aloft our lighthouse of the night, showing the way to Carlisle and a hotel we knew with a 24 hour reception—a place we had stayed before.

We stopped five or six times during the drive, for Olivia to take a rest from holding the torch. Cold and exhausted, we finally arrived and booked in to the hotel for two nights just before four in the morning, although most of the first night had already gone. We left the Austin 7 in the underground car park of the hotel, hoping, when it was reported stolen, it would remain safely hidden until we had moved on.

The hotel bedroom was a welcome and warm sight after a long and difficult night.

'Max, we are running out of time, I don't think we're going to make it. It's already five on Friday morning and we haven't been to bed yet. We have to be in Cliff in a little over three days. Oh, and we have lost another car, unless you intend taking the Austin 7 all of the way to Scotland?'

'I'm glad you haven't lost your sense of humour,' I responded. 'Anyway, you think the M20 will be waiting for us in Scotland? I'm really sorry Olivia, but I need to tell you something. I'm struggling and feeling very unwell and quite heady, which is upsetting my balance. I am afraid tonight has taken too much out of me; it might have been the cold on the drive. I think I am done for on this adventure and you may have to go on without me.'

In her warm and caring way, the woman I have loved most of my life said, 'It will be okay Max; tonight would have defeated people half our age but, here we are, you and me. Partners. Let's get some rest and clear our minds. I'll set the alarm for midday and we'll see how you're feeling then. If we need to stay here an extra few days, then so be it.'

Olivia helped me to undress and guided me gently to the bed. For the last couple of weeks the memories and insecurities of my age had been forgotten. This was the first time I had felt unwell since leaving the nursing home but, now, feeling dizzy and nauseous, and being helped to lie down, the truth was difficult to ignore. What had possessed me to ever believe we could do this? A dull pain twinged in my chest and with it arrhythmia. I felt my heart as it raced and missed beats. *Should I tell Olivia? Should I ask her to call an ambulance? I'm going to die,* I thought. I said nothing and decided; *what will be will be.*

Olivia, despite her own ordeal and fatigue, lovingly sat beside me and stroked my head. A tear formed and trickled from my eye and I felt its path as it slowly journeyed down my cheek, falling away before I could taste it upon my lips. To the rhythm of Olivia's hands I slowly drifting off, content with the life I had lived.

***

Inspector Axel

'Inspector Axel, are you still there?' said the voice on the other end of the phone.

Heavy with slumber I replied, 'Yes, I'm listening, it's 1.30 in the morning and I was asleep. What do you want?'

'Yes, sorry for ringing so early, but we thought you would want to know. Olivia, one of the people you are looking for, has just called *999.*'

The name *Olivia* removed any semblance of sleep from my brain. I sat straighter in bed with my full attention now focused on the phone call.

'She told the emergency services operator that the people in the place where they are staying are in imminent grave danger.' The voice on the other end of the phone described what had transpired between the operator and Olivia.

'How long ago was the phone call?'

'A matter of minutes, sir.'

'How long until we can get someone there?'

'An armed response unit will be at least 35-40 minutes.'

'We don't have five minutes.' I growled down the phone. 'What about your normal nightshift patrols?'

'About ten minutes,' came the reply, followed by, 'you do understand in Britain they are not armed!'

'Okay,' I said, 'let's do what Olivia wants and try and scare them off. Light and sirens all the way; perhaps the noise will carry and buy us a little extra time. If you have a staffed fire station in the town, turn them out as well, lights, sirens and bells. Oh, one further thing, it's a long shot, but ring RAF command, authorisation code—Charlie Delta 1723. I understand they use the Lake District for low flying exercises, so see if they have anything up in the air on night exercises near Windermere. If they do, tell them low and loud. I want you to wake the town, ring the neighbours if you have to—it's the only solution I can think of. Max and Olivia must be protected at all costs. Remember, don't intercept them but, if by chance you can follow them, without their knowledge, that would be sensational. If at all possible, do not detain them.'

'I'm relaying your instructions as we speak,' came the reply. 'And sir, there is a plane waiting to take you to Edinburgh—you're not to return to London. Exeter is to remain the command post.'

'I understand,' I said and hung up the phone.

Chapter 12
The Extortion

This is the BBC's midday news. We are still standing by to take you to a live news conference called by the Chief Medical Officer and the Secretary of State for Health.

In other news today. A mother, charged with the attempted murder of her autistic son told a court she had not given him at least five months of chemotherapy medicine because she was afraid it would kill him.

Kristen LaBrie, 38, of Salem, Massachusetts, said she mostly followed doctor's orders during the first four phases of treatment for her son, Jeremy Fraser. She stopped giving him his cancer medications during the final phase of his treatment because she 'didn't want to make him any sicker' she said at the second day of her trial.

Good news for those of you following the adventures of Max and Olivia, our nursing home escapees from Australia. In a statement today Inspector Axel of Interpol, who has been assisting our local police in their search, said Max and Olivia were found yesterday at 4.10 in the small village of St John's Well, Police are still trying to piece together their movements. Anyone with any information should contact crime stoppers on 0800 555 111.

'Did you hear that Max? On the TV—the News. They are saying we've been found. Do you think it possible they have the wrong people?'

'I heard it,' I said, feeling much better than when I had gone to bed. 'I'm guessing that was no mistake and they are trying to send us a message. Did you hear; St John, 4:10 and "Well", as in drinking well, from the scriptures?'

'Do you think it's a trap, or at least a strategy designed to get us to drop our guard? Or do you really think this Inspector Axel wants to help us?'

'Your guess is as good as mine,' I began, but before I could continue, our attention was drawn back to the TV.

We now take you live to a statement being made by Andrew Lansley, Secretary of State for Health.

'Good afternoon. Thank you all for attending at such short notice. I am here with the Chief Medical Officer.

Earlier today I was advised that a bacterium, a penicillin-resistant superbug has escaped from the hospital environment and is at risk of spreading within the broader community of

London. There have been no confirmed fatalities. I repeat; no confirmed fatalities but, as a precaution, we are declaring a health emergency.

We will take questions at the end of the conference, so please wait until then. Can I now hand you over to our Chief Medical Officer? Professor...'

I looked to Olivia. 'Do you think it's possible?'

'I don't know,' she replied.

I picked up the TV remote control, turned up the sound and listened.

'Thank you Andrew. As most of you will understand, we have known about antibiotic-resistant bacteria or superbugs, as we commonly call them, in hospitals for a long time. Over time, some have mutated to be resistant to all known antibiotics.

'A number of days ago, a new mutation of a known bacteria, Methicillin-Resistant Staphylococcus aureus, or MRSA, was detected in three of our major hospitals. Generally, we believed these bugs spread through person to person contact. So you get the contagion by touching another person who has it on the skin. In this case, however, we believe this contagion is being spread like the flu virus, by droplets made when people cough, sneeze or talk. As a consequence it has spread outside of the hospital environment.

The initial presentation of the infection is small bumps resembling sores or boils, accompanied by fever and rashes. What is both unusual and alarming about this mutation is its virulence. Following the initial symptoms the patient will experience necrotizing pneumonia and infective endocarditis; pneumonia affecting the respiratory system and endocarditis affecting the valves of the heart. Finally the other vital organs will be affected. As you would all be aware, particular mutations seem more attracted to certain people; that is, antimicrobial resistance is genetically based.

We believe people 65 years and older will not be affected by this outbreak and, just as importantly, we understand this bacterium can live for only seven days from its original mutation. A total of seven days means that, in five days' time, it will no longer be infectious and it's spread will cease. If we can contain it now, the number of people exposed will be significantly reduced. We are therefore imposing what some may see as extreme containment measures. As of midnight, for the Greater City of London, with the exception of emergency service works and people over 65, all citizens are advised to stay at home and in doors. No public transport will operate and all airports will be closed.

Stay indoors and you will be safe; this will all be over in five days' time. We will have further announcements to make later today.

We are also requesting that no one leaves London or travels to the Capital. This will ensure the safety of people both within and outside of London. The Prime Minster will be remaining at Number 10 and the Queen will be in residence at Buckingham Palace.

The incubation period for this particular strain of MRSA is approximately 36 hours. This means we won't understand the magnitude of the contagion until sometime tomorrow. Anybody experiencing symptoms is to remain at home. Ring 999 and we will come to you. You are not to go to your local doctor! You are not to present at the Emergency Department of a hospital! I make this point absolutely clear—call 999 and we will come to you.

'Are there any questions?'

On the TV screen, we watched as a flurry of hands went up and people called out over the top of one another. Finally, the Secretary of State for Health pointed to someone and said, 'Yes, Stephen from the *Daily Telegraph*.'

'Thank you. What is the mortality rate for this superbug?'

The Chief Medical Officer replied, 'We don't know!'

Stephen from the *Daily Telegraph* continued, 'You must have some idea of the number of fatalities you are expecting. Twenty, fifty, hundreds, thousands?'

The professor looked to the Secretary. The room fell silent. The Secretary nodded.

'It will be in the hundreds—possibly more,' said the Professor.

With that answer, the room was again a flurry of noise, with people calling out questions and hands raised.

Again, we watched as the Secretary of State for Health scanned the room before pointing to another journalist.

'Jenny Holt, ABC Australia,' said the questioner. 'Is it true that this was a terrorist extortion threat and you were given the opportunity to pay a ransom for the superbug not to be released?'

'That is not the case.'

Last question,' said the Secretary pointing to a journalist at the back of the room.

'Petra Harrison, from the *Independent*,' she introduced herself. 'If, as you say Secretary—no one has yet died, how do you know that this bacterium can be fatal? And, the obvious follow up questions—if I may. How do you know it is only virulent for seven days, that it has spread outside the hospitals and finally won't affect people over 65 years?'

The professor looked to the Secretary, who accepted the cue and said, 'We have our very best scientist working around the clock on this and that is the advice we have received. It is also our scientist who has recommended the containment measures that we are announcing today.'

'I'm afraid we can't take any more of your questions now. Can I thank you all again for attending. As I have said, we will be making continuing announcements during the day and over the coming days.'

Switching off the TV, I looked to Olivia and said, 'There, I think, is the answer to your question about Inspector Axel. It would be my guess that the news story about us was really a message and they want us to make contact. Perhaps the Government knows we may be able help them— whether they know about Janus or not, we can only speculate.'

'His name sounds very familiar. Isn't he the person "Cliff" told us about, the man who investigated us after the accident in Europe?'

'Olivia, you're absolutely right but, if you also remember, he's Kate's father and that's my problem. It's a real possibility he is the one chasing us and not as a police officer. Don't you think it's an unlikely coincidence? He investigated us in Europe, is Kate's father and is now leading the search for us in the UK? I don't believe in coincidences.'

'That's all true Max, but it could just as easily be explained by his father—Jean Axel. And anyway he's not going to harm his own children, is he?'

'I know, I know, but until we understand more, I don't think we can afford to trust him and, who's to say, Kate and Edward were actually harmed. That could have been a trick. What's really worrying me is this so-called superbug. Is it an accident, or was it caused by people chasing us? Have they unleashed some kind of biological weapon on London? If it is them, there's one thing for sure. They will redouble their efforts either to stop us or to get Janus for themselves.'

'Max, do you think it's possible that there is another Janus machine, with a key?'

'I was thinking the same thing myself; how else do you get a bug to leave people over 65 years alone or to lose its virulence after seven days? It's the perfect extortion tool. I suppose, in the end, it's irrelevant; they will want to stop us or get our machine regardless.' With that said, I slowly rose from bed and found that I was still a little unsteady on my feet but determined to go on with the mission.

With Olivia's help I dressed and, together, we went downstairs for lunch. Our minds were preoccupied with the best way to travel undetected to Scotland. I could manage only a light lunch but felt better for having eaten. I was improving with every passing minute.

'Max, we are running out of time. I suggest we simply order a taxi and have it drive us to Edinburgh. Once we arrive, we can go to the railway station and see if the M20 is parked there. If not, we have to risk hiring a car. I don't think it would be a good idea for you to go stealing one this time, not unless we absolutely have to. From Edinburgh we drive up to Anstruther and find somewhere to stay the night. First thing Saturday morning, we go to the bunker and find the Janus Machine. If it's hidden anywhere nearly as well as the key was, even with the clues, it could take us a couple of days. That will leave us all day Monday to get back to Cliff.'

'You make it all sound so simple and I hope you're right. Listening to you, I can agree with everything except for the taxi. Ringing a taxi may be too risky, particularly if we are asking to be driven all the way to Edinburgh. If I remember correctly, there's a business and corporate executive chauffeur service in town, so let's see if we can hire one of their cars to take us. I'm sure, if I offer them cash, they will be most obliging. If we can't get them, then it will have to be a taxi.' I waited for Olivia to consider my suggestion.

'Okay, I agree, a chauffeur service would be more discreet and much more to your taste,' she said with grin. 'Are you thinking of using them to take us all the way to Anstruther?'

'No, I agree with you on that; to the railway station only. We need to make our own way to Anstruther.' I looked at Olivia, took a deep breath and then said, 'I'll go and settle our account and ask reception to call the chauffeur service. One way or the other, by the time I come back, we will be leaving.'

'Max, I'm a little scared!'

Taking Olivia's hand and looking deep into her eyes, I said, 'I know, so am I.' Letting go of her hand slowly, I stood and walked toward reception. By the time I returned, not fifteen minutes later, our travel plans were organised. A chauffeured car would pick us up in thirty minutes.

The trip to Edinburgh, once negotiating the traffic had been factored in, took a little over two hours. We asked to be taken to the Balmoral, a beautiful Victorian hotel, only a short walk from the station. In keeping with our deception we went inside for a glass of wine and waited a good half an hour before leaving and making our way towards the car park. 'You do know the car won't be there?' I said.

'As you have said before… but you know what I think.'

'Yes, I know. I'm not very trusting.'

'I tell you what Max! If the M20 is there, I get to drive.'

'I suppose it's too late to change my mind. You know you haven't driven in quite a few years.'

'Don't be silly, Max. If you can do it so can I and, besides, it's an automatic, so how difficult can that be?'

How difficult indeed… I mumbled to myself.

Looking for the car proved more like searching for a needle in a haystack. We had to walk each lane methodically one at a time. Just when I was about to call it quits, there she was, as Olivia had said.

'I'll have the spare keys please, Max.'

Inside was a note from Jess and David which read;

Sorry about yesterday. Car broke down and had to be fixed overnight. Hope you managed to find you way here.
Good luck with your book.
Love Jess and David

'What did I tell you Max?'

'I know. You win—as always. Let's see how well you can drive.'

Unlike me, on my first drive after the accident in Europe, Olivia showed no hesitation. The only thing that delayed our progress was my navigation skills. The car ran faultlessly along with Olivia's driving. Along the way, to be sure we were not being followed, she turned on and off all manner of minor roads. Nothing filled the rear vision mirrors and it was just on dinner time when we finally arrived in Anstruther.

Anstruther had been one of the sea ports from which we conducted our clandestine missions during the war. Coming back always brought mixed emotions, some not so pleasant. It was here, towards the end of the war, I withdrew from a mission because of illness. Of the crew that left on that trip, none returned. Every man perished and, but for fate, so should have I.

Olivia brought the M20 to rest near the harbour. I bowed my head and, in silent prayer, remembered the friends I lost that night. I gave thanks for my life and the extra time I had been given.

'Where do you want to stay?' asked Olivia.

'I haven't seen that place before,' I said, pointing to a nearby building. 'Not as a hotel, anyway.'

'Okay,' said Olivia. 'The Waterfront looks perfect.'

Unlike in Windermere, our surveillance entering the Waterfront and then, later on that evening, revealed nothing of suspicion. Everything of that night was unremarkable, which was mildly unsettling in itself. Even the reports coming out of London were, considering the circumstances, benign. There were no reports of mass panic or hysteria and no rush to leave the city before the curfew came into effect. It seemed that everywhere was waiting in expectant foreboding and we, like London, were on edge.

Considering the day ahead, Olivia and I slept well. The previous night, over dinner and before going to bed, we talked very little. Other than driving to the bunker we had made no plans or contingencies for what lay ahead. Having woken at seven, I looked out over the water, and saw it was going to be a fresh but magnificent day. The sea was at peace, in a tranquil state of calm, beguiling the day ahead. Unusually for Scotland it was a bright and cloudless day.

My health had now fully recovered and, after washing and dressing, we went downstairs for breakfast just on eight. Entering the dining room, with the exception of the TV, on which the BBC was running continuous news coverage of the events as they unfolded in London, we found the room eerily silent. The first reports of people known to be infected with the superbug came in as we sat down. The other guests, along with the hotel staff, were glued to the TV screen—totally absorbed.

Good morning to those of you who have just joined us on this most difficult and distressing of days here in London. Repeating the news from earlier; we can confirm that the Department of Health is reporting that they have received over 1500 calls for assistance in the last hour. They have not confirmed how many of those calls are actually MRSA related. Nevertheless, on a BBC Facebook page specifically set up for people wishing to discuss the superbug epidemic, we have unconfirmed reports of 350 fatalities.

Speculation, after the extraordinary allegations made by an Australian news reporter during yesterday's press conference, that this superbug is actually a terrorist attack, will not go away. In what's seen as a highly significant move, Number 10 has softened its wording when responding to the claim. They are no longer categorically denying the possibility of a terrorist attack. Rather—they are now considering all possibilities. We will be joined a little later in this live coverage by Dr Williams from the Centre for Conflict, Security and Terrorism to discuss the ramifications of a biological terrorist attack.

With the incubation phase for those first infected only recently reached—that is—a matter of hours ago, we are expecting, based on current unconfirmed reports, the number of people who become critically ill to be very high. We are now joined by epidemiologist Professor Vasanthi Roye from the University of—sorry, we will return you to that story shortly. In breaking news, the Prime Minister will address the nation at ten o'clock this morning. It is expected that he will confirm that the United Kingdom is under attack.

Drawing my attention away for the TV screen, I looked to Olivia who, like me, was dumbfounded. 'It's 350 deaths and this is just the start. By the time this is all over, it could be in the thousands.'

'If it's a terrorist attack, when will it be over?'

'Three days' time so they say.' Changing the subject, I asked, 'Do you think we can ask for some breakfast or should we leave and allow them to keep watching the TV?'

Ordering something to eat proved a welcome relief for all of those in the dining room. People turned their attention away from the constant news and the room began to fill with the sounds of conversation. Strangers and friends alike began discussing and then speculating on the unfolding events. I heard an older man, over 65 years and a retired nurse, contemplating driving to London to offer assistance. 'The bug won't affect me and I think the hospitals are going to need all the help they can get. I'm surprised a call hasn't gone out for us retirees.'

'It will,' responded the person to whom he was talking.

Next to us, two forty-something ladies were having a different conversation.

'You can't ask that,' one of them said.

'I can and I will,' came the reply. 'We have a right to know if anyone here has been in London during the last three days. They need to be locked up, before they can infect us!'

Shaking my head slightly, I said to Olivia, 'It's time for us to leave.'

With a heavy sense of trepidation, we rose and walked towards the door.

'Not staying to watch the news?' called the manager, a handsome man somewhere in his early twenties.

'No, I'm afraid we have some other commitments,' I called back.

'Ah well, I suppose it doesn't affect you old people. We will definitely see you tonight then.' With that said, he went back to watching the TV and conversing with those around.

Outside of the hotel, the street was deserted; not a person or vehicle stirred. Before making our way to the car, we studied our surroundings in case we were under surveillance, but everything was extraordinarily still.

'Do you want to drive? I said. To which Olivia replied, 'With your navigation proficiencies, which proved worse than mine, we may well end up back in London. Perhaps it's best- no. Perhaps it's a necessity - that you take the wheel.' She gave me a cheeky grin before saying, 'This time we need to be extra cautious - if we think we are being followed, we don't attempt the retrieval. It's best it stays hidden and, if something were to happen to us, perhaps Cliff has some other operative who can complete the mission. No matter what, Janus must not be compromised. Do you agree, Max?'

For the first time on this trip, seated in the front of the M20, waiting to go, felt like something from my old rally driving days. The adrenalin is pumping, butterflies are in your stomach and you wonder—*what the hell am I doing*! But the countdown continues, 5...4, you pull your racing harnesses even tighter, 3....2....1, and then, despite the fears, you go. At that moment...the second you leave the start line, all thoughts of apprehensions are left behind and you become totally focused on the job at hand.

This is how it was now.

'I agree,' I replied to Olivia. 'What's your plan?

'Okay, my idea is that we take the long way to the bunker; this will give us ample time to see if we are being followed. You drive via Crail and then double back using the B940 before we go up onto the B9131. If it's still all clear—then we go in.'

'You know I can't outrun anyone in this thing?' I said, starting the car.

Olivia did not answer but stared into the distance, looking out through the windscreen.

The drive to the bunker was as disconcerting as stepping outside the hotel. The roads were empty, so it was easy to surmise that, as in the hotel, everyone was watching the events unfold in London. We were headed to what is now a tourist attraction, a secret bunker built under a farmhouse and used during the cold war. What was not commonly known, however, was that the bunker existed long before the cold war—a place we frequented on many occasions as part of our covert work.

Like the road, the tourist attraction was deserted, although the sign said it was open for business. Stopping in the car park and looking out the window, we saw nothing that looked familiar. It had been so many years since either of us had been here that we had virtually no memory of the place at all. A few old derelict military vehicles were scattered about the fields next to the old farmhouse. The whole place looked like a left over movie set from a 1960s nuclear disaster film.

We looked at each other and took a deep breath as we readied ourselves to leave the car. I was about to open the door when Olivia asked. 'The clue; what do you think we're looking for?'

'I've gone over and over it in my mind. *"If you knew the gift of God and who it is that asks you for a drink, you would have asked him and he would have given you living water."* It's a passage from *John 4:10*—my best guess is that we are looking for something to symbolise John; perhaps an eagle? Could be something to do with water, as the passage—on the surface at least—relates to water from a *Well*. Perhaps the Janus Machine is hidden in an old well. It's difficult to tell until we get inside and start looking around.

'Oh, Olivia, can you grab the torch we took from the old Austin before you get out? We might just need it.'

When we opened the door and stepped outside on to the asphalt, the place felt even more deserted. The security system was child's play as nobody expected anyone to break in.

Switching on the lights and passing through the heavy metal doors which separated the farmhouse from the bunker, we found that it was much bigger than either of us expected. The bunker was spread over two levels. 'You were right Olivia; this could take a couple of days. I suggest we split up. You take the first floor and I will take the second. We should make a note of anything, absolutely anything, that could be part of the clue. We meet back here and then together, we go back and check them out methodically.

'I suggest we take one of those maps, the ones kindly marked, "How to find your way around Scotland's Secret Bunkers".' Pointing to a pile of maps made handy for any tourist about to embark on their discovery tour, I continued, 'Let's meet back here in, say, two hours, unless one of us discovers anything really promising.'

'Good idea,' she said.

I picked up one of the maps. 'Oh Olivia, would you believe it? Look in the index, number 34 on the lower floor. Secret Passage!'

'Go on, get on with you. I'll see you in a couple of hours,' came the reply.

Although the lights were on, the moment I was on the lower floor, by myself, the place became surprisingly spooky.

More than once I thought I saw someone in a doorway but, when I reached the room, it was empty. Alone on the floor, I heard the sound of whispering voices, or did I imagine them… When I entered the old radio room, the hairs on the back of my neck stood on end and I shivered as if there was a presence. Forcing myself to cross the threshold, I continued the search and, finding nothing, I left.

Room by room, my examination revealed nothing. Checking my watch I saw that it was time to meet Olivia. Perhaps she had been more successful. Secretly, I would be pleased to no longer be on my own. *I'm a brave man*, I said to myself, *but I couldn't stay here overnight*. I don't believe in ghosts but this place was definitely haunted.

'Any luck?' I asked Olivia, having made my way safely back to the entrance.

'Nothing, although there is a chapel and it may be worth another look. Otherwise, nothing caught my attention. Oh, there were some sinks with taps—that's water I suppose.'

'All right, let's check the chapel; it seems the most obvious place to start. If that doesn't throw up any surprises, I think we should go to the very bottom and work our way back, one room at a time. By the way, you didn't happen to see any ghosts on your travels?'

Olivia looked at me dismissively before replying, 'Now then Max—you're not going senile on me. Are you?'

'No, no. Just asking.'

The chapel was a long, narrow room and we concentrated our search on the exterior walls but everything appeared solid. The lectern, being an eagle, was a prime suspect. We checked on it, in it and under it, but came up with nothing. Having ruled the chapel off our list, we went downstairs and to the very back of the bunker. Starting our search afresh and, in keeping with Olivia's observation, we gave special attention to anything with water.

In the plant room, tucked away in the corner, were some exposed water pipes leading to a wash basin complete with a couple of taps. Directly behind the sink and, on the wall, were some old discoloured tiles. A couple of times I turned away from the wash basin only to find myself drawn back to it.

'What is it?' asked Olivia.

'I'm not sure. There's something about the tiles. They have birds on them. Do you think, rather than an eagle, we are looking for birds?

'Okay, let's assume for argument's sake, that you are correct—what do we do?'

'There's something else about them, look; three tiles across and four down, it might be some kind of key pad? Maybe it's the verse 4-1-0.' I reached across to the tiles and applied pressure in that combination. They certainly didn't move in and out like phone buttons, but there was some give there nevertheless.

'They moved, Olivia, though that combination didn't work but they definitely moved.'

'Try 1-7-2-3, the date from the gravestone.'

After I pushed firmly on the tiles with the new combination, as if they were a key pad, the room was filled by the sound of moving masonry. A rush of musty air came from a door, as the area behind the wash basin swung inwards to reveal a stone staircase spiralling downwards.

Taking the Austin's torch from Olivia's hand, we crossed the divide and headed into the unknown. Shining the light down the stairs, we could see what looked like a cave entrance below. The stairs were carved into the rock, possibly centuries old. Ever wary of slipping and, having to occasionally hold onto one another for balance, one slow step after the other, we descended.

What, from above, looked like a cave entrance was a short tunnel, at the other end of which stood a wooden door. Despite a key being in its lock, the door pushed open easily to reveal a rocky chamber. Crossing inside, we stopped to scan the space below. The cavity walls appeared to be natural rock and vanished into the distance. On its floor and within our vision with the torch, there was the remnants of an ancient civilisation, perhaps early *Picts*. Piles of old stones made the outline of what could have been past dwellings and, from our vantage point slightly above, the structures were built round a circle of rock which surrounded a hole.

'That could be our well,' I said before cautiously entering our forgotten world.

The short path down was rocky and uneven and our knees and lower backs felt the strain as we battled slipping. 'Where's your walking stick when you need one?' I jested, trying to lighten the enormity of the moment.

The hole was larger than it appeared from the doorway. Running around its edge and cut into its wall were more stairs, spiralling downwards for about twenty feet before finishing on a small and narrow landing. It was difficult to make out by shining the torch down from above, but there appeared to be a small sized gap carved into the rock face on the ledge. The hole around which the stairs were carved seemed to go down forever and the torchlight just disappeared into the abyss. When Olivia dropped a stone into it, we never heard it hit the bottom. Falling here would be a long and frightening death.

Standing at the side of the hole and having given up on listening for Olivia's falling stone, I said, 'Only one of us can go down; it's too narrow for both of us. You will have to stay behind, in the dark.'

'That's a joke; with your balance you won't even make it halfway down. Anyway you know I'm frightened of the dark.'

'Who's holding the torch?

'Who forgot to get new batteries? It's almost dead.'

'Good point, but I still have the torch.'

'Don't you fall you stubborn old bugger. I'll be really pissed off if you leave me here all alone in the dark. Stop! Wait! Max, you won't be able to carry the torch and the Janus Machine if you find it. The steps are too narrow. Give me the torch and I'll shine the light down for you.'

Olivia helped me over the edge, holding my hand and then my shoulder until I could lean against the inside wall of what was really a deep pit rather than a well. I inched my way down the stairs. The light from Olivia was marginal and it was more a case of feeling my way than seeing.

A light breeze circulated up from deep within the hole, not enough to make you fall but sufficient to make the descent a little more challenging. Reaching the platform, the light from Olivia's torch focused on the small wall cavity which was pitch black inside. I slid my left arm up the wall and reached in. I felt about but found nothing. 'It's empty,' I called up.

'Try looking for a trigger. Maybe there's something to open another passage?'

Reaching back inside, it took a bit of scratching about until, finally, I felt something. Getting a purchase, I pulled what may have been a lever and almost instantaneously lost my balance. The narrow hole, in which I had my arm extended, moved downwards. Fortunately it stopped after a matter of feet, revealing a much larger cavity. Taking a second or two to regain my composure, again I searched the space. This time I felt something and, using my fingers to walk around it, gradually pulled a box into view. Although the light was poor, I could see that it was the box that held the Janus Machine.

'It's here,' I cried. 'I'm coming back up.

Then, it went pitch black and I froze,

'Olivia,' I called out. 'Are you all right?'

The scrap of light came back.

'Sorry, I slipped.'

Carefully, having removed the box, and keeping my back against the wall, I turned round on the narrow ledge for the ascent.

I had no choice but to put the box in my left hand and, holding onto its handle, hang it out over the edge of the well. As with the descent, I leaned in against the wall for balance. The weight of the box made the climb difficult and, on a few occasions, I had to swing the box in front of me, putting it on the narrow step so that I could rest. I was relieved when I felt Olivia's hand take my shoulder, steadying me, and helping me out of the well.

'Hello sweetie, you have led us on a merry chase.' With these words three flashlights switched on.

Looking about, I saw Olivia was standing in between two armed men who were on the other side of the well. The woman who'd spoken and the person who must have helped me out of the hole stood a few feet away from me.

'Oh sweetie, the cat got your tongue?'

'Who are you?'

'Now, that's better. Manners; I do so often forget them in these times of excitement. I'm Claudia. Over there are my associates Semyon and Vladimir and you are Max and Olivia. Sweetie, you have something that I want.'

As she spoke I extended my hand over the well, dangling the box above the abyss.

'You British are so melodramatic. Sweetie, you misunderstand me. I need to make myself clear. We don't want you or anybody else to have it. You can drop it if you like but then, I'm afraid, I will have to kill you. If you give it to me, sweetie, I think we can let you live. This is just business after all.'

My mind was buzzing. If what she was saying was true, I was in a no- win situation. *Stall;* I said to myself; *give yourself time to think.* The weight of the box was getting heavy for my arm and I brought it back to rest beside me.

'How do I know I can trust you—after what you did to Kate and Edward?'

'That was your fault, sweetie. You were about to tell them about Janus and we couldn't have that. I know, sweetie, because we were listening. All we ever wanted was to follow you to the hiding place and then wait until you recovered Janus for us but, no, you had to go gallivanting around the countryside causing absolute chaos. If you two could have kept your silence, no one would have died.'

'And Windermere? We didn't tell them anything.'

'That was a silly mistake; my masters were becoming impatient so I thought we could do a good old fashioned snatch-and-grab and extract the information from you. However, you proved far more resourceful that I had expected and we even lost you for a while. Predictably, you eventually turned up at that old Russian car onto which we had put a GPS tracking device, and here we are. A happy little family.

'What about Elinor?' Olivia asked from across the well.

'I'm sorry, sweetie.'

With the news of Elinor, the conversation began to stall before I said, 'I thought you already had one of these?' I held up the box. 'I mean it was you that created the so-called superbug spreading in London wasn't it?'

'Sweetie, you do want to ask a lot of questions. I suppose at your time of life there's not much else to do. Okay sweetie, yes we made the superbug and no, we don't have another Janus Machine. You're so naïve, Max; this is what modern crime looks like. We have our own biological weapons team just as we have our own cyber extortion experts. We make billions hijacking people's computers or infecting them with ransomware. Typically we ask for hundreds or sometimes thousands of pounds to unlock their encrypted data. With superbugs, if you want to call them that, we can hold entire countries to ransom, for billions. We don't want anyone to die; to the contrary! The better economically a country is doing, the more money we can extort. You British are so arrogant and stubborn; a stiff upper lip and all that crap. The Yanks paid up but not the Brits. We had already demonstrated our capabilities. Britain knew what we were capable of and we warned them that, next time, the consequences would be severe. Ten billion is all we asked but the price has now gone to thirty billion.

'Your scientists will combat our attack and, while they do that, we are working on new variants, which takes us time and money. We don't want to cause mass casualties. A country must believe there is some hope and, in the end, we want them to pay… let's call it an annual insurance policy. With Janus, the work is already done and, no matter how smart your scientists are, we can always come up with something different. We will have a guaranteed income for life, from all the major economies. On the other hand, if you have Janus, it will be like having a virus protection system, a firewall on your computer. Every now and then we will still get through but it will be more difficult. So you see, if we have no choice, the only real thing we want is for you not to have Janus. If we have it, it's worth hundreds of billions of pounds.'

'You need a key and without the key the Janus Machine is useless.'

'Sweetie, we've had a key for a very long time, well before even my era. The second key, so I have been told, was never destroyed but that's enough talking; it's time for our exchange. Janus for Olivia.' With that Claudia signalled to the men standing next to Olivia. I watched as one of them levelled a gun to her head.

'This won't work you know; the governments of the world will get together. You can't hide those sums of money and that will be the end of you. Let her go; there's no point!'

'Max, we *are* the government, you stupid senile old-has-been,' she snapped. 'This is far bigger than just money. Now I will give you to the count of three. Three—two.'

A red dot from a laser sight flashed momentarily into Claudia's eyes before vanishing back into the darkness. She stopped counting. A voice I vaguely recognised called out from the shadows, somewhere near the door above. 'I think it's time to leave, Max and Olivia.'

'Sweetie,' replied Claudia. 'This is what they call a Mexican standoff. You may be able to shoot me but my men will have time to kill Olivia. I don't think you are in a position to negotiate.'

'Max,' came the voice. 'You come with me.'

'Go on,' said Olivia, 'you have to leave me.'

'Sweetie, listen to me very carefully now. I will let you go so you have time to think this over. I want you to bring me the Janus Machine at...' She stopped talking to look down at her watch, and continued in a calm and unflustered voice. 'At four o'clock this afternoon. It's now one-thirty. By the time you get back to the Waterfront Hotel, there will be a message waiting for you with the location of our exchange. The machine for Olivia;

if you don't bring the machine, Olivia will suffer a long and painful end. We will starve her to slow death but keep her fluids up so that the agony is prolonged. When she finally slips into unconsciousness, there will be no morphine to ease her suffering. As she gasps in those dying breaths, intravenously we will give her more fluid so her lungs begin to drown. It will be your worst nightmare, a long undignified and unbearable end. If, on the other hand, you get the silly notion of attempting a rescue, perhaps with the assistance of the British Government, we will inject her with one of our old viruses. Again it will be a slow and excruciating passing. Don't forget, we have access to satellites, so we will see if you try anything stupid. You can bring your friend, but no one else. Do we understand each other?'

'Max...' said the voice from above.

With no alternatives, I turned to walk into the darkness.

Three green tubes of fluorescent light tumbled through the air, landing on the ground in front of me. They lit the way ahead for a careful climb. Reaching the door and tunnel I could just make out the silhouette of a man.

'Close and lock the door; it may slow them for a minute or so if they try and chase us.'

I did as directed and, when the door was closed, the bright beam of a torch came to life, lighting the way in front. Still the man's back was to me but I felt sure I knew him. It was not until we entered the bunker and its rooms filled with light that I could see his face.

'Jana, is that you?' Without giving him a chance to reply, I added, 'It can't be; where's the beard? You look fifteen years younger.'

'Hello old boy; no time for questions. I'm afraid we need to get out of here. If they can pop us off to get Janus—I'm sure they will.'

Jana moved quickly but had to stop and wait for me to catch up. Reaching the heavy steel door he pushed it shut but did not lock it. Looking about and seeing the master switchboard, he pulled all the fuses. The building and the bunker descended into darkness. Once outside he beckoned me to his vehicle.

'I want to take the M20,' I said.

'It's got a GPS tracking device on it,' he responded.

'I know.'

His face betrayed confusion, but quickly changed to acceptance. 'Okay, I'll meet you at the hotel.'

I followed Jana back to the hotel and, while I parked at the front, he hid his car from view. Three minutes later and almost right on two o'clock we were seated in the lounge. My mind was full of questions for Jana but they were outweighed by Olivia's predicament and the events unfolding in London, a constant reminder of which played on the TV in the background.

'What are you doing here—no, don't answer. Sorry Jana, but I'm not as good at this kind of stuff as I used to be. Give me a couple of minutes to gather my thoughts. I need to take a short walk to clear my mind; then I'll be back.' But rather than leaving

I continued speaking. We have to save Olivia; that's my first priority.'

As I began to stand, Jana replied, 'I understand Max. Will you let me call someone who may be able to help us—Inspector Axel?'

'Inspector Axel?' I said with some alarm. 'Olivia and I are worried he's working for the organised crime gangs.'

'I can assure you that's not the case. Let's just say, I've had some first-hand experience with Mr Axel. If you can just wait two minutes, I'll give him a call. You can listen to the conversation; it might help to set your mind at ease.'

Hesitating, I put my hand on the table and gently lowered myself back into the chair.

Jana took out his mobile phone into which he dialled some numbers before lifting it to his ear.

'Pierre Gicquel,' began Jana. 'Good afternoon Inspector, now that I have your attention. We had the pleasure of meeting in Clyst Hydon and then again under more difficult circumstances in Mawnan. I'm here with Max.' Jana stopped speaking briefly and I assumed Axel was asking a question. 'No, no Inspector, nothing like that. Max and I need your help. Where are you?' After waiting for the reply, he said, 'Excellent, St Andrews,' repeating the location for my benefit. Jana then proceeded to briefly describe what had occurred in the bunker but left out the part where I had found the Janus Machine. He added instead, 'Olivia has the final piece of the puzzle; we need

Max and Olivia together to find the Janus Machine. As you can appreciate—you must come alone and unfortunately we have very little time. Can you be here by, um, two-thirty? Thank you, Inspector. Oh Inspector, we think they are working with a foreign government, so be extremely careful.'

'That was very clever,' I said to Jana, who smiled.

Standing once more and rubbing my forehead with one hand and carrying the box in the other, I said, 'I'll be back before two-thirty. I need some time to think.' As I made my way to the door the voice in my head kept saying over and over again, *there must be some way of getting her out alive* before being interrupted by the hotel manager.

'Excuse me; a phone message came in while you were out.' In his outstretched hand he held a piece of paper.

Feeling the weight of my age and unable to think clearly I turned to the manager and said, 'Thank you, would you mind giving it to my friend over there?' pointing to Jana and continuing on my way out of the hotel and onto the street.

Chapter 13

Showdown

'Here he is,' I heard Jana say as I walked back into the hotel lounge. Jana was still seated at the same table at which I left him. He had been joined by another man, to whom he introduced me. 'Max this is Inspector Axel, Inspector Axel, this is Max.'

Ignoring the formalities and without bothering to sit down, I pointed to the stairs and said, 'Gentlemen, would you like to come up to my room? Perhaps the environment may prove a little more conducive to our conversation.'

Once in the room, we made ourselves as comfortable as the surroundings would permit. I sat on a chair, Jana on the only other chair and Inspector Axel on the bed.

'How are we going to get Olivia out?' I asked.

Inspector Axel pointed toward the box which I had placed near my feet and said, 'Is the Janus Machine inside?'

'It is,' I said, but, not wanting to focus the discussion on the box, I continued, 'Somehow we need to keep the Janus Machine and rescue Olivia. I assume the note, the one I asked the manager to give you,' I added, looking to Jana 'was the location of where the exchange is to take place?'

With an air of frustration showing in his voice, Inspector Axel said, 'You said on the phone that you didn't have the Janus Machine.'

'I didn't say a thing, it was Jana who lied. But, now you're here.' Again refusing to be drawn into a debate, I said, 'Do you know where the exchange is to take place?

Inspector Axel waited before answering, probably considering the predicament and weighing his options after being lied to. Finally he sighed before saying, 'Yes. Jana and I have already looked at it on Google Earth.'

'It won't be easy,' interrupted Jana. 'From what we saw, it's an old farm house on a slight rise in the middle of open fields. It's at least 600 metres, maybe more, from the nearest cover and there's only one track in. A perfect place for an exchange assuming they have helicopters. It would be nearly impossible to overrun without being seen.'

'I understand that we have to get Olivia back,' said Inspector Axel. 'But if we are going to succeed, you must trust me—let me organise some help.'

'I agree with him Max; we won't be able to do this on our own. If you make the exchange there is no guarantee that they will release Olivia and, if I was a betting man, they will take you both hostage so they can escape.'

'Max,' continued Axel, 'I can access satellite photographs and, in twenty minutes, we can have the very best of personnel standing by. If you want to go it alone, I promise not to interfere—but think about it. If you go in without some kind of back up, you can't win. There is no easy way out of this, if at all.'

I decided to inject a little humour, which was my way when the severity of a situation was overwhelming my thinking. 'What about the old secret escape route which runs from the edge of the fields and comes up in the cellar beneath the cottage?'

'You're thinking of some fictional plot from a spy novel,' replied Axel in a way that indicated he was not sure if I was joking.

'Okay, how about the cache of guns and explosives you have in the boot of your car?'

Now it was Jana's turn who, after sharing a nursing home with me for the last two years, was a little more accustomed to my bouts of sarcasm. 'Ah, that would be from one of those Hollywood blockbusters.'

'Go on Inspector,' I said with all seriousness returned to my voice. 'What are your thoughts?'

'Very well,' he said, shaking his head and obviously wondering what on Earth had just taken place. 'We may have to play this a bit by ear. There is so little time to organise anything, which I am guessing was their plan in the first place. A couple of options have come to mind. We place marksmen around the perimeter; 500 to 600 metres is within their range. If we get a clear shot at all of the terrorists at the same time, we take it. We could also consider putting a couple of men in the boot of your car. Use it a bit like a Trojan horse to get them closer to the house. The final thing I am considering is using men in camouflage to slowly bridge the open space undetected. We could then storm the house and take them using stun grenades and the like. I won't really know until we have a proper look at the place. There is one thing I am certain about; they will be expecting you to try something and will have planned some counter moves. Perhaps if you use the car, the one Jana said has the GPS tracking device on it, they might be a little less suspicious and drop their guard—although I doubt it.

'There is one thing that I *can* tell you Max and Jana. If they get the Janus Machine, even if you are all taken hostage—we won't be letting them leave. You do understand that?'

I nodded in silent acknowledgement. Axel stood and, from his pocket, he took a two way radio. 'Here, take this so that we can talk because, I'm afraid, I have to go back and make some plans with people who do this kind of thing for a living. I'll let you know what we decide on. Looking at the time we have left, that may not be until you're driving to the exchange point. Good luck and dump the radio out of the car window sometime before you go down the driveway.' With that Inspector Axel headed toward the bedroom door.

'Inspector,' I called as he was leaving. 'I was really sorry to hear about Kate and of course Edward.'

He acknowledged me not by words but by folding and then biting his bottom lip while looking briefly down.

'One more thing,' I continued. 'Can I have your mobile phone? You can keep the SIM. I only want the phone.'

Without a moment's hesitation and without asking questions, he took the phone from his pocket, removed the SIM and threw the phone across to me. Then he was gone, leaving Jana and me alone. After a moment in silence I looked to Jana and said, 'I need some wire.'

The trip from the hotel to the farm house took only twenty minutes. Jana drove while I cradled the box and spoke via the radio to Axel. We paused before starting the 500 metre trek up to the house, not only to dispose of the radio, but to ready ourselves for what was to come.

'Are you ready?' I asked.

Jana didn't reply, but nudged the M20 gently forward. As it slowly picked up speed, I took the opportunity to scan about, trying to spot our marksmen, but nothing seemed out of the ordinary. If the inspector had not said that they were there, I would have assumed we were alone.

Jana kept a steady pace as we approached the farm house. From the car, we could see three armed men and two helicopters, one either side of the house. If there were more armed people inside, it was impossible to tell. There were no outbuildings, no trees and no stone fences. The house stood all alone.

Stopping five or six metres short of two of the men, who seemed to be our welcome committee, Jana switched off the engine. Taking a couple of deep breaths, we both left the vehicle, me holding the box and Jana his rifle. We looked to each other for reassurance then moved off towards the men. One approached us while the other stayed behind—watching with his levelled gun. The approaching man walked straight past us. I turned and watched as he inspected the back seat of the M20 before lifting his gun and discharging three rounds into the boot.

'What was that for?' I demanded.

Ignoring my outcry, he levelled his gun and indicated for us to walk towards the house.

'Stop,' said the other man as we approached. 'Spread your arms and legs while I check you for wires.'

We did as we were told, Jana still holding his rifle, which seemed of little interest to our guards, and me, the case. With the pat down over, he took Jana's phone, before saying 'Okay, move on.'

The entrance to the stone house opened onto a large room with doors leading from it on the left and right and one to the rear. A desk sat roughly in the middle, behind which sat Claudia watching a computer screen. Two empty chairs awaited us in front of the desk. The room was well lit by two small windows, one either side of the entrance but, to my dismay, Olivia was not present.

'Hello again sweeties; come in and sit down but Jana, if you don't mind, please leave your rifle by the door.'

Jana did as he was told and we moved on into the room.

'Where's Olivia?' I snapped.

'All in good time, sweetie. Be seated gentlemen, please,' she continued, pointing to the two vacant chairs. 'Now, where's the Janus Machine?'

I held up the box.

'Excellent, Max. Now, let me explain, sweeties, how this is going to work,' she said, turning the computer screen to face us as she spoke. There on the screen, via a live feed, was Olivia, tied and gagged.

'It all very simple sweetie. You give me the machine and, in exchange, I tell you where Olivia is and, before you make up some cock-and-bull story in the hope of stalling so that you can be rescued, Olivia has...' Claudia looked down at her watch. '...exactly twenty-three minutes before she dies. As we speak, the house where she is—is filling with gas.'

A long pause followed and, when I was just about to speak, she continued, 'In...' and she looked down at her watch again, '...twenty-two minutes and thirty seconds, an automatic timer will strike a flame and, just like Kate and Edward—Boom.'

I jumped out of my seat, startling one of the guards, who immediately levelled his gun and moved in front of the window.

I had to cover Claudia from any snipers sighting her from outside until I knew where Olivia was being held.

'Semyon,' said Claudia calmly, 'Max has been naughty and brought some friends. Cover the windows and tell the others to keep out of sight; we may be expecting company. Max you have—let me see, oh yes twenty-one minutes and thirty seconds left. It will take say nineteen minutes from here to reach Olivia. The Janus Machine. Please.'

'How do I know you will let her go?'

'Sweetie, you don't, but, as you can see—you have no choice. The Janus Machine please.'

Moving back from in front of the window, with Semyon pulling the curtains closed behind me, I carried the box holding the Janus Machine and placed it carefully on the desk in front of Claudia. In doing so, I pushed one of the buttons (BEEP) of the mobile phone which I had secured to the front of the box. Wires ran from the phone, vanishing inside.

Claudia looked from the box then back to me.

'What is this phone doing on the front?' she said in an angry voice.

'I have just triggered a mercury tilt switch,' I said coolly. 'It's attached to explosives for which you can thank Inspector Axel. He, along with some of his men, is waiting outside. 'This— *sweetie*—is how it's going to work. You will release Olivia to Inspector Axel and, once I have proof that she is okay, I will open the box and the Janus Machine is yours. It's all up to you now. We are willing to die along with Olivia but—if you want it—give her to Axel and I will open it. It will be yours! You still have to get away, but I assume you have made contingency plans for that.'

'Sweetie, I have truly underestimated your tenacity. She's in Elie. Do you have Inspector Axel's number?'

'I do,' said Jana with some urgency. Reaching for his mobile phone and finding it missing he remembered it had been taken during the *pat down*. 'One of your baboons has my phone.'

Calmly, as if unfazed by the dwindling seconds, Claudia commanded, 'Give him the phone.'

Vladimir, who had remained standing beside Claudia, threw the phone to Jana who caught it and dialled Inspector Axel.

'It's Jana; there's been a development. Hold the line.' He handed the phone across to Claudia. She described the house where Olivia was and told him how to find and then disarm the ignition system.

'You have less than eighteen minutes and don't forget, Inspector, wave to the camera.' After a short pause Claudia laughed before handing Jana back his phone.

***

'I'll do more than wave. If anything happens to either of them, no matter where you are or where you go, I will hunt you down.'

She had already hung up with a laugh before I could finish my empty threats.

'Colleen,' I called to a young detective who was working with me. 'You need to drive while I use the phone and radio. You have seventeen minutes to get us to Elie. 'Come on; run.'

She looked at me in mild confusion, as if unsure what to do.

'Run to the car,' I yelled.

From our observation spot, where we had been watching the house, even sprinting, it took over a minute to reach the car. From the passenger seat I looked at my watch for the first time—by my best estimate, there were fifteen minutes and thirty seconds remaining.

The car accelerated from where it had been hidden and jumped onto the road before speeding away. With Colleen driving furiously, I made a series of frantic phone calls. 'She's in a white house in Ferry Road,' I shouted down the phone. 'What do you mean it will take twenty minutes to get a car there? We don't have twenty minutes. *Think man, think, there must be something else you can do*—' were my last words before hanging up the phone. Watching out of the windscreen as the scenery sped past, we came up behind a slow moving truck.

'*Come on, come on—go round,*' I said aloud but more to myself. 'Put the lights and bells on,' I said heatedly.

'You don't have lights and sirens in this car,' came Colleen's edgy reply.

'Toot the horn and flash your lights then, try and get past.'

Colleen obliged but this seemed only to raise the ire of the occupant and the truck slowed even more. The road straightened but although it was two way, the width of the truck made seeing and passing difficult. Colleen stuck the nose of the car out from behind the truck, only to bring it swinging rapidly back in order to miss an oncoming vehicle. On the third attempt she pulled onto the wrong side of the road and accelerated our little buzz box, a 1.6 litre non turbo sedan. As the passenger side of the car cleared the truck, I could see that the road was clear but that the overtaking distance before the next corner was limited. Colleen changed down a gear and the engine screamed as we inched past. About halfway through the risky manoeuvre, a car appeared from around the corner. At the speed we were fast approaching each other it was closing rapidly; too late to brake—we were committed. Changing up gears, the car lurched forward and I could see Colleen desperately flashing the headlights as we careered towards the oncoming car. The approaching vehicle responded by flashing its lights, as if it were in a game of chicken. Colleen kept her foot buried into the foot well and we continued to increase speed as the distance between us and the approaching car narrowed. With less than a metre to go before impact, the truck moved rapidly to the left and our nemesis to the right. Colleen, without lifting her foot from the accelerator, went down the middle and the vehicles passed three abreast to the sound of our passenger side mirror being torn off by the truck.

Once past, the conditions on the other side of the truck were almost perfect for racing; the road was dry and flat with gentle sweeping corners. The overtaking manoeuvre must have taken some of Colleen's confidence as we slowed notably. Watching our progress I became more and more irritated.

'Come on Colleen, put your foot down.'

'Sorry sir, but we can't help if we are dead.' As she said this, another slow vehicle came into sight—another car to pass.

'Okay you're right—sorry. As fast as you can then.'

Looking again at my watch I saw that there were only six minutes to go. I knew that we were not going to make it. A sense of nausea swept over me; here I was, helpless in the passenger seat of a car and there was nothing I could do. It was only going to be a matter of minutes; the difference between life and death but we were too far away and the task now impossible.

***

Max

'Sweeties, eighteen minutes is such a long time when you're waiting and we still have an agonising ten minutes to go. What shall we talk about next? I know. Tell me, Jana. Why can't we find anything out about you? Other than going into Bellbird Village not long after Max and Olivia, you're a mystery to us.'

'Am I now?' responded Jana. 'I hope to keep it that way.'

'Come now, if Max blows up the Janus Machine because our intrepid Inspector Axel can't save Olivia, I may have to kill you. There's no harm in telling us something. Oh and that name sweetie—Jana. It's like something out of a B-grade movie. I'm surprised Olivia and Max weren't onto you straight away. Janus is a Roman God and so is Jana—God of secrets and mysteries, no less. If my memory serves me well, the God was a woman. So, sweetie, a strange name to choose. Come on then, between friends—who are you really?'

I could see Jana wondering if he should answer but, after a matter of only seconds, he said, 'That's the problem with you modern folk, if it's not on a computer it didn't happen. I'm there but on some old and dirty archived dossier, down in the bowels of a derelict building. After all of this time the notes have probably been destroyed.'

'Who would have kept a dossier on you, sweetie?'

'Well, that depends on which government you work for.'

Sweetie, we don't actually work for the government. We have—how would you describe it—more of a symbiotic relationship, a mutual understanding. For our services we get money laundered and cleaned, information, passports, assistance from time to time and protection. In return they get what it is they want.'

'Which is?' pressed Jana.

'Sweetie, I see no harm in telling you because there's nothing you or anyone else can do about it. We are all playing a part in a much bigger game. A plan to weaken NATO, Britain and the US alliance. No one wants a war because that's not good for business but, by using some good old fashioned gun boat diplomacy and manipulating opportunities as they arise, the balance of power in Europe will change. There are invisible but well understood lines that are drawn on a map that can't be crossed. The time is coming, however, to restore the old lines. The Bear is on the move.'

'Russian Mafia working in cahoots with the Russian Government; I should have guessed,' said Jana.

'For Russia the timing is perfect,' continued Claudia, ignoring Jana's comments. 'Flexing her muscles in this, a period of unprecedented instability, she will take advantage of the impact of the Global Financial Crisis in Europe, the rise of *Isis* and the *Arab Spring* uprisings in the Middle East and the *Rise of China* in Asia.

'After the Global Financial Crisis, some of the economies in Europe are weak and, in particular, Portugal, Ireland, Italy, Spain, and Greece. If the EU wants to keep its common currency, they will have to lend to those countries; to Greece in particular, massive loans, worth billions, while demanding austerity measures in return. The people of Europe won't want to loan those sums of money and the people in the receiving countries will think the austerity measures unfair. The first real cracks and, all of their own making, will begin to show in the European Union.

'The Arab uprising, along with *Isis*, has the potential to destabilise much of the Middle East. Conflict has already flowed over into Syria. Because of fracking, America, in the future, won't need to import oil from the Gulf; this makes the Middle East less important to them. With its navy facility in Syria at Tartus, Russia is always going to support the Syrian government and will be prepared to use its military assets to protect its interests. The West will be frightened of a direct conflict with Russia over Syria, while Russia pretends to be fighting with the US on a common enemy of *Isis*, all the while really shoring up its interests in Syria.'

'The Syrian conflict and the fight with *Isis* has the potential to create the biggest refugee crisis the world has seen since WW2. Millions of refugees will flee to Europe. This will place the Union under extraordinary pressure, to the point where it could collapse.

'*Isis*, like the *Taliban* before them, will declare a religious war—Islam against the West. Overwhelmed by immigration and with threats of terrorist attacks, Europe will become increasingly xenophobic and intolerant. Its citizens will demand their governments close the borders and stop the refugees, to stop the foreign invaders from coming in and taking over their country. For those European countries with a high Islamic population like Britain, France and Belgium, internal tensions and threats from home grown terrorists will make them look inwardly even more, further intensifying unrest within its population. The Euro Zone will squabble even more, torn between their individual state interests and that of the Union as a whole. Europe's and NATO's capacity to act collectively will be virtually destroyed.

'While this is occurring, Russia will flex its muscles to unnerve Europe. The manoeuvring to redraw the old *Cold War* lines has begun.

'The Ukraine joining NATO or the EU is out of the question. Russia will use the threat of this to destabilise the Ukraine peninsular; it will not use tanks but, with people fighting for their right to remain a part of Russia, it will then annex the Crimea for peace and security reasons. Russia will never give up *Sevastopol*, the home of Black Sea Fleet. NATO and the Yanks will jump up and down and squabble amongst themselves but they will do nothing.

'Continuing to flex its muscles, Russia will blatantly tease European, Britain and the Scandinavian countries by sending fighters into their air space and by sailing ships and submarines through their waters. NATO, has dramatically cut its defence spending. This has pissed off the Yanks, who already think NATO is a scam of sponging countries. They will receive no sympathy from the USA.

'As Uncle Sam finds itself drawn more and more towards Asia, with the rise of China and in particular the South China Sea, it will expect Europe to pull its own weight.

'As the tensions between the US and China rise, Russia will increase its pressure by escalating its incursions into Europe. The Scandinavians and the other so-called neutral countries will become the first to capitulate and become more malleable to Russia's wishes.'

Rolling my eyes at the utter self-indulgent rubbish, I said. 'You can't expect us to believe there's some big conspiracy going on between Russia, China and who else you mentioned?'

'Sweetie, there are no conspiracies; this is taking advantage of events that are forming, what do you call it? Ah yes—*A Perfect Storm.*'

'Go on then,' I said, a little dismissively. 'What happens next in your fairy tale?'

'Civil unrest, perhaps even armed insurgencies will spring up. When they occur in old Russian satellite states, aided of course by Russian manpower, money and resources, Europe will be too paralysed to respond. Russia will be free to annex Poland, Romania, and Hungary for their own protection. The invisible lines on the map will have been redrawn and no one will do anything about it—except maybe for Britain!

'You may not realise it sweetie, but everybody in Europe, and even the Americans, hate the British. Our friends in the Russian Government don't want the Brits to feel nostalgic for WW2. Britain, on its own, is no threat to Russia but, if Britain intervened in, say, Poland, the rest of NATO may reluctantly follow and eventually the US. As I said, no one wants a *Hot War*. This is about redrawing the old lines.

'Russia wants to, let's say, encourage Britain to mind its own business, which is where we come in. All we are doing is asking Britain to pay an annual insurance premium.'

'Extortion is more like it,' interrupted Jana, only to be ignored again by Claudia.

'An insurance premium makes it more difficult for Britain to afford its new *Successor Class* submarines and will encourage it to scale back its defence spending even further,' she continued. 'As I have already told you, we don't want to harm the economy, otherwise how will you pay? I see us a bit like a central bank; we can raise and lower the premium to help your economy along. In the end, it will come down to a matter of priorities for the government. It won't be us who dictates how you spend your money but I know what your citizens will say. If it comes down to a choice between submarines and hospitals—how do you think they will vote?' Then, if it came to intervening in Poland or schools—how will they vote? I do so much love democracy.'

'It's a perfect symbiotic relationship—Russia gets a weakened Britain and we get money.'

'I thought you said the US has already paid up?'

'Max, everybody has to pay; the US, Canada, Brazil—it's all a matter of how much!'

'Doing what you are doing will force Britain to spend more on security, not less,' said Jana.

'Exactly, sweeties. Homeland security and not armies, ships and planes. Britain will isolate itself more and more from Europe, which is what we want.'

'Russians will eventually turn against you,' I said.

'Max, sweetie, of course they will but, by then, we will have amassed trillions and own pharmaceuticals, weapons and telecommunication companies. We will be whatever the next Google or Facebook is and won't care about the government. We will be pulling the strings because money talks. Biological weapons and even Janus will become yesterday's news. It's all a matter of economics.'

Jana looked to Claudia and said, 'You could make millions by using the Janus Machine to cure cancer, malaria or AIDS and that's just a start.'

'Jana,' replied Claudia, her voice filled with cynicism. 'Hope and fear Jana—it's about hope and fear: if you cure something there's no fear—people are willing to pay for hope.

'But Jana, I've digressed, it's your turn in our little game of show and tell.'

Jana again thought for a second before deciding he should continue speaking. 'Until a couple of years ago, when they needed an *old* person to keep an eye on Max and Olivia, I was just a discarded relic, a leftover from the cold war. Then, out of nowhere, a call came from MI6 and I found myself stuck in a home watching Max and Olivia. Over time, I was forgotten again.

'For a while, I thought I was going to die of old age myself in that home before anything happened. You,' he said looking across to me, 'got frailer and frailer and, although I saw you check the newspaper every morning, I watched as your life slowly slipped away. When the message to retrieve Janus did finally come, I didn't think you could do it and that the secret would die with you.

'Here we are and, by *God*,' he said, with a slight chuckle in his voice, 'did you take some following!'

'If we are all to die today—for you and Olivia—it's better here than in a home. For me… I know it's the wrong thing to say, considering London and everything else that's happening, but the last three weeks have put meaning back into my aging bones and I won't forget it.'

'Oh forgive me sweeties; I'm almost feeling sick. Can I remind you that, no matter what happens, you have lost? What a waste! If you had just given me the box, Olivia would live and none of this would be happening.'

The final minutes were taken in agonising silence. Watching the computer monitor, I saw Olivia seated motionless, her eyes staring straight ahead. I didn't know whether to watch the screen or to look away.

With two minutes to go I couldn't control myself any longer. 'Jana, ring Axel…I need to know.'

'Are you sure that's a good idea Max? You may slow him up.'

'Go on; do it,' I persisted.

Taking the phone from his pocket, Jana dialled Axel and almost instantaneously the phone was answered. I listened as Jana asked, *where are you?* Following what seemed the longest wait in my life, Jana shook his head - no. He hung up.

Time had run out, 5-4-3-2-1(BOOM). But, the explosion I was anticipating didn't happen. There was no boom and Olivia stayed seated, staring straight ahead and alive. We watched as a man I didn't recognise untied her. She waved to the camera before being rushed from view.

'Now that was a surprise, sweeties.' Claudia's words were cut short by the ringing of Jana's phone. I can only think that Claudia was as curious as the rest of us to know what had happened—she waited patiently for the call to end.

'An off-duty police man living in Elie. They rang him at home and Olivia is safe.'

'Excellent. The Janus Machine if you please Max,' said Claudia.

I reached across to the box where it rested upon the table and ripped the mobile phone from its surface.

'It was all a hoax,' I said. I undid the latches while Claudia and Jana watched on in anticipation. I lifted the lid to reveal what was inside; a pile of old books.

'Where is it Max?' spat Claudia with venom.

Looking at my watch before facing Claudia I replied, 'The Royal Mail got picked up a little over an hour and a half ago. I guess by now it's somewhere in Edinburgh and will soon to be on a plane to London.' It wasn't actually going to London; I said that only for impact, and to keep the *Agency* and its nondescript house in Cliff secret.

Claudia was still for a moment, saying and doing nothing, before taking, from her side, a Glock pistol. Pulling the hammer back for effect, she pointed the muzzle straight between my eyes. Olivia was safe, Janus was safe and I wasn't going to give her the pleasure of flinching. She held my gaze and, in my peripheral vision, I saw as her finger pulled slowly back on the trigger. It was difficult to resist the urge to close my eyes but neither of us blinked. Then, without warning, she pulled the gun away from my face and said, in a voice restored to her normal calm and overly polite way, 'You may have won, but tell me—what do you have to look forward to? Nothing! Max, you have nothing! Go back to where you came from and spend the remainder of your miserable life in a nursing home.'

'Boss,' interrupted Semyon. 'The diversion for our escape starts in two minutes.'

'Thank you Semyon. Max sweetie, I've changed my mind –I've other plans for you. Semyon tie Jana up. Max is coming with us.

'Where are you taking him?' I heard Jana ask.

'Sweetie, you will have to wait and see.'

THE END

www.ingramcontent.com/pod-product-compliance
Lightning Source LLC
Chambersburg PA
CBHW031038120726
47905CB00007B/2238